WOLVES OF CHAOS VALLEY

CHAOS BITTEN

RAVEN WOODWARD

This is a work of fiction. Names, characters, businesses, places, events and incidents are either the product of the author's imagination or are used in a fictitious manner. Any resemblance to actual persons, living or dead is purely coincidental.

Cover Design by Pixie Covers

Editing by: IDK Art

For the ones that have to hide their wild side.

Callahan Pack

Carvingwood Pack

Blackclaw Pack

Shadow Ridge Clan

Ivywood

Friar Pack

Dockhills Pack

Soul Reaper Pack

Dread Cany Pack

Crimson Hill Pack

Silver Falls Pack

Ashbourne

ARS HOLLOW
PACK

GREYWOOD
PACK

HIGHCREST
PACK

BEAR ROCK
PINES

BLACKTHORN
PACK

ONE
USHERS
ACK

BLOOD
HOLLOW

IREWOLF
PACK

HOGAN CLAN

BLOODMOON
LAKE

HAITOKE

ONYXPAW
PACK

WOLFSBANE
PACK

CRIMSONPAW

DARK RIVER
PACK

10 MILES

CHAPTER ONE

Dani

The early noon sun beating down on me was stifling. Sweat trickled lazily from my neck to my back, dampening my loose tank top. Panting and grinning a wide, feral smile, I lunged forward, diving under the fist thrown where my face had just been.

My own punch landed on a set of bare, sweaty abs, knocking my opponent back a step. Using the momentum, I swung my leg out, preparing to knock him off his feet. He leapt over me with ease, a growl echoing in his chest.

The people gathered around watched with tense stillness that spurred me on. Rising to my feet with fluid grace, I just barely managed to side-step the brutal kick that would have easily knocked me out cold. Catching him by the ankle, I yanked it up, then twisted.

The muscled man grunted but caught himself on his hands before springing upright once more.

We were both out of breath; this dance of ours having gone on for far too long. Depthless amber eyes tracked me with the hunger of a predator as I paced, trying to level out the rampant beating of my heart.

"What's it going to be, Dani?" he taunted. "Surrender?"

I scoffed. "Not a chance."

His answering chuckle was cut off when I dove toward him, faking left. He read my move and crashed into me, gripping my wrists so I couldn't strike. We landed in the dirt—a round of whoops and jeers went up from our audience.

Syracuse Milton held me pinned for several moments with both his hands and his penetrating honeyed stare. A smirk twisted his lips.

"Gotcha," he rasped.

I blinked demurely. "Did you?"

His eyes widened a fraction of a second before my knee came up between his legs. At the last possible moment, he rolled us both, managing to escape a particular type of pain, leaving me to straddle him.

Shaggy brown curls matted to his forehead with sweat; Syr's throat bobbed. "That wasn't nice," he teased.

I winked. "Surrender yet?"

His gaze lowered to my mouth. "I've never minded surrendering to you."

My grin slipped and brows dipped. Deciding he was likely just sick of the stalemate we'd been stuck in for nearly an hour, I peeled my sticky body off my best friend, offering him my hand.

"Good, because you stink," I lied, wrinkling my nose for added effect. Truly, he smelled divine—like sunshine in a meadow. Why hadn't I noticed that before? He got to his feet, barking a laugh before pushing my shoulder lightly.

He was certainly bigger than I was—especially in the last few months I'd noticed his lean form bulking up—I was just glad I could hold my own against him. The applause faded out around us, and I met my father's gaze from across the fenced-in ring. His brows were a flat line that made my stomach dip slightly.

We exited the sparring area—me climbing over the wooden beams, while Syr simply stepped over them.

Tall people, I grumbled internally.

A few of the pack elders clapped my best friend on the shoulder, telling us both how entertaining it was to watch the two of us train. We'd been doing it since we were kids, but our matches had grown steadily longer, usually with no clear victor. Regardless, it was fun. A way to let out the pent-up aggression that simmered in my veins.

We grabbed our bottles of water from the grass. I guzzled most of mine in a few swallows, reserving some to dump over my head.

A happy sigh escaped me as the cool droplets dripped down my body. Wiping the water off my eyelids, I blinked my eyes open, finding my friend watching me intently.

"What's up?" I asked. His eyes were on me more than usual today. Or maybe it was just my imagination.

My words seemed to snap him out of whatever trance he'd been in, shaking his head as though to clear it. "Nothing. I thought I left a bruise on your cheek, but it was just dirt."

I laughed. "It's a little late to care about bruising me, Syr. You've been doing it since we were five."

He smiled. "Pretty sure I sport more injuries from our matches than you ever do."

Before I could respond, his attention shifted to something behind me. "Sir," he said, and my father's presence warmed my back.

Our alpha rested a hand on my shoulder, giving it a slight squeeze. "Great match, you two. You seem to be equals in every way, though I could have sworn I saw you pull back a little, Milton."

My jaw dropped and I whirled to face my father, irrational anger swirling through me like a tornado. His challenging expression, however, had my mouth snapping shut.

"With all due respect, sir, I've never held myself back in the ring," Syr answered, his tone clipped.

I blinked, still fuming at the insinuation that Syr had let me win. We knew each other in and out of the ring better than anyone else knew us, and I wanted to believe Syr had never pulled any punches for my sake.

"Are you holding back, Syr?" I demanded. "Because you know I don't want you coddling me. Just because I'm daughter to the alpha doesn't mean you need to restrain yourself. You know I can handle it."

My best friend scrubbed a hand over the back of his neck. "I'm not *letting* you win, Dani. Hell, keeping up with you is exhausting."

I let my shoulders relax slightly, casting a suspicious look at my father who was looking at my friend as though he was trying to dissect him just with his eyes. I wasn't sure if he was stirring up trouble or trying to rile me, but whatever his motivations, I never wanted anyone to treat me like I was fragile.

And my father knew that.

Sighing heavily, I grabbed Syr's hand. "Come on, let's go help set up the bonfire for tonight."

"Actually, I think your mother was wanting to see you," the alpha said, stopping me.

"Okay, I'll go see her." I nodded, pulling my best friend in the direction of my house, hating the way I zeroed in on a drop of sweat that wended its way between perfectly carved abs.

Seriously, it would be impossible not to notice how stacked the guy was even if he wore a snowsuit. Being wolves meant I was entirely familiar with Syr's nudity.

And it also explained why every single female in the pack vied for my best friend with a hunger that made me want to wolf out.

He threaded his fingers through mine, effectively dispelling my lingering jealous thoughts and making my stomach swoop. Glancing sidelong at him, I noted the hard expression he wore. It was so at odds with his usually playful demeanor.

We practically sprinted through the throng of people carrying supplies around for the festival later tonight. His scent wafted to me and my mouth watered.

Ugh, I really need to get laid, I thought as I swallowed my extra saliva. Clearly my ladyhood was feeling neglected.

My mother stood on the porch, hanging a colorful banner

between the beams on her tip-toes.

Syr let my hand go to help hoist the ribbon up and tie it in place. She laughed. "Thanks, Syr. I was silly and didn't think to bring my stool out." She cast me a warm smile that I tried to return, but my lips wouldn't cooperate.

At only five foot three myself, I was used to having to depend on tall people for so many menial tasks, and my mother was an inch shorter than I was. Stalking up the steps, I pressed a kiss to her cheek.

"Dad said you wanted to see me?"

She brushed a few dark strands of hair that had escaped her messy bun from her face. "Yes, can you and Syr run to town to get some things?"

I shrugged, glancing to Syracuse who finished retying the other side of the banner higher up so no one—mainly him and my dad—hit their heads on it.

"Happy to, Mrs. Carvingwood." He pressed a kiss to her cheek as well before escaping back down the steps. She swatted at him anyway, shaking her head and smiling wide.

I got the list from my mom and followed Syr to his truck. The list was far too long for the backpacks we'd usually use when shifting into wolf form and running the fifteen or so minutes to Ivywood. The second he turned the beastly vehicle on, the speakers blared with Bad Omens before he turned the volume down, low enough to talk if needed, but loud enough to comfortably just listen. It was exactly what I did as we drove down the gravel road toward town.

Just as we passed the sign welcoming visitors to Ivywood, I

turned the music down further.

"What did my dad mean about you taking it easy on me?" I asked.

He glanced fully at me with a single brow raised. "You're still weirded out about that, aren't you?" He chuckled, shaking his head.

I pursed my lips a moment before saying, "If he thinks you're holding back then others will too. Last thing I need is for people to think I'm weak. It's bad enough the pack leader's only child was born a girl; if they suspect at all that I'm second best, it'll be seen as a weakness in my father and make it next to impossible to take over when he's gone."

Syr gave me a bemused look. "Dani, no one with even half a brain would think you're weak. You kick everyone's asses, not just mine." I must not have looked convinced because he sighed. "Obviously I don't hit as hard as I would in an actual fight but the rest of it is me giving it everything I have."

I rolled my shoulders back, accepting his answer. For now. He shook his head again. I knew I sounded petulant but there was so much pressure on my dad as it was. With there not being a Chaos for over nine years, things were tense.

Each year at the beginning of summer, a full moon settled over the entirety of Chaos Valley, sending nearly every unmated wolf into a frenzy where they took their mates—in the most primal sense. It was a tradition that we wolves had become accustomed to and looked forward to.

That is, until it stopped. I was thirteen when the last one took place. Though it was a long time ago, I could still vaguely recall the energy and anticipation that thrummed through those that were of age.

Now, without it, wolves took mates that were not their *fated* mate. Abductions were a growing problem where women were auctioned off to desperate wolves. Our pack had several teams that sought out those auctions, breaking them up and executing the wolves responsible, but the trail had gone cold two years ago.

With summer right around the corner, we arranged a weeklong festival that helped serve as a distraction. Still, I heard the discontented whispers. If there was a new alpha, maybe the abductions would stop. Maybe the Chaos would return.

My teeth ground together just thinking about my father being challenged. He was the perfect alpha whether they saw it or not. A change in power wouldn't bring the Chaos back; they had to know that.

We pulled up to the convenience store and my gaze immediately snagged on the two sleek black motorcycles parked a few spaces down.

My mood soured and I groaned.

Syr clearly tracked where my eyes had gone because he growled, "Fucking Dockhills. What are those bastards doing all the way up here?"

"The Pack Games aren't for two weeks, there's no reason they should be here." I got out, slamming the door shut behind me as the engine switched off and Syr followed.

We started inside, Syr pushing a cart so I could toss what we needed in as fast as possible. Up and down the food aisles, I tossed bags of chips in on top of the gallons of soda that lined the bottom, all the while feeling on edge.

The Pack Games was a competition of sorts held between the packs west of the Reaper's Spines. Dockhills was about as far south as you could go within Chaos Valley and they were filled with arrogant jerks who all thought they were better than everyone else. They'd won the games nearly every year for the past decade—or rather, their alpha had. This year I'd beat him though.

I refused to see the leader of the Dockhills Pack's smug expression one more time. The infuriating male was none other then—

"Ah, if it isn't the Little Wolf and her bodyguard," Donovan drawled in a voice that was both silk and jagged glass.

The alpha was as tall as Syracuse, though where Syr was hulking muscle, Donovan was leaner. It made his sharp jaw and wicked grin that much more intimidating, but I refused to be affected by him or his stupid face.

"If it isn't the biggest dick from the hills," I said with faux surprise.

The petite blonde that appeared at his side smirked. "You've already used that insult," Autumn Lefair—Donovan's beta—said with a smirk.

I shrugged. "That must be because you're so forgettable."

Donovan chuckled; a dark sound that rumbled in his chest like thunder. "You keep telling yourself that, Daniella." His dark green eyes slid down my body slowly, and his lip curled. "Clearly you lot still prefer to roll around in the mud."

I didn't need to glance down at myself to know I was still

wearing a thin layer of dirt from my earlier sparring match. While Donovan looked pristine in dark denim jeans, and a black T-shirt that hugged his toned chest beneath his open leather jacket.

Honestly, if he wasn't such an asshole, he'd be completely mouth-watering. Too bad it was impossible to see past his inflated ego.

"And yet it's you who plays the dirtiest, eh, Dickholes?" I said sweetly, before attempting to maneuver around him. The rumors of his pack cheating in the games went without any sort of proof year after year, but I couldn't help throwing the accusation in his face.

Donovan stepped directly in front of me, leaning down to whisper, "I hear you like getting fucked in the mud and grime like a squealing bitch in heat. Want to meet me around back to—"

My fist swung without thought, but before I could make contact, a strong hand ripped me back, then Syr was in Donovan's face, snarling.

"Get the fuck out, Dockhills. No one wants your kind here."

Donovan's grin was unnerving. "Whatever you say, lap dog," he told Syr. Switching his gaze back to mine, he strode past me, invading my personal space as he did. "I'll be seeing you very soon, Little Wolf," he purred.

His scent made me think of rain and pine trees mixed with pure, male musk—the result made an odd sort of heat settle low in my gut. It annoyed me that I liked the smell so much, and I ground my teeth together to keep from inhaling it deeply. Autumn caught my eye as they strode down the aisle. She winked, sashaying after her alpha in tight black skinny jeans that hugged her every curve.

My fingernails bit into my palms and I spun, marching toward the checkouts. There was no way I could stay in this building with those two insufferable jerks. Syr watched me closely as I piled the belt with almost everything on my mother's list.

Sorry, Mom, I thought wryly, *you'll just have to do without cheese.*

CHAPTER TWO

I passed her once more, sending her a wink that made her full pink lips purse in irritation. Her scent seemed to chase me even when she was on the other side of the shop. She smelled like vanilla, woods, and that meat-head who always followed her around. It made my wolf want to come out and tear his throat out.

She won't be his much longer, I thought with primal satisfaction.

Just the thought of her belonging to me—kneeling in front of me with my cock in her beautiful mouth—had my body hot with arousal.

"Ugh," Autumn wrinkled her nose. "You can stop giving off pheromones; *I'm* not going to mate with you."

I shoved her shoulder hard enough to send her stumbling a step, but she laughed, swatting at me good naturedly.

Even though Daniella Carvingwood was nine years my junior, she was a hell of warrior. Never, in the past four years had she passed up an opportunity to go up against me in the Pack Games. She was fierce, and there was a reason she'd earned her pack's number two spot. Watching her strong, lithe body flex and move was the reason I kept coming back. The sight of her furious face every time I bested her was just an added bonus.

And what I was about to do would ensure she fought me at every step of my diabolical plan.

My blood was still heated when we exited the shop. I hadn't planned to run into Evan Carvingwood's only daughter this soon, but I never could turn down an opportunity to rile her up. Autumn smirked sidelong as we walked to our parked bikes.

It made my semi-hardened cock deflate. "What?" I asked through gritted teeth.

"I'm not sure who gets under whose skin more. You or her." A laugh bubbled out of her, and I rolled my eyes.

"I enjoy fucking with her," I said as though that dismissed her claim.

Autumn snorted. "While giving her your I-can't-wait-to-fuck-you eyes."

A growl shook my chest. "Don't make me kick your ass, Lefair," I snapped.

She chuckled again, checking over her shoulder to be sure we were alone before she said, "Are you ready for this?"

"Of course I am. But make sure you find a way to distract her while we're in our meeting. She won't let me within a mile of her alpha if she catches my scent." My second nodded, blowing a bubble that popped soundly. I don't even know when the fuck she started to chew gum, or where she'd gotten it.

She probably had me pay for it, I realized too late.

My gaze casually roamed over the small town's daily bustle; the majority of its population was human, though they knew about our kind and respected us. However, it looked like every other town we'd gone through. "Evan Carvingwood is going to angle himself right under my boot by the time I'm through with him. Only when he's sufficiently crushed and the pack destroyed will I be satisfied."

Just then, the object of my lust and her lap dog emerged, heading for the ugly green truck to load groceries in the back. It took less than a minute for her to scent me, then her violet eyes were narrowed on us both. I grinned.

Get ready, Little Wolf, I thought. *The game just changed.*

CHAPTER THREE

Dani

While we loaded bags into the back of the truck, Autumn and Donovan sat on their motorcycles like they were thrones overlooking the whole town.

Donovan's lips curled up at the corners when he saw me glaring in his direction before both engines roared to life. When they began to speed away, I flipped them off, hoping they saw it. I might have been imagining it, but I could have sworn his shoulders shook with laughter.

It doesn't matter, I told myself. *At least they're gone now.*

Whatever reason they'd had to be so far north to begin with, I didn't know, and I could tell from the puzzled look on Syracuse's face that he wondered the same thing. As Carvingwood beta, I would have known about an inter-pack meeting.

When we were settled in the truck, we began the journey back to Carvingwood territory. The music was kept off, and the air seemed unusually tense. Sure, it probably still had something to do with my fuming over Donovan, but Syr's shoulders were tight, and his scent had changed.

Before I could ask what was up, he spoke.

"Have you ever thought about just taking a mate, even though they may not be your true mate?" He kept his gaze firmly fixed on the road, but I blinked at him in surprise.

"No," I answered after a minute. "Even if there's not another Chaos ever again, I don't think I could ever take a mate that wasn't meant to be mine."

He turned his gaze to the side of my face and I turned to meet his eyes. "But what if you knew the two of you would be good together? Don't you worry about the pack going extinct?"

I exhaled a heavy breath, feeling like his first question held more weight than he was letting on. "Just because *I* don't want to, doesn't mean others won't. Plenty do. But what if I took a mate and then the Chaos hit, revealing my true mate? Seems like a mess to me."

He frowned. "But if there's not another Chaos in our lifetimes you'd die alone because of a 'what if.'"

A thread of irritation wound through me, making my blood heat in my veins. Why did he care all of a sudden? "I won't be alone, I have you and the pack." A thought occurred to me and my stomach dropped. "Are you considering taking a mate?" I asked. For some reason, the thought of him being mated with someone made an ache blossom in my chest. I knew in part it was because we had been best friends since we were kids, and him being mated would feel as though I'd lost him.

He would belong to someone else.

And that hurt far more than it had any right to. It was selfish to begrudge him any future happiness simply because he wanted a mate.

He shrugged. Though his attention was on the winding gravel road, white dust kicking up on either side of us and nearly blocking out the sight of the trees, I could still vaguely make out the way his jaw tightened.

My heart pinched. "Did you have your mind set on someone in particular?" I tried to think back on the past few weeks, if he'd been spending more time with anyone than usual. He'd had lunch with Maeve after fixing her porch railing the other day, but they'd been casual friends for years. She was slightly older with a three-year-old from a wolf who'd died on a mission to find and stop the auctions.

In such a small pack, it was hard not to know everyone. Almost every other moment Syr and I had spent together, unless he had been meeting up with her late at night.

A flare of irrational anger burned in my chest. It made my skin ache with the need to shift forms. I inhaled slowly, easing away the tension coiled in my muscles.

"Maeve is sweet and all, but I don't think she's right for you," I said, trying to sound like his best friend and not a jealous lover.

Syr looked at me like I'd just spoken in a different language. "Maeve?" he asked incredulously. Then he shook his head and scoffed. "There's only one person I'd consider mating with, Dani." His cheeks pinkened the moment he spoke the words and it took my brain a second to catch up.

Did he mean me? I wasn't completely stupid, I noticed the lingering glances and the way his eyes jumped to my mouth sometimes when I licked my lips or bit my bottom one. But was I reading too much into it? I mean, he was a guy and as far as I could tell, he hadn't hooked up with any of the girls in town or in neighboring packs in almost a year. Maybe he was just lonely.

Speaking of, it had been a while for me too. *I should probably sort that out soon*, I thought, making a mental note to do a forest hunt later this week. After the festival, but before the Pack Games.

Of course, I'd have to make sure Donovan was gone because the last thing I wanted to do was run into *him* on a late night hookup.

"Dani." The rumbling word beside me was half-growl, half-plea. A plea for what, I wasn't too sure.

Our eyes met and his pupils had turned to slits, his irises silver. His wolf was just beneath the surface. My heart picked up speed. "Are you about to wolf-out? Do you need me to drive?"

His nostrils flared before he put his window down, breathing in the forest air. He stayed like that for several minutes, then flicked his window back up, rolling his neck from side to side.

I lifted a brow when he still hadn't offered an explanation. "What the hell was that?"

Syr tightened his grip on the steering wheel. "Nothing. Just need to work off some steam."

We pulled into the village, cutting off my reply. The truck rolled slowly over the stone path. People milled around with decorations, bundles of wood for the bonfire, food, and tablecloths, setting up for the festival that would start tonight and carry on for days. We parked in front of my house at last, and I hopped out to grab the bags.

As much as I wanted to push my best friend for more information, the tight set of his shoulders and the way he pointedly stalked away from me with most of the bags clamped in his fists, told me it was best left alone.

At the base of the steps that led up the porch, I caught a whiff of a familiar scent and my brows drew together. The air was a chaotic mixture of so many smells that I brushed it off with a shrug, then headed inside.

My parents weren't in the house, but Aunt Clarissa and Uncle Jess were, slicing and chopping vegetables. I pecked them both on the cheek before I shuffled the ingredients onto the countertop.

Syr muttered something about needing to go help his father before he took off back out the door. I watched him go, staring after him even once the door had closed.

"Such a lovely boy," Aunt Clarissa mused. "He'll make some woman a very happy mate."

I groaned. "Ugh, no more talk of mates. I can't take it."

Uncle Jess chuckled. "Why don't you go clean off, eh? We've got this."

The suggestion seemed nice, so I nodded. "Where did Mom and Dad go?"

"They had a meeting. I don't think it was expected though. Your dad was certainly in a huff about it," Clarissa said mildly, chopping a carrot into slices.

I bit the inside of my lip, wondering if the elders were giving him a hard time again. They wanted a team of researchers to go across Chaos Valley and try to figure out why there hasn't been a Chaos in nine years. But Dad knew it was fruitless. Whatever magic controlled the moon and caused the Chaos to take place was certainly not influenced by anything we were or weren't doing.

To an extent, however, I understood the desperation. If another one never took place again, wolves would be forced to accept mates through tying ceremonies that were just simple ceremonies proclaiming your choice of mate.

It was part of the reason why I didn't want to force anything. I didn't need a mate to become the pack leader one day, which was what I wanted, but the smallest hint of curiosity crept in every now and then.

What would it be like to have a mate? To be so thoroughly bound and tied to someone that they could hear your inner thoughts. My parents were all sorts of in love and mushy. It gave me something to look forward to when I was young, but once the Chaos stopped showing up, the dream faded little by little.

Now I existed with the contentment of knowing it may never happen. Hell, even with the Chaos, you weren't guaranteed to find your mate. Some never did.

But Syr's questions and his behavior on the drive back made me wonder if he felt the urge to mate stronger than I did.

I waved to my aunt and uncle before slipping out the door and down the steps. Weaving through the crowd, I made it into the trees, shucking off my clothes to shift.

My paws hit the cool earth and I raked my claws into the soil slightly. A satisfied growl reverberated in my throat and I took off at a light sprint through the forest.

Ducking under low-hanging branches, I felt the scrape of pine needles through my fur. My limbs ached to go faster, but before I knew it, I was at the edge of the river. Slowing, I followed it slightly east, coming to the decent-sized pool with low, burbling falls.

Just as I sat back on my haunches, letting myself return to my human form, a head broke the surface in the middle of the pool. A golden mane of hair fanned out in the crystalline blue water, and eyes to match its rippling surface. They shone in the sporadic rays of sunlight as they found mine.

Autumn. Fucking. Lefair.

A smile curved her plump pink lips, and she swam lazily toward the shore, standing up in the shoulder-height depth to reveal the tops of her very naked breasts.

I stood there gawking like a freak, also completely butt-ass naked. "What are you doing here?" I demanded, folding my arms over my chest.

"Well, well, no wonder your bodyguard is so taken with you. Those tits are spectacular." Her voice was husky, and it did weird things to my belly.

Truthfully, I'd hooked up with a female once before, and it had been hot, but I liked dick too much.

I glared. "What. Are. You. Doing. Here?" I repeated, low and harsh.

Autumn sighed, leaning back into the water. "Donovan had

a meeting with your pops. I'm just wasting time. It's not like your packmates are very…welcoming."

"Well get out," I demanded. "There's a reason why we don't want you here. And that includes in this river."

Her laugh was throaty, but she ignored me, turning to stroke lazily to the falls before tilting her head under the spray.

I ground my teeth together, taking a few steps back before running toward the edge. Diving hands first into the cool, fresh water, I opened my eyes, watching the tiny fish before me scurry away. Taking my time to walk my hands along the rocky bottom, knowing nothing untoward hid between the cracks and crevices, I wished I could hide under the water for hours.

Long enough for the Dockhills beta to get the fucking message and leave me alone.

When my lungs began to burn, I kicked my legs, propelling me to the surface. Sucking in a lungful of air, I pushed the errant strands of my midnight black hair from my face.

I didn't hear Autumn anymore, and spun, looking for the witch. When I didn't immediately spot her, I grinned to myself, triumphant.

Then a shadow stirred beneath the surface, a body shooting toward me. I dove out of the way, only for Autumn to pop back up, right in front of me. She smirked like a sly cat with a wriggling mouse caught between its paws.

"If you think you can outswim me, you clearly don't remember the laps race from the games last year."

I scowled. "An unfair advantage considering the Dockhills Pack is bordered by a massive lake."

Her eyes sparkled with amusement. "I could teach you a few things, Carvingwood," she purred.

I wrinkled my nose in disgust. "Are you seriously hitting on me? You know I prefer my fucks with cocks, right?"

She snorted. "I could make you forget about that useless appendage in a single night."

My useless, neglected clit decided that moment to throb. I seriously needed to get laid. And my pussy needed to get the hint that it was not going anywhere near a Dockhills loser.

"I'm good, thanks. I'd rather eat every pussy from here to the Badlands than ever touch yours." Leaving her with that mic-drop moment, I moved toward the edge to scrub the dirt off my skin. I'd still need a shower when I got home since the run back would just make me dirty again.

This was supposed to be my alone place where I could go to think and just breathe without the stress of the pack being on the verge of fracturing. But this stupid bitch just had to go and fuck it up.

But the niggling question at the back of my mind finally pushed its way to the forefront. When I spun, I found Autumn along the opposite bank floating on her back. Pert, pink nipples pointed to the sky. She literally had no shame. Not that shifters ever really did, but Autumn was a kind of bold that people either aspired to, or were violently discomforted by.

Sensing me watching her, she found her feet, casting me a knowing smile.

"What business does your alpha have with mine?" I asked.

She clucked her tongue in admonishment. "I'd have told you if you'd been nice."

Before I could either spew vitriol or choke her to death, Syr appeared through the trees, fully dressed but slightly winded.

His eyes went from Autumn to me, and agitation shown in everything from his balled fists to his darkened expression. "Your parents want you."

CHAPTER FOUR

Dani

I climbed out, forcing myself not to try to hide my nudity, though Syr looked away, holding out a folded towel to me. He'd carried it in human form, the extra set of clean clothes tucked inside.

I took it wordlessly, pulling the clothes out and setting them on a rock while I wrapped the towel around my body. Wringing out my hair, I asked, "What's going on."

"Well, I'll take that as my cue to leave, since my alpha is going to be needing me very soon," Autumn chirped far too gleefully as she pulled herself out of the river.

She wrapped a towel she'd clearly brought with her around her own body before stalking toward the trees, a bag slung over her slim shoulder. Catching my eye when she passed, she blew me a kiss that made me roll my eyes.

I waited a few minutes for her to get far enough away before I started to dress. My feet were still bare, but that was nothing unusual.

Buttoning my jeans, I gusted a breath. "So what's up? Did Alphahole tell my parents I tried to punch his smug face?"

"I don't know," Syr said tightly. I spared him only one more glance before tossing the damp towel over my neck.

We started through the trees, picking up speed the deeper we went. Brittle needles crunched under my feet, though I barely felt it. Leaping over roots, I held tight to my towel, reveling in the cool air that rushed over my face and tugged at my damp hair.

The edge of the forest came into view, marked by my pile of discarded clothing. Slowing, I snagged them from the ground, shaking them free of debris. Syr was unusually quiet, his playful demeanor somber.

Knocking my shoulder against his, I smirked. "Too bad you ran off instead of coming to the water hole with me."

It was our spot. A place we'd hung out together for over a decade.

He grabbed my arm, forcing me to face him. "Whatever reason Donovan has for being here can't be good. The games aren't meant to start for two weeks."

I shrugged. "Maybe he wants to propose some new trade or something."

Syr rose a brow that said, *you really can't be that stupid.* "Dockhills doesn't trade with anyone. They're the biggest and most self-sufficient pack. They only compete in the games to show off, not to build relations."

I shrugged. "I'm just trying to be pragmatic."

"They both looked too self-satisfied. Whatever it is, it's not good," Syr answered.

We stopped at the entrance to the town hall, a plain building built to look like a large, brick house; the steepled roof pitching it higher than any of the other houses for the sake of distinction.

Syr grabbed my hand, threading his fingers through mine before pulling me forward. I hadn't even realized I was digging my heels in until that moment. With a sigh, I followed, pulling the door open when we reached it.

Javier, my dad's oldest friend, stood just inside the doors. He flashed me a blinding white smile, his mocha eyes alight with a brilliance that dazzled both males and females alike.

"Hey, princess," he greeted. "They're just through there." Indicating down the hall.

"Do you know what it's about?" I asked in a hushed voice.

His smile faded. "I heard bits and pieces."

My stomach churned with nervousness. Straightening, I marched toward whatever accusations the Dockhills alpha wanted to throw my way. I wouldn't be cowed by him.

Syr reached the door first and pulled it open. Three faces turned toward me, one of them looking utterly punch-able with a grin curving his lips at the sight of me.

"Come in, Dani," my father said. His expression gave nothing away, but my mother bit her bottom lip. Something she only did when she was agitated.

When Syr attempted to step in after me, my dad held up a hand to stop him. "Just Dani, I'm afraid."

My brows creased and I looked over my shoulder at my best friend. His gaze—fixed on Donovan—was lethal. Grabbing his hand, I gave it a reassuring squeeze. "I'll see you in a bit."

"Take Javier and the two of you do a perimeter sweep." My father's voice held the command only an alpha could give.

Syr lowered his glare, nodding once—almost imperceptibly. He turned, pulling the door shut behind him. Locking me in with Donovan Dockhills.

"Let's sit," my mother suggested, steering her husband by the arm toward the sofas. At the back was an empty, stone fireplace.

Taking a seat across from my parents, Donovan dropped onto the cushion beside me, far closer than I'd have liked. Dad rested his forearms on his knees and sighed. "I know you're aware, as well as the rest of us, that we haven't had a Chaos in nearly a decade."

I nodded, feeling wary of the strange topic.

Dad continued. "With wolves either choosing not to mate or fruitlessly waiting for their fated mate, it's affected the birthrate in all the packs in Chaos Valley."

"To be frank, at this rate, the wolves will become extinct," Donovan interjected.

My hackles rose and I stood. "You had better not be suggesting what I think you're suggesting."

"Sit down, Daniella," my mother ordered, but not unkindly. There was an apology in her eyes.

Deep down, I knew what was coming, but I couldn't will my body out the door.

"Donovan has come here to ask for your consideration as his

mate." My father spoke, but I barely heard the words that followed. "The two of you would produce strong wolves. Capable of leading future packs. The union would be forfeit in the event of a future Chaos should either one or both of you were to be properly mated to another. In exchange, the Dockhills Pack has agreed to share resources, including trained wolves to help hunt down those organizing the mate auctions."

My head whipped to the side as I fixed an incredulous look on Donovan who lounged in the high-back chair with ease.

"So let me get this straight," I cut in. "You'll only help stop the trafficking of humans and wolves if I agree to carry your pups?" My voice bordered on hysteria.

Donovan's face was finally void of amusement, switching to intensity while he rose to his feet. Eyes blazing like twin flames, he stepped closer until he was very clearly invading my space before saying coldly, "Just because I never agreed to teaming up with Carvingwood doesn't mean I haven't scoured the valley for auctions and kidnappings. I'm willing to work together seeing as we'd have an alliance of sorts." His lips curled, baring his teeth. There was nothing friendly about his smile, but I didn't back down. We kept our eyes locked on each other in challenge.

"How does this benefit my pack? We don't need anything from you," I snapped.

"Donovan has access to useful technology which would allow us to gain information on strongholds without going in blind. His pack also developed communication devices that allow for distress signals to be sent to other pack members when senses fail. That way if any of our own are taken, we can locate them easily."

Folding my arms over my chest, I cocked a hip to one side. "And why not make that available for everyone anyway? That's not something you should be keeping to yourself if you care at all about the future of wolves."

Donovan lifted a single dark brow. "Do you think any of that is cheap? It costs more than your pack would ever be able to afford and just handing it out would more than bankrupt my own pack."

My heart twisted painfully. That sort of technology was invaluable. Last year we lost twelve girls—some minors, and some new into early adulthood. We recovered only two of them. It haunted my parents every day knowing daughters and wives were sold into the hands of wicked men.

"I'm not going to be your breeding machine. You could use any one of the hundreds of willing bitches always following you around, you don't need me," I answered stubbornly.

"Daniella." My father spoke my name firmly but so quietly I might have missed it since Donovan chose that moment to chuckle.

I pivoted my entire body toward my parents, pleading with my eyes for there to be some way—any other way—to make this deal that didn't involve selling my body. My mom looked remorseful, but my father just looked irritated.

Was he seriously expecting me to do this?

"What if the mating was broken after five years?" my father asked, looking at me but his words were meant for the infuriating male behind me.

Donovan rested a hand on my shoulder, gripping me tightly

before yanking me back against his hard chest.

"Breaking the mating bond is not an option, Evan. I will mate for life. If, by some miracle, the Chaos were to take place during our lifetimes and Daniella were to be mated to another, I would agree to a separation. But the bond must remain."

Whirling, I knocked his hand off my shoulder and snarled. "I would rather die than be your mate."

His lips pursed, eyes flaring with bright. "Would you rather our packs die? Would you sacrifice the humans in the nearby towns who have no means of defense? And your own packmates, would you allow them to be taken for the sake of keeping away from me?" The dark, rough quality of his voice had the hairs on the back of my neck standing on end.

I wanted to say yes, that none of those things meant anything to me, but he knew as well as I did that there was only one way forward.

"You're despicable," I growled.

His lips tugged up to one side. "You have no idea, Little Wolf."

Shooting a look at my parents that no doubt showed everything I was feeling, I stormed out, running down the hall and back out into the evening set alight by the setting sun.

My wolf tore free, ripping my clothes to shreds and my paws were moving, carrying me into the forest. A shout followed me, but I ignored it, pounding the ground to get me further.

How could my parents ask me to do this? To bond myself to a man that I couldn't stand. To carry his pups and be some dutiful alpha's mate. That wasn't me.

Rage tore through my chest, dragging a low snarl from my

maw. Night was settling on the Valley, casting the trees in long, eerie shadows.

The rushing of water over rocks sounded from just up ahead, growing louder until the edge of the bank came into view. I picked up speed, the tension in my limbs growing as I prepared to leap over it.

A furry body crashed into mine right before I could launch myself into the air, sending us both tumbling. I lashed out with bared teeth, sinking into golden, familiar fur.

The yelp of surprise came a moment too late. We rolled off the edge, clawing for purchase on the rocky side before cool water rushed up to greet us. I melted back to human in an instant, the surface of the current pushing me down while I held my breath. My feet worked for several seconds until they hit the bottom and I propelled myself back up, gasping when air caressed my face.

I swam to the side, latching onto the rocks for support. Syr paddled toward me, shaking his shaggy brown hair out like a dog, sending droplets flying. "Where the hells were you planning on going once you crossed the river?" he demanded, though he didn't look mad. His arms and legs worked, allowing him to tread water.

"My parent are selling me off to the alpha of Dickhills," I said with a bitter laugh by way of answer. "They want me to be his mate and carry his pups like I'm some kind of brood mare."

Syr went still. "Why?" His voice was half growl, half rasp.

My body shook from the adrenaline still coursing through my veins. I shrugged. "He has technology we need and apparently I'm the price."

I still didn't understand why. Sure, I was the daughter of an alpha, but I wasn't the only one. Other pack alphas had daughters similar to my age.

"What if you took a mate?" Syr said slowly, his dark brown gaze boring into me. "He couldn't claim you if you were already mated."

I scoffed. "Well for one, some wolves have more than one mate, so I doubt that would deter him, but who would be stupid enough to bond to me just to save me from Donovan? It's not a fair trade."

"I would." He answered quickly and so passionately, I sucked in a sharp breath. Staring up at him, clutching the jagged rocks while the river tugged at my body, I saw the change in his demeanor. The way his chest puffed up the way males did when they were trying to show a potential mate they would be cared for.

"Syr," I whispered, "you can't mean that."

His brows crashed down in a frown. "Why are you so fucking dense, Dani? I've been practically waving a neon sign in front of your face for the past year that I want you."

My eyes widened, attention switching from his intense stare, dropping to his full, sensual lips. We suddenly seemed so much closer. If I leaned in just a little, those lips would be on mine.

He seemed to be on the same wavelength as me because his head tilted down ever so slowly. I blinked, clearing myself of such an absurd notion. My toes fit between the stones under the water before I pulled myself up, climbing out as fast as I could manage.

The clearing was almost completely dark now, with stars beginning to dot the deep purple sky above. Beside me, Syr hopped onto the bank, both of us naked. He grimaced down at his forearm which bled lightly from the bite I'd given him when he scared me. It would be healed within minutes now that he was out of the water, but still I felt bad.

"Sorry about the bite."

"Don't worry about it," he answered flatly, getting to his feet.

The flex and pull of his muscled chest and arms drew my attention, making my stomach flip. I'd seen him without a shirt hundreds of times, but I couldn't deny that it felt different now, especially after his declaration. Striding toward the hollow in the tree where extra stores of clothes and blankets were kept, he brought back two woolen blankets and some clothes.

We dressed in silence and I wrapped the blanket around my body, even though the temperature was still stifling. My gaze caught on the sinewy movement of muscle on Syr's back as he tugged a shirt on over his head.

Both sets of clothes were ill fitting, but they just had to get us back to the houses.

"Come on," he said, turning, but not looking at me. "We need to get you back before your parents come looking for you."

I nodded, heading through the trees with him. The awkwardness was near suffocating, but I didn't know how to fix it.

Before reaching the edge of the forest, I grabbed his hand, tugging him to a stop.

"If there was anyone I'd want to choose as my mate, it's you, Syr. I was just…thrown. I mean, we've been friends since we were kids—"

"You don't have to explain, Dani." Syr's voice was gentle as he cupped my face, rough palm scratching but feeling…right against my skin. "With or without the Chaos, Daniella, you'd be the one for me. My mate, whether chosen or fated."

My eyes stung with unshed tears. I leaned into his palm, clutching the blanket tighter around myself. "You know I love you, Syracuse Milton," I breathed. "But I can't get out of this deal."

His throat bobbed and I could see emotions brewing within the depths of his dark eyes. He stroked his thumb over my bottom lip, sending a shiver down my spine. "You don't know me at all if you think I'm going to just hand you over to that bastard."

I let out a humorless laugh. "We need this technology." I shook my head. "It's not about what you, or me, or what we could be in an ideal world. This is a sacrifice I *have* to make in order to make sure no more women in this pack are lost to the rogues. We'd be able to find them right away and save them."

Syr's jaw tightened visibly, but he nodded in understanding. My chest ached with the loss of my best friend, because after tonight—his confession—things would be different no matter what. Not to mention the fact that I'd have to move south.

But also, I felt keenly the loss of what might have happened if I hadn't charged out of the river. If under different circumstances, I'd allowed Syr to kiss me—if I'd accepted his offer and became his mate—how different my life could be in comparison to what it soon would be. But even if he'd come out and asked me in his truck earlier, I would have said no.

I'd be alpha when the time was right, but I'd envisioned Syr at my side. We'd talked about ruling the Carvingwood Pack together since our friendship had first taken shape. But as mates? It hadn't occurred to me until this moment.

When I was walking toward my future with a man I would rather stab than bed.

A figure sprinted into the trees, coming toward us, and I scented Javier before he appeared. He looked uneasy when he took us in, gaze flicking to our wet hair and the blanket I held around myself.

Clearing his throat, he shifted his bulky, muscular frame from one side to the other before saying, "Your mother is requesting you hurry home to get ready. They'll be making the announcement right before the bonfire."

I swallowed hard, then nodded. Syr squeezed my arm, giving me a gentle smile before releasing me. Javier waited for me to pass him, walking me to my front door as though I might run again.

With my hand on the doorknob he said, "I know what you're giving up for your people. You've always been brave and kind, even though you hide it behind your tough girl façade. You'll make an incredible leader."

I scoffed. "I'll be a terrible breeding machine. Donovan Dockhills will regret his decision to buy me like an item. I'll make sure of it."

Javier flashed me a grin that was all teeth. "See that he does, girl."

CHAPTER FIVE

Dani

My mother shoved me into the shower, threatening to cut off the supply of hot water if I wasn't out in twenty minutes.

I used all twenty, staring through the steam-filled room, letting my resolve solidify.

The price for the technology we needed might be my body, but I'd be damned if I took his demands lying down. No, the price for me would come with hellsfire, teeth, and claws.

Think you can bargain for my submission, Dickhills? You've got another thing coming.

When I stepped out of the shower, I wrapped myself in a plush, deep-purple towel before padding out of the bathroom, immediately spying the silver dress laid out on the bed. It was covered in glittering rhinestones that made up swirling, chaotic patterns. The slit on one side was thigh-high and the entire thing was strapless.

"Wow, Mom, why not just send me out in my underwear," I groused. The dress had been an impulse purchase when I'd gone shopping with some of the other girls. I'd doubted I'd ever find an occasion to wear it, but clearly my mother had found such an event.

Too bad I still had no intentions on wearing it. I strode over to my walk-in closet and pulled the door open, going straight for a sheer, lowcut black top, a pair of tight, sexy leather pants, studded combat boots, and a matching leather jacket.

I dressed quickly, smirking at the image of myself in the full-length mirror. My blood-red bra was just slightly visible beneath my shirt, and my breasts were pushed up high. Feminine and badass. It wasn't far from my normal attire, but if Donovan expected me to waltz around in a skimpy dress and act like the simple female that would happily spread her thighs for that prick, he was in for a rude awakening.

The faintest sound inside my room caught my attention and I whirled silently, grabbing one of the knives hanging on the wall. Creeping toward the closet door, I paused, waiting.

The scent knocked into me at the exact moment a massive dark figure lunged around the door. Donovan's hand gripped my throat, pushing me into the wall right as my blade kissed his neck. His other hand held my wrist captive above my head.

He smirked down at me as though he'd fully expected my reaction.

"What the fuck are you doing in my room?" I snarled.

Leaning down, his nose brushed my cheek and I heard him inhale. "What was my future soul tied doing with the bodyguard down at the river?" he asked instead.

My heart beat hard in my chest. I let the edge of the knife dig into his skin a hint more, feeling satisfaction when the skin split just a little, and a bead of crimson welled to the surface. "Are you spying on me?" I asked incredulously.

His nostrils flared, golden eyes burning brighter. "I can smell him on you still," he rumbled, his voice part growl and menace.

The corner of my lips kicked up. I thought about playing him and lying about what transpired, but his fingers tightened in warning.

"Don't fucking lie to me, Little Wolf," he drawled. "I'll know if you do."

I shook my head. "Is this how it's going to be, Donovan? You threaten me, expecting me to cower at your feet? Because I won't."

He chuckled—a dark sound that was somewhere between velvet and a thunderous crash of waves. It sent a tendril of heat licking through my veins, settling between my thighs. His lips caressed my jaw, skimming back toward my ear and an unbidden shiver rolled over me. "I have no interest in women without teeth. I'll threaten you all I like because I know it makes you wet."

I glanced down, seeing the evidence of his own arousal plainly straining against his jeans and ground my teeth. Without warning, I threw my forehead forward, cracking it against his nose. He swore, but didn't release me, instead drove his hips into mine, grinding his hard length against my damned, traitorous pussy.

My clit throbbed and I had to fight the urge not to lean into him. Blood trickled from his nostrils and with a satisfied smirk, he took a step back, letting me go.

"In front of your pack, you'll smile and pretend this is what you want. Because if you don't, the deal is off. You'll spend the evening at my side, playing nice. When the first shipment of communicators arrive in the next week, we'll have the ceremony. You can be every bit the ungrateful, loathsome bitch I know you to be, but we will complete the bond before we journey south."

When I opened my mouth to argue he held a hand up, cutting me off. "If I had it my way I'd rip those tight fucking pants off you and bend you over this dresser right here, but I'll give you a few days to accept what's coming."

I shook my head in disgust. "You can't force me to have sex with you. I'll tear your fucking throat out if you come near me."

Donovan stepped into me again, forcing me to crane my neck to meet his swirling, molten gaze. "Keep telling yourself that, Little Wolf. Every time I get close, I see your pupils dilate. I hear your breath hitch when you scent me. And I can smell when you're wet for me, like you are right. This. Second." He inhaled deeply as if to emphasize his point. "If I dipped my hand down those impossibly tight pants and slid my finger inside you, you'd be a moaning mess. I've had my eye on you for the past three years and it's obvious you've been watching me. I came here to take what I want. And I *always* get what I want."

He stepped away, leaving me with rage churning my gut and my heart racing faster than my wolf could run.

And fuck that infuriating man straight to the hells because I could feel the slickness between my legs. I hated that he made me respond to his cruelty in such a way.

What did it say about me?

"Fuck off," I said through gritted teeth. "I may have agreed to this deal, but I'm not letting your nasty ass dick inside me until I'm damn well ready."

He barked a laugh. "We'll see how long it takes before you're begging me for it." With that he turned, striding away from me as if I didn't have a knife in my hand that I could bury into his back. "I'll see you out there in ten minutes."

He lifted my window, slipping out into the night that was lit with hundreds of string lights. I stomped over to it, slamming it closed and flicking the lock to ensure he didn't have access to my bedroom again.

I scanned the grounds right outside, but he was nowhere in sight. My mother chose the next moment to burst in.

"What in all the name of Chaos are you wearing?" she screeched. "And your hair!"

I let her push me along to the bathroom where she helped curl the mane of wild waves, spraying them with enough hairspray that I'd have to take two more showers just to get it all out. While she stood in the corner, arms folded over her chest and lips pursed, I applied some dramatic, sweeping eyeliner to the tops of my lids, a light shimmering shadow, and lip gloss.

When I was done, I spun, giving my mother a questioning look. Her shoulders sagged slightly, expression softening.

"Oh Dani," she whispered. "You know your father and I love you, right?"

I bit my bottom lip, not trusting myself to speak and nodded.

Tears brimmed her eyes. "We never would have even considered such an offer if there was another way. Trust me, we've looked into that sort of technology several times this year, but none of it was accessible or affordable."

Taking a deep breath, I said, "I know. Whatever it takes to keep this pack safe, I'll do it. I wanted to be alpha, and this is exactly the sort of decision they'd make."

A tear slipped down my mother's beautiful face. She rushed to me, wrapping me in her arms. I buried my face into her similar dark curls, breathing in the scent that had soothed and comforted me my whole life.

We held each other for several moments and I willed myself not to cry. I wouldn't break down over this. I couldn't.

When we broke apart, I offered my mother a reassuring smile. "It's going to be okay, Mom. I'll come visit as often as I can."

She looked skeptical, but nodded. Taking my hand, we left the bathroom. At the front door, she gave me a light squeeze.

Then we each pulled our shoulders back, lifting our chins to face what was to come. I let my gaze harden. Until I was in front of everyone, I'd remain me.

He couldn't take away the hatred I felt boiling in my blood, no matter how much my body craved him.

I just needed to hold onto that hatred if I was going to survive.

CHAPTER SIX

Dani

Lights strung between trees and houses illuminated the path. Chatter created a layer of noise that was highlighted only by the odd hoot of an owl.

Mom took the lead, winding us deeper into the town. Hundreds of people waited in the center, standing around a massive tower of logs and twigs. I scanned the crowd for Syr, spotting him near the center-most structure. Our gazes clashed, and I felt every ounce of his raw anger. It wasn't directed at me, I knew, but I couldn't help the desire aching within me to fix it. Of course, the only way to do that would be to send Donovan packing, and I couldn't do that.

Beside Syr, in the gazebo wrapped in lights, stood three familiar figures. My father and Javier stood on either side of a figure that somehow exuded superiority. Somehow, the shadows clung to him.

But I could see the heat burning in Donovan's molten gold eyes. The intensity of his stare combined with the muggy night air had my own temperature rising.

When we approached the steps, the dull roar of voices and laughter died down to silence so acute, our footsteps seemed to boom through the area. I kept my chin up, looking past my father, as far from Donovan as I could without making it incredibly obvious.

My mother approached, and Dad pecked her cheek, roping an arm around her waist before pulling her tight to his side. I took my place beside her, thankful I no longer faced my betrothed of sorts.

"Carvingwood!" Dad boomed in his alpha voice, demanding every eye and ear be focused on him. "Tonight we celebrate the arrival of another summer. As is tradition, we use the coming weeks to focus on our pack as one family, as well as the unity among the other packs of Chaos Valley. Though we all feel the loss of the Chaos strongly, we must continue to forge our paths forward. We will not sit by and waste our precious years of growth, innovation, and development longing for an event we cannot control.

"To adapt to these changes the world has forced on our kind, it is wisest that we embrace whomever we choose as mates, rather than relying on fated mates to be revealed."

A murmur of discontented voices slipped through the people standing out, looking toward my father—their leader. But he seemed unfazed, pushing ahead with the point I knew all too well was coming.

"To prove that the rise of our imminent future is for every unmated generation, my own daughter, Daniella—" He reached across my mother, grabbed my arm and pulled me in front of him. Donovan stepped up to my side, weaving his fingers through mine. Sparks shot through my body and my breath caught."—will be bonded to the Alpha of Dockhills."

There was a brief pause, apprehension clear on their faces. But when Donovan lifted our hands, smiling wide and victorious, the town center erupted in cheers. Clearly they bought his act, but I knew the truth.

Giving my hand a squeeze, he hissed, "Smile, Little Wolf," out of the corner of his mouth.

I squeezed back, hoping to crush his fingers to dust as I pasted on a pleasant smile that may have even passed for one of excitement. Donovan simply chuckled that irritatingly sensual sound.

My gaze snagged on one face that had come into view, and my heart sank. Syr's glare was angled directly at Donovan, who either didn't notice, or didn't care. He whipped around, carving a path through the throng until he was out of view.

"And now," my father announced, "we will light the bonfire."

When everyone's attention shifted to the pyre, Donovan and I let go of each other's hands like they were poisonous.

The flame was tossed onto the pile and almost instantly, it caught, blazing bright and hot. Instead of fearing it, however, I wished it would slink across the ground and devour me whole.

Donovan leaned close, his breath feathering the top of my head. "Stay close, Little Wolf."

I wanted to snap at him, even if it was with my fangs, but I didn't get the chance to do so before I was shuffled down the steps and into the heaving mass of people eagerly waiting to congratulate us.

Women hugged me despite never having done so before, while men clapped Donovan on the back like he'd slain a dragon or something. Some of them were amongst my father's guard, like me, trained to protect the pack. Maybe in their eyes, after having their asses handed to them by me over and over, I was something like a dragon needing to be brought down by some valiant knight.

My anxiety increased as the night wore on in a blur of drinks, snacks, and dancing. Donovan and I had gotten out of most of the dances until a slow, smooth, and sensual song began to play and my mother pushed me toward him with a whispered, "Just this one; you're starting to look suspicious."

I clamped my jaw shut hard to keep from spilling every curse word I knew when Donovan smirked down at me, taking my hand in his, the other snaking around my back and pulling me flush against his chest.

His subtle, masculine scent enveloped me, and I took the opportunity to take in the black T-shirt that wrapped around his muscled chest beneath the leather jacket he usually wore.

Internally, I rolled my eyes at myself because it didn't matter how good the prick looked or felt beneath my fingertips. He'd still bargained for my body. I hated him, and that would never change, even if he stood in front of me completely naked.

"Imagining me without these clothes, Little Wolf?" Donovan teased and my eyes flew wide, snapping up to his.

Before I could stammer my denial, a flash of surprise flitted across his gaze. He tsked. "So you *were* imagining me naked." His smile was wide and mischievous. "I have to admit I'm surprised—"

"You don't know shit, Donovan," I snapped. My cheeks heated against my will, and I hoped he was too focused on stroking his own ego to see it.

He barked a laugh before dipping his head to speak against my ear. "I can assure you, the reality is better than the fantasy."

I scoffed, pushing away from his hard chest. The sudden action drew several confused gazes and I hastened to make an excuse. "Sorry, I'm feeling a bit light-headed. Too much wine, I'm sure. I'll be right back."

I hurried from the clearing, snagging a glass of water from a tray carried by a pretty, petite blond girl who was only twelve or thirteen years old. She startled at my aggressive momentum, but I didn't falter.

Through the town toward the forest, I followed Syr's scent, already knowing where he would be.

I climbed up the rough limbs with ease, my hands and feet knowing where to move instinctually. Through the thick shield of needle-covered branches, the bottom of the treehouse came into view. Rungs appeared, nailed into the trunk for support when the bigger limbs thinned.

I smelled the faint taint of smoke in the air just before my head popped in through the opening. It was far darker up here above the lights, making the orange glow of Syr's lit cigarette visible.

I sighed. He didn't smoke often, usually just when he was stressed. I didn't mind the smell, and climbed up into the wooden structure, making my way to where he sat, with one knee bent, the arm holding the cigarette resting on top. Wordlessly, I sat on his other side, laying my head on his shoulder.

We didn't speak, but I heard everything he wanted to say. I wished I could give him what he wanted, but more so, I longed for the freedom I'd had this morning before all of this had happened. Less than a day ago, I'd believed I'd make my own way, choosing what lovers I wanted and perhaps taking a mate if I ever fell in love, but now I was little more than the currency used in a business transaction.

There was no more freedom for me—at least for now. If anything, I was more anxious for a Chaos to take place at some point in my life. If a true mate was revealed, then I would be free.

Well, free from Donovan.

A high-pitched squeal rocketed up past the open window, followed by a pop. Bursts of color painted the sky, one after the other.

Syr draped an arm around my shoulders, though it felt possessive. My own dominance made it difficult not to shake him off, but I conceded this small gesture for the sake of argument. I'd never be his the way he wanted me to be, so if just for a moment, we could pretend we were just a boy and a girl with nowhere to be but snuggled up together like we had a thousand times before, watching the fireworks.

When they ended and cheers rang up from the ground, I yawned. Syr pressed a kiss to my temple, and heat spilled through my limbs like honey.

"Let's get you to bed before the whole pack notices you're

missing," he said gruffly.

I nodded, following him down the tree. He walked me to my front door in silence, but stopped at the bottom of the porch. My brows dipped together, but I reined in my hurt. It would be considered inappropriate now for him to come in and stay in my bed with me, but part of me didn't care because my bonding with Donovan wasn't real.

Physical touch was essential for wolves. When we were younger, Syr and I had curled up together during sleepovers often. It happened less frequently now that we had others fill our beds from time to time, but I found myself wishing for his heat and comfort.

Maybe then I wouldn't feel quite so alone.

We said goodnight and he vanished down the pathway, hands stuffed into his pockets. In my bedroom, I stripped down to nothing, then slipped on a loose band T-shirt. Not bothering to shower out the super-glue-like hairspray, I crawled into bed and let sleep claim me.

I ran through the forest, feeling the slap of branches against my skin, twigs tearing at my clothes. My hair. Mist crawled lazily over the reaching, twisted roots on the soft ground.

Chest heaving with labored breaths, I glanced over my shoulder. Three dark forms sprinted after me, their eyes glowing with menace. Hunters stalking their prey. I could hear them getting closer, yet their movements were near silent.

My heart hammered—a drum beat sounding the rhythm of my demise. Inside, my wolf was howling to be set free. But I was too far from home. If they caught me, I'd be naked. Vulnerable.

And I could feel their hunger. It was me they craved.

Just a little further, *I urged, forcing my body to carry me faster. Instinct helped me navigate the unfamiliar surroundings. Yet no matter how hard I pushed myself, I couldn't seem to lose my pursuers.*

The moment the first one shifted, snarling his rage, I choked out a desperate cry, allowing my own transformation and hoping it would be enough.

My paws flew over the dirt and rocks with greater ease, and the sound of three beasts thundering after me had me winding between narrow gaps, zigging and zagging with all the effort my training had afforded me.

A howl of frustration and warning rose up through the trees. It was further behind than before, which was all that mattered. Internally, I cheered, but didn't let up my pace.

You can't run from me, Little Wolf.

I heard Donovan's voice in my mind and sat bolt right up in bed, blankets tangled around my waist. My breaths were desperate gasps for air, lungs tight.

Slowly, I registered my darkened bedroom.

And the cool breeze that had my curtains fluttering slightly. My frantic heart stopped dead.

Had the bastard been in my room when I slept? I wasn't sure how that was a possibility considering I'd locked it myself before leaving.

I tossed off the blankets holding me hostage and stomped over to my window, slamming it shut. After locking it once more, I glared down at the ground below, but it was of course, empty.

Settling back in bed, I allowed my heart to steady, convincing myself to get a few more hours of sleep before I had to be up in the morning.

It took at least an hour to let the haunting dream—which was no doubt a projection of my current state of mind—fade away and for sleep to claim me once again.

CHAPTER SEVEN

Syr

I tossed and turned, replaying the night's events over and over in my head. If I'd just fucking sucked it up and asked her to marry me like I'd planned weeks ago, Donovan wouldn't have been able to blow into Carvingwood and blackmail her into tying herself to him.

He was going to take her away from me. The only thing I held dear in this life.

Dani was a beacon of light in the darkness after my father died. A raven-haired beauty that could light up a whole fucking room when she smiled.

She was my moon in the darkest part of the forest. The stars lighting my way.

I rolled over, reaching under the bed for the old, tattered

shoebox. Setting it in my lap, I turned on the lamp above my side table.

Lifting the lid, I stared down at the faded pieces of folded paper. They weren't organized, so I selected one at random before setting the box aside to unfold the paper. The young, choppy scrawl told me it was one of the first notes Dani and I ever exchanged back in elementary school.

Dear Syracuse,

I hope my mom packed something good for lunch today, I'm starving. What did your mom pack for you?

I hope your after-school detention isn't terrible. You really shouldn't have hit Michael when he kept yanking on my ponytail. He thinks he's big and bad, but I bet he'll cry like a little girl the first time he shifts. Hey, maybe I can stay after school with you!

I chuckled at Dani's words, though I'd read them a hundred times over. Setting that one aside, I reached for another. This one was clearly written later, the date at the top made my stomach clench.

Syr,

Okay, I hate seeing u look sad so I'm gonna distract u. R u ready? I am so sore from training yesterday. My dad and Javier have been kicking my ass. Wanna go for a swim later? U can have dinner with us, we can do homework together and then u could stay the night if ur mom says it's okay.

Now smile dammit. If u don't, I'll have to stand up on the desks n dance. And no one wants to see that.

Love, Dani

P.S. Do you miss him?

My breath stalled in my lungs as I swallowed hard. It was the anniversary of my father's death. Whenever the date got close and my mood shifted, she always seemed to sense it and knew exactly how to cheer me up. She got me through some of the hardest days of my life.

I shuffled through the notes and plucked a third from the box, relaxing against the headboard of my bed.

With the smaller scrap of paper open, I scanned the now elegant hand-writing of a young woman.

Hey. Yeah, I'm ready for the pack run tonight but I can't sleep over after. I have a date tonight. Movie night this weekend though! Xo

I felt the punch of jealousy hit me even harder than it had the first time I'd read it. The paper was crumpled from the times I'd balled it, preparing to throw it away, but I never could. It was that weekend we'd stayed in, watching movies until the dark part of the morning. Her slender frame was curled up against my chest and I'd heard her murmur my name in her sleep.

I had no idea how long I'd stared down at her full pink lips parted with sleep, daring myself to kiss them. But I'd determined the first time I kissed her she'd be fully conscious and willing.

A growl rumbled in my chest as I threw the sheets back, getting to my feet in a huff. I threw my jeans on, though I wasn't planning to wear them long.

Outside, music still played softly in the square. The more rowdy party goers were still in attendance, but I passed by the side of the house, dodging their notice. Once out of view, I removed what little clothing I wore and called forth my wolf.

A rumbling shook my beast's chest and then I was running into the forest. My paws pounded the moss-covered floor, snapping twigs and pine needles. I ran hard, pushing my body to get it all out.

She will never be mine.

He stole her from me.

She'll be gone forever. Far from me.

A howl clawed its way free, and I bayed to the moon all the pain and loss that swirled through me like a tornado, tearing the air from my lungs and trying to suffocate me.

And for a moment, I wanted to let it do just that.

Then I dug my claws into the dirt, halting my manic run as though I could flee the future hanging over all our heads.

She wasn't his yet.

I still had time.

Trotting back into the town, I wove through the darker parts while hope pushed away the agony of potentially losing Daniella.

My wolf sat back on its hind legs, and I stared up at her window, willing her to wake. To open the window and let me come in like I did most nights.

A dim light flicked on as though by my command. I paused, cocking my head to the side. Had she sensed me? Was she having a hard time sleeping too?

I scented the bastard only a moment before I heard his voice. Whirling, I bared my teeth at the shadows, knowing he was there.

"Now what would the lap dog be doing outside my future mate's window?"

I wanted to claw his voice box from his neck. A snarl was my only answer.

Donovan stepped into the dimly illuminated pathway, smirking. His hands were in his pockets, and he stopped beside me. He gazed up at the window for a moment.

"If you do anything to interfere, I'll string your entrails from her window. And if the idea of her having to see that every day until we're in Dockhills isn't enough, just know that the bargain struck with your Alpha is contingent on her remaining untouched between now and then. If your pack loses this deal, you'll be left to fend for yourselves against The Silver Vipers and The Bone Crushers."

He lingered only a moment more after dropping that fucking bomb before he slid back into the darkness where he belonged.

The asshole.

My eyes shut, and a deep primal ache took root in my gut. I wouldn't do anything to cause Daniella harm.

With a final glance at the now darkened room, I padded back to my house, letting Donovan's words play over and over in my mind until sleep finally claimed me.

CHAPTER EIGHT

Brax

An eagle shrieked somewhere above the treetops, hidden by the early, misty morning. I stalked lightly through the forest, keeping my ears trained for any other sounds. The trail of footsteps left in the damp soil were still plainly visible, though they'd been left the day before. My hand inside my pocket wrapped around the warm locket.

I'm close, Esme, I swear it. Sending my thoughts to the trees where the eagle above might carry it into the afterlife, I set out once again, hunting my prey. Rogue bounded ahead, sniffing the trail, his brown tail swinging contentedly.

The hound was good company and seemed to like my wolf more than my human form. When I needed to make up a great deal of distance, we'd run together as beasts.

We kept a steady pace, pausing to ascertain the distance between us and the enemy. Their scent was weak but growing stronger with every hour. Tire tracks with the occasional footprints told me there were seven people. A truck pulling a trailer, if I was correct. When the day dissolved to night, we set up camp.

I could hike for days with only small breaks here and there, but Rogue, stubborn though he was, was thirteen and needed his rest. Besides, we both required to eat if we were going to be able to take down an entire ring of traffickers.

A few hours later, after hunting for our dinner and getting a fire hot enough to cook, I heard the faintest gurgle of a stream nearby. Rising to my feet, I cast a glance at Rogue lounging near the fire, still gnawing on a whole roasted pheasant.

"Stay, Rogue," I ordered in my best alpha voice.

He gave a grunt that I took to mean acknowledgement. Nodding sharply, I plucked my dagger from the dirt beside the rock and headed toward the sound of fresh water. The dirt caked to my sweaty skin was beginning to itch, and I was fairly certain the last time I'd washed was four days ago.

My wolf senses allowed me to navigate under low-hanging branches and between the thick underbrush.

When I emerged in the relative clearing, the moonless night cast its speckled navy blanket over the water, allowing only the slightest shimmers as it flowed over rocks. I stalked toward it, using the long weeds for handholds to step into the cool stream.

It only reached my waist, but I wasted no time cleansing my clothes, then stripping them off and tossing them to shore. The silken purple flowers that lazily waved in the gentle breeze were a type of buttercup that could be used for soap.

I snagged several, rubbing the petals into my skin to try to freshen my scent. Even a human could likely smell me from a few miles off.

Using a few more to rub against my scalp, I massaged the scented flower through the dark strands of my hair. The smell—something akin to vanilla—drew up a vague memory, though I couldn't place it.

After soaking for far too long, I waded out of the stream and wrung out my garments before pulling them back on.

Back at camp, Rogue was snoring, the fire reduced to embers. I rolled out my bed pack near the hound and settled onto it, letting the faint warmth from the fire dry my sodden clothes. Slowly, my eyelids grew heavy, the tantalizing scent lulling me into sleep.

I was back at the stream, but standing outside it, looking down. The moon ahead shone bright and full; very unlike how it had been earlier. And the clearing was larger, the pool deeper. The back of a naked woman was illuminated by the brightest rays of silver. Her hair was dark and black, like mine.

Cocking my head to the side, I breathed in the serene setting, watching the girl wash herself like some sort of creep.

But it was that scent.

Vanilla mixed with something else.

It was mouth-watering.

I cleared my throat, hoping not to startle the female. She jolted, whipping around in the shoulder-height water.

But when she faced me, she stole my breath away.

Shining eyes almost purple in the dim lighting and a face that was formed by the wings of my gods. Those eyes narrowed in accusation.

"Who the fuck are you?"

Her voice was velvety, yet her words so jagged and vicious. I couldn't help the way my brows shot up on my face. Then, I smiled. A fiery goddess bathed in the splendor of night.

And gods damned, she smelled like sin and divine perfection. Though her features seemed hazier than they did a moment ago, I could tell she was a fair bit younger than me.

"I am Braxton. I have traveled from the far north. What is your name?"

Scooping her mane of hair over one shoulder, the girl left the other exposed and deliciously bare. My mouth watered.

"I'm Daniella," she said skeptically. "Why are you here?"

I opened my mouth to explain, taking a step toward the calm waters to join her, when screams started.

The goddess of the stream didn't seem to hear them. And I knew why. I knew these screams. I'd heard them every night for the past decade.

I rushed forward, throwing myself into the stream, but it vanished beneath me and my body hit hard ground. A hiss of pain escaped me, while tongues of heat lapped at me, singing my flesh—burning through my clothes.

All around, fires raged. Daniella was gone.

They devoured homes while the villagers ran scared through the streets. Wicked men riding roaring motorcycles tore after my people. Shots rang out and one cry sounded above the rest.

It made my heart constrict as it always did.

Esme's pain carved through my body as I scrambled to my feet and ran. I knew where she'd be. At my family home in the middle of town.

I glanced only once at the lifeless body of my brother, Fenrick. Seeing his glassy, unblinking eyes yet again and knowing I was too late, only made my desperation to get to Esme before it was too late.

There was blood outside the door. Crackling, monstrous tides of bright flames climbed the walls. Acrid smoke billowed from the open windows upstairs.

A flash of her golden-brown hair and soot-covered skin as she tried to scream out the window for Mimi. For Fenrick. For me. Choking for air.

It cleaved my fucking soul into an innumerable number of fragments. And as I sprinted up the stairs, hearing the entire structure groan, about to give way, I knew I was too late.

But I kept running, my wolf bursting to the surface to try to get there faster.

When the house gave way, crumbling beneath the devil's fiery grip, I bellowed her name. The weight of it all came down on me, crushing my body.

Bones snapped, and unlike my true memory of that night, blackness did not sink its inky claws into me, pulling me down while my body healed some of the more serious injuries.

I crawled through the wreckage, broken, and screaming her name.

And again, where my current reality differed from my memories, I didn't have to search for hours only to come up empty handed. This cruel, twisted part of my mind had her small, cold form sandwiched between charred beams, and I pulled her free, cradling her to my chest. The guttural scream of a man who'd just lost everything poured into the night soaked with blood and fear.

My pack was attacked. Women and children were stolen; but most were dead.

My family was dead.

Esme was dead.

My eyes opened, but the cruel, haunting images didn't fade so soon. Like most mornings, I spent the first few hours reliving it all. Rogue stayed close, sensing my need for someone.

Anyone.

Because I was left alone in this fucked up world.

But I was not without purpose.

The men that stormed in, shredding my life to pieces weren't the worst of this world.

Because a man with an insatiable thirst for vengeance was a terrifying thing indeed.

CHAPTER NINE

Dani

I woke early to use up all the pent-up fury simmering in my veins on the training field. After the nightmare, I'd sunk back into my dreamscape. Just me in the cool river, bathing in the moonlight when one of the most breathtaking men I'd ever seen had approached.

His eyes—like the dark, starry night sky. They were mesmerizing. The ink that coated most of his dark skin, sliding like claws around his narrow waist. His dark hair that held a feather and several stones made him look wild. But there had been a sadness in his gaze before his features had morphed into pure terror.

And then he'd vanished. The dream had been hazy right up until I'd turned and saw the brutal man standing over me on the bank. He was intensely vivid, like I could have reached out and touched him for real.

It made sleeping more than a few extra hours next to impossible, allowing me to be the first one out of the house. My mind had raced.

Braxton, he'd said his name was.

Of course my mind had conjured up the most tantalizing morsel of a man after everything with Donovan and Syr. That was just my luck.

I sprinted through the obstacle course, diving beneath two flying blades that would have sliced me in the middle if I'd been standing a moment longer. Rolling back up to my feet, I whipped my torso around, sending my own knife flying. It hit right between the eyes on the target with an audible *thunk*.

A blast of flames roared toward me from a hidden cannon in the fake bushes and I lunged to the right with a choked gasp. Running again, I leapt over the axe that shot out at calf level. Sweat trickled down my forehead, stinging my eyes.

I heard the creak of another target flying toward me and I sunk my other blade into its center. Unsheathing two more, I kept my eyes peeled for more traps. Perhaps setting the course on its hardest setting hadn't been the wisest idea.

A net fell from above, narrowly missing me when I dove out of the way.

Targets shot up left and right.

Throw.

Turn.

Strike.

Spin.

Throw.

Dodge.

With my final blade in hand, I knew I was at the end, but it was too dark and there had to be at least one more trap. Creeping forward, I held the knife at my side, ready to let it fly if necessary.

A figure shot out from between the simulated trees, but it wasn't a target. The clang of a sword meeting the edge of my blade made my ears ring. I gritted my teeth, holding the attacker's sharp point from impaling my skull.

The barest hint of light illuminated the sharp features of the man baring down on me, and I snarled.

"What the hells are you doing here?"

Even in the dim lighting, I saw the curl of his lips. "I got bored just watching," Donovan answered simply.

I twisted, knocking my body into his as hard as I could, forcing him back a step and allowing me the distance I needed between us. My senses were dulled where he was involved.

"How long have you been watching me?" I demanded.

He swung the sword for my neck, and I used the hilt of my dagger, hitting the blunt side. That swung it away from my body while I took another step back. My legs hit faux greenery, letting me know the edge of the training course was just behind me.

"About an hour," Donovan said at last.

I huffed in frustration. "That's creepy as fuck."

He snorted a laugh. "There are windows for observation. So, clearly not that creepy. Besides, now that you're mine, you'll be watched constantly. Not just by me, but by my enemies as well."

I stumbled on my forward attack, and he took that opportunity to swing. Ducking just in time, I swiped the dagger for his shins. He leapt back, but I managed to nick the skin, earning a hiss of pain.

I got to my feet, baring my teeth in fury. "I." Swinging, for his chest, I advanced. "Am." Slash. Step. Jab. "Not." Swipe. Step. Kick. "Yours!"

My wild, uncontrollable anger made me reckless, but also relentless. Donovan took each of my attacks in stride, dodging and stepping back in time with my movements. As though we were a brutal dance of blades—swaying and writhing closer to bloodshed.

Donovan lunged a step, capturing my wrist. He stopped the blade less than an inch from his eye. "Think again, Little Wolf. The deal is made."

My knee came up in a petty move, but Donovan caught it with one hand beneath my thigh. I only had a split second to register why his smile turned wicked, my eyes widening before he yanked my leg high. I went back, landing on my ass, but I used the momentum to roll, swinging a leg out. It knocked Donovan back too, sword hitting the dirt path.

Lunging like a crazed woman, I scrambled onto his chest, digging my knees into his biceps, dagger clutched in both hands and raised above his chest.

His grin was cruel. Sadistic. I hesitated, because even though I hated him, putting the knife into his heart was a step too far. In an instant, he rolled us, pinning me on my back, the blade's edge pressed to my throat.

"Never. Hesitate," he breathed, lips hovering above mine.

My lip curled. "My humanity got in the way for a second. Won't happen again."

Our legs were tangled together, and I could feel every inch of his hard body pressed against me, including his growing erection. The realization sent tendrils of heat pooling at my core. His nose nuzzled my lower jaw and I heard him breathe me in.

Then his tongue licked up my cheek, making me gasp. Though my pussy gave a sudden throb, I swung my free fist for his jaw, connecting with a satisfying crack. He reeled back, growling low in his throat.

I got to my feet just as he did, and we stared each other down for a long minute. For a moment, given the sawing breaths his chest heaved with, I thought he might lose control of his wolf. His eyes were pools of liquid gold that scorched my body and heated my blood in ways I didn't want to acknowledge.

"Care to take this inside?" he asked, then paused. "Or we could deal with this right here. I know how much you like the dirt."

I quirked a brow at his statement, though my cheeks heated. "How could you possibly know what I like when you haven't taken two fucking seconds to think about anyone but yourself?"

He flashed his teeth in a smile. "You'd be surprised by what I know about you, Little Wolf."

My eyes narrowed. "You've not looked my way more than a handful of times my entire life. And each instance was simply for you to gloat about how much better your pack is."

Donovan rolled his eyes before bending over to collect his sword from the ground. "Perhaps it's you who hasn't spared a single moment to consider those around you. Or maybe you just see what you want to see and ignore the rest." He strode toward me, but I didn't move. I wouldn't back down. Not now. Not ever, so long as I drew breath. "Every year before the games you've taken some inconsequential wolf—or worse, human—to your bed, reeking of their scent for days on end. Yet here I am, weeks before the event and the only stench lingering on you is one that hasn't tasted that pretty pussy of yours."

I folded my arms over my chest. "How do you know I just haven't been fucked this week?"

The flash of possessiveness in his eyes made my heart stutter in my chest. *Damn, useless organ.*

"Your room is absent of any other males' scent."

I shrugged. "Could have just washed my sheets."

He smirked, not taking the bait. "No, I can smell your arousal, Little Wolf. You're ravenous for a hard fuck."

The bastard was right, and I hated it. "Well I still have a few days," I sneered. "Plenty of time to find someone to…help me out."

His hand was around my throat in an instant. Maneuvering his leg behind mine, he tried to force me onto my back. I used the momentum, twisting, and bringing Donovan's large body over my shoulder. It was awkward with someone so much taller and heavier than me, but it worked.

Well, that is, until he gripped my hips and pulled me down onto him, then rolled, hands flying out to capture mine and hold them hostage above my head. I huffed, wiggling against him to try to find the space for an opening, but all I could feel was Donovan's cock straining against his jeans.

"You're *mine*, Little Wolf," he said, the start of a growl rumbling in his chest. "If you need to get off, it'll be me you use. Do you understand?" His gaze bared down on me with its intensity.

I rolled my eyes. "No need to get all primal, we aren't fated mates."

His nostrils flared and I sensed he wanted to wring my neck. *Ha. Good.* With his knees caging my thighs, he kept most of his weight off me, but there was still no easy way out of his hold. He was incredibly strong.

Vaguely, I registered faint footsteps coming toward us. Donovan seemed unaffected, though I knew he heard the newcomer.

"Wow. This is hot," Autumn purred, coming into view. She smirked down at me, wearing a plain pink crop top that showed off her toned stomach. "I think you're missing a trick though. It's much better without clothes."

I made a choked noise that was somewhere between disgust and disbelief. Without wasting another second, I shifted, my wolf forcing him to break his hold. I kicked my back legs at his chest, knocking him off me completely.

His eyes blazed like fire, a snarl curling his lip. "There's nowhere to run that I can't find you," he warned.

I ignored them both, loping out of the training building and back home to get some clothes. Mom was in the kitchen making breakfast, the scent of sausages and buttery biscuits filling the air.

"No claws on the floor, Daniella, you know that," she scolded, barely glancing up as I passed.

I snorted in confirmation, transforming in the hallway so as not to parade my nakedness around the whole house.

"Get dressed and come help with breakfast," she called after me.

I sighed, heading straight for my shower to rinse off the sweat from the rigorous training. My eyes closed as I soaped up my body, recalling the heat of Donovan pressed against me, his solid, muscular frame pinning me.

A distinct throbbing started in my clit and I stifled a groan. I really did need to get laid, or I was going to die from sexual frustration. There was no time to ease the ache, so I rinsed my body and got out, toweling off as best I could.

I dressed in jeans and a loose black T-shirt that had diagonal slits running down the front and back, giving glimpses of the black lace bra beneath. When I was dressed, I snagged a hair tie from the dresser, working to braid the entire length of darkest-night black hair as I strode back out to help Mom set the table.

I made quick work of it, hurrying to the coffeepot to fill my mug with the steaming hot brew. After dropping a sugar cube from the bowl beside the pot into my drink, I took a sip of the dark liquid, and hummed in satisfaction.

Dad emerged from the hall where his office was moments later, paying more attention to the papers in his hands than the rest of us. Mom steered him toward his seat, placing a gentle kiss on his cheek. He looked up then, catching her eyes and grinning.

Now that I was old enough, I recognized the glint in his gaze.

"Okay you two, you had all night together, simmer down," I said, busying myself with the mug of happiness.

Dad sent me a wink before going back to read the documents in his hands. His brow furrowed. Mom set the last sausage patties onto the heaping plate and took her seat.

"What are those, dear?"

Dad glanced up at me, a look of apology staining his handsome features. "Order form for suppliers...For the Mating Ceremony."

My breath hitched. "Can't we just keep it private?" I asked, sounding far more panicked than I'd have liked. "Everyone already knows it's happening. Besides, he is supposed to have witnesses here. And people to celebrate with—"

"You forget that several members of his pack are journeying here now. They'll arrive in time for the ceremony. It was part of Donovan's conditions," my father answered, shuffling the pages.

"I'm sure it was," I grumbled.

"As was the tattoo as proof of selective mating," my dad added, pointedly avoiding my gaze.

My veins were flooded with ice. "Excuse me?" I croaked. "A tattoo?"

"Lots of couples do it," my dad said. "It's not a big deal."

The rage that barreled through me settled into a quiet calm.

"Eat before the food gets cold," my mother admonished. I knew she was just trying to keep me from storming out into the woods again, but she needn't have worried. I planned on having a little chat with Donovan soon.

After eating and cleaning up, I frowned, noting the time was already nine in the morning, and Syr still hadn't come over. Normally, we trained together in the mornings, but occasionally, he had to help his grandfather with the livestock.

We didn't have much, what with wolves regularly traversing the town, but kept in the stables were pigs, chickens, and a few sheep. I headed out of the house, prepared to head to Syr's grandfather's house, but stopped dead when the breeze carried two painfully familiar scents to me.

From the training field.

I jogged down the dirt road, hearing the grunts and sounds of fists on flesh before I came to the enclosed sparring ring. A crowd was already gathered around to watch—more people than usual, I noticed.

Squeezing my way through the people with murmured pardons, my stomach dropped when I took in the sight of Donovan and Syracuse facing off.

Syr's nose was bleeding and there were two purple bruises on his face—which meant they were fresh as his accelerated healing would likely have them healed in a matter of minutes.

Donovan didn't look quite so bad, but his lip was split and a single cut on his right cheek marred the golden perfection of his skin.

Both males seemed to sense me because they stole glances in my direction, while keeping the majority of their focus on each other. I inhaled sharply through my nose before letting it out in a large gust of air.

They were going to kill each other.

Circling each other slowly, fists up to protect their faces, they moved like water, muscles flexing with each subtle movement. Then, they attacked in a flurry of limbs. It was clearly shaping up to be an excellent match. They stepped, struck, dodged, stepped again. Over and over with neither one pulling ahead.

Their breathing was hard, and my own chest heaved with uneven breaths. Watching them fight was nerve-wracking.

Intoxicating.

There was no doubt they were each great soldiers, made for fighting, but when Syr's fist cracked into Donovan's cheek, my heart swooped with the insane urge to check that he was okay. His head snapped to the side and fresh blood poured from the wound.

I couldn't move, watching and waiting for one of them to call their stalemate. A flash of golden hair caught my attention as Autumn leapt over the fence, joining in the ring with a wicked grin.

I narrowed my eyes at the girl, climbing over the wooden posts to land on the solid dirt-covered arena.

Autumn moved her focus from approaching Syr, to me. I stalked toward her, ready to send my fist into her face. The men paused to gawk for only a second before another crunch of bone reached my ears. I flinched, but before I could check who had sustained the injury—the audible hiss of pain indistinguishable above the roaring of blood in my ears.

The blonde cracked her neck, rolling her shoulders back in a show of swagger that I didn't care for. She was still dressed like a teenager about to go to the mall, not a woman about to be matched in the fight of her life.

I knew not to underestimate her. She was Donovan's beta for

a reason, but she was a participant in the Pack Games, and I'd seen her fight.

Neither of us uttered a word, Autumn's grin still firmly in place when we both shot into action. She threw the first hit and I dodged, ramming my shoulder into hers to knock her back several steps.

I didn't let up, stalking her down and throwing punch after punch. Some landed with cracks, my knuckles barking in pain, others she managed to dodge. Whirling to get out of my striking range, she fought to catch her breath.

The blood marring her beautiful face was only secondary to my satisfaction. It was the absence of her usually smug attitude that had me preening.

I shook out my hand, wishing I'd had time to tape them. But it didn't matter. My injuries would heal before I had time to even clean them.

So I leapt for the girl again, a feral noise of bloodlust erupting from my lips. She snarled, kicking me straight in the chest.

I went back, hitting the ground and my lungs struggled to take in the air they needed for several seconds. Unable to wait, I got back to my feet and lunged again. The ferocity of my attacks grew, but Autumn held her own.

Distantly, I registered that the men had broken apart and now watched us. For some reason, it only drove me harder.

With a brutal kick to her kneecap that shattered the bone and joint, causing her to scream in agony, I jumped on top of her. The rage I felt brewing inside me tipped over the edge.

All semblance of tolerance fled and the beast inside me took over. The need to hurt and maim was like a disease, spreading through my veins at an alarming rate.

I wanted to punish her—punish him—for the fucked up deal I was trapped in. For the Mating Ceremony I didn't want. For the loveless, miserable life I was being forced into. My fists rained down on her face, not stopping even when the blood was hot and thick, droplets hitting my face and burning my eyes.

It wasn't the pretty beta I saw beneath me. A smug grin, dark hair, and golden eyes filled my mind, but it was impossible to stop. The body beneath me didn't struggle against me, but still I unleashed my fury, screaming it for all to hear.

Hands gripped my biceps, ripping me off the girl, but I kept swinging, managing one good punch to someone else's face before they were caught in an impossibly strong grip and wrenched behind my back.

I let loose a feral shriek.

Familiar honey brown eyes filled my vision, hands cupping my face. "Hey, Dani, what's going on?" Syr's soothing, raspy voice asked. "This isn't like you, babe."

The fire roaring in my blood began to cool as my surroundings came into focus, and with it, the man crouched over the unmoving girl lying on the ground.

Donovan's dark eyes were unfathomably cold when they met mine. He looked down at the girl that I suddenly realized wasn't moving. If she even breathed, I couldn't see it.

Had I killed her?

But no, Donovan stroked her cheek, murmuring something to

her that I couldn't hear.

Around us, people's eyes were wide, filled with both concern and…fear.

"Is she okay?" I asked. My voice sounded strange to my own ears.

"Yeah," Syr said, wrapping me into his arms. I buried my face in the crook of his neck, but over his shoulder, I found Donovan watching us. Eyes narrowed and murder written on his face.

"Come on, let's get out of here," Syr suggested, clearly sensing that the alpha was pissed. Whatever his reaction had been while I'd accidentally beaten Autumn into unconsciousness, I didn't know.

Syr took my hand, and we fled the training arena, heading straight for his truck. We got in, and he sped down the road, weaving through the town at a speed that broadcasted we were running away from something, but I didn't care.

Soon we were on the road, and all that could be heard was the crunch of gravel beneath the tires. And my thunderous heart.

"He's going to void the arrangement," I whispered after several minutes of riding in silence. Angry tears burned my eyes.

Anger with myself for letting my emotions get the better of me. I'd never turned into a monster in the ring before. It was where I cleared my head and let off steam, but even when faced with much weaker opponents, I never injured them to that extent.

I covered my face with my hands, allowing a sob to wrack my whole body. Donovan would leave, taking his technology with him and all of this would be for not. And the likelihood was that he wouldn't return for the Pack Games either. Not that I cared about that even half as much.

But I'd screwed up. Less than a day after the deal was struck, I'd found a way to so thoroughly piss off Donovan that I had no doubt would reap consequences for years to come.

"What are we going to do?" I asked, my chest tight. "We needed that technology, and now it'll be gone. It's all my fault."

Syr was silent, though I didn't need him to answer.

Finally, he said, "I need you to tell me what happened. I've never seen you black out like that before. It was like you weren't even in your head. You were just on autopilot and couldn't switch off."

I lowered my hands, wiping away the errant tears. With a nod, I stared out the window. "My parents told me that Donovan required a mating tattoo in order for the bargain to be complete. I was so mad…" A violent shudder ran up the length of my spine. "I lost control."

Finally managing to gather the courage, I looked at Syr, expecting to see judgement or even disappointment. Instead, his eyes were distant narrowed on the road, but it was like he saw right through the dirt and gravel. He nodded. "It all makes sense now."

I scoffed. "What I did was horrible, Syr. No one in their right mind could justify that."

He blew out a long breath. "Sure. What you did was fucked up. But the situation you're in kinda warrants a little fucked up. She'll heal. Honestly, by morning she'll be almost as good as new. A little sore, but fine. You definitely broke her nose and possibly her eye sockets, so those might take a little longer for the swelling to go down, but she's not human."

"If she were human, she would have died," I said in a cold, dead tone.

"But she isn't," Syr said firmly. We entered Ivywood, slowing to the town's speed limit before he parked outside the ice cream parlor. He pushed his door open, then turned to face me. "Here." Fishing a water bottle from beneath his seat, he handed it to me, along with napkins.

Pulling the mirror down, I checked my reflection, noting the blood splashed across my face and grimaced.

I got to work wiping my face down, tossing stained wads to the floor until Syr nodded in satisfaction. It was on my clothes too, but only truly visible on my jeans, which could be explained away by simply reminding anyone that dared comment on the fact that we slaughtered livestock on our territory.

Humans knew better than to question us anyway. They didn't necessarily live in fear of the resident wolf-shifters, but they minded their own business when it counted. I appreciated the fact that we could live in harmony, knowing other places in the world didn't have that same luxury.

He got out, rounding the truck before opening my door and taking my hand. "Come on. You need this."

I let him pull me from the cab, but I wasn't under any illusions about this being anything more than a distraction, and a few miles between Donovan and I. Hopefully, that meant he wouldn't come for me just yet.

We entered the ice cream place hand-in-hand until I spotted a booth. He let me go to it with little hesitation and I sank onto the creaky leather with an audible sigh.

A few of the patrons glanced my way, each of their gazes snapping away when my eyes scanned the small building, then moved to the parking lot and beyond.

I couldn't see him, but I swear I could feel his wrath from here.

It was only a matter of time before he found me, and then I'd have to face what I'd done.

CHAPTER TEN

By the time I'd left Autumn with the healer wolf and began my hunt, my thundering pulse had dulled to a low roar. In animal form I kept to the forest, tearing over the rough ground hard and fast.

She'd nearly killed my beta.

I would make my Little Wolf bleed for what she did.

At least I know for certain she's a Carvingwood through and through. My father had met that same fate—only no one had seen it coming. The dirty tricks Evan Carvingwood had used wouldn't be repeated. I'd made sure of that.

Spying the end of the tree line, I transformed, pulling the pack of clothing off my shoulders before slipping it on as quickly as I could. Laced up in sleek Doc Marten boots, I marched out of the forest, coming to the town's main road with war thrumming through my veins.

I'm coming for you, Little Wolf, I vowed maliciously. A smile curled my lips as I spied her profile in the window of an ice cream parlor. She and her lap dog sat at a table. A bowl of ice cream melted in front of her, untouched.

Her head turned in my direction, as if sensing me, and I retreated behind a car in the parking lot. My heart still thumped hard with the need for vengeance. After a moment, I peered around the vehicle to see if she'd detected me, but they were speaking to each other, seemingly unaware.

Rolling my neck, I waited out the next ten minutes of their sporadic conversing—a little pissed I couldn't hear what he said when she finally cracked the slightest smile. What right did she have to smile right now? And what the hell could he have possibly said to make her do so?

Her rage was lethal. A beautiful, disastrous weapon.

I wanted to punish her for taking it out on Autumn. I also wanted to bend her over that table and fuck her senseless.

What I had planned, however, would be payback enough.

Finally, they rose from the table and strode from the ice cream shop, walking so close I could have sworn he grabbed her hand. When their backs were solidly to me, I saw their twined fingers. The easy way they walked together as though they were a couple.

It made my hackles rise—the wolf in me snarling with the urge to rip them apart. I forced myself to trail them until they disappeared into the movie theater. Imagining them curled up together, watching a movie and his slimy hands on her body had my chest rumbling with violence.

I snuck around back, finding a worker sitting on a crate, smoking. He eyed me with well-placed suspicion when I stalked up to him. It was clear he knew what I was.

"Fifty bucks for you to let me sneak in and make sure my sister's boyfriend isn't getting handsy." I pulled the bill out and waved it in front of him.

He quirked a brow, taking a drag of his cigarette before saying, "Cheaper to just buy a ticket."

I shrugged. "I don't need one. I'm not staying."

"You gonna cause me problems?" he asked.

A dark laugh escaped me. "Not if I don't have to."

He nodded as though he understood what I was saying. There was no way he had any clue, but I gave him an amicable smile. Standing with the cigarette clamped between his lips, he unlocked the door, allowing me to slip inside. I gave him a nod of thanks, relinquishing the cash before taking a deep breath.

Her scent, mixed with blood was a tantalizing beacon in the air. I followed it as far as I could, deciding to duck behind the wall near the women's bathroom. I'd wait her out. Chicks always had to pee the second a movie was involved.

The women that passed stared like they were in a trance, milling in and out without ever knowing a predator stood so close. It only took fifteen minutes before her scent wafted toward me—stronger than before.

When she turned the corner, I lunged from my hiding spot.

Her eyes went wide, body switching to defense mode. I knocked her attempts at defense away like gnats flying too near me before crushing her body against the stone tiles. My blood pumped hard, heating my limbs, and before I knew what I was doing, my mouth crashed down on hers.

Her lithe body struggled for only a moment before her fingers twined into my hair, tugging on the strands, and making me growl into her mouth. She kissed me back with the ferocity of a panther trying to subdue its prey.

But I was prey about as much as she was. Gripping her ass, I lifted her up, and she responded by wrapping her legs around my hips, grinding against me.

I wrapped one hand around the length of her black hair and pulled, forcing her head back before nipping the column of her throat. "Were you hiding, Little Wolf?" I rasped before crushing my lips to hers again in a bruising kiss.

She pulled back, breathing heavily. "You're assuming," she panted, rolling her hips against my now throbbing cock, "that I'm afraid of you, *Dick*hills." Another upward thrust from her hot cunt made me growl low. Smirking she said, "I think it's you who should be afraid."

A slow smile curved my lips. I let her drop to her feet and she gasped, using the wall for support, but her smile remained. Letting claws descend from my fingertips, I ran them from the curve of her jaw, slowly to the base of her throat, then lower, using just enough pressure to make the skin redden.

My lips curled in satisfaction at the sight.

"If you think this means I'm going to let you brand me like some common cattle, you're wrong," she growled.

Gripping her throat with my claws still extended, I leaned in, my lips hovering above hers. "It's non-negotiable, Little Wolf. Without my tattoo, this bargain is void."

She placed her hands on my chest, batting her thick, dark lashes. I wanted to drink in the heat of her—the scent that had my cock so fucking hard it hurt. Without an uttered word, she shoved me, forcing me to take a step back as her expression turned to stone.

"Drop dead, Dickhills." She strode away, swaying her hips like she'd just won the war.

I watched her go, grinning to myself. I'd just sent her back to her pining lap dog with my scent all fucking over her.

Little by little you'll become mine, Daniella, I thought with pure, primal satisfaction before I left the theater the way I'd came.

CHAPTER ELEVEN

Dani

I was still a little dazed from Donovan's aggression, and maybe a little horny. Okay, a lot horny. The feel of his mouth claiming mine, his palms and fingertips searing my skin in ways that felt more like a brand than the one he was demanding.

Ugh, I thought, shaking myself from my lust-haze as I stalked down the steps in the dimly lit theater. *Fucking Alpha Dickhills and his feral, animalistic ways.* What was so wrong with a ring or a necklace as a symbol of commitment? A tattoo was archaic, and forcing anyone to endure it was a violation of their basic human rights.

I'd kill Donovan before I allowed him to mark me in such a way.

Syr's face whipped toward me before I reached our row, his eyes flashing wolf-silver. My stomach dropped and I froze, realizing what

I smelled like. *Who* I smelled like. There was nothing I could do about it now, I supposed. We're going to be mates anyway, so Syr would have to get used to the two of us being around each other.

Maybe not the making out part. I cringed inwardly.

I avoided my best friend's burning, penetrating stare as I took my seat beside him. His hands gripped the armrests so hard I heard the plastic groaning, his knuckles white. My mind was so far from the film playing, even though I stared at the screen. Laughter came from all around us, but the heat and anger radiating from Syr was just as distracting as recalling the feel of Donovan's body against mine.

Finally, I abandoned the idea of sitting here, letting my best friend seethe. I gripped his shirt and pulled him up with me, dragging him from the theater. By the time we emerged out onto the street, the air was as hot as the sun beating down on us and Syr's body was expanding. Contracting. His bones cracking audibly. His wolf form was on the brink of winning the struggle, shudders racking his large frame.

"Seriously, Syracuse Ryon Milton," I growled low to keep the humans wandering by from hearing. "So help me, you better get yourself under control or I will beat your ass."

Syr snarled, though it sounded like one of frustration at his own inability to calm the fuck down than it did my chastisement. I glared up at him, arms folded across my chest.

"What the hell is your deal, anyway?"

He tangled his fingers in his shaggy brown curls and muttered, "Your scent." The words were garbled from the mouthful of fangs he hadn't quite managed to get rid of.

I sighed, glancing around the street before grabbing his hand and pulling him away from the theater towards his truck. Once we were both securely inside, I turned toward him. "I'll be bonded to Donovan inside of a week. I'm going to smell like him occasionally, it can't be helped."

Syr leveled me with a venomous glare, staying silent for several moments. Just when I thought he was about to say whatever it was that was bothering him, he scoffed and shook his head. "Well he didn't kill you, clearly. So what did he say? Actually, I'm guessing there weren't a lot of words exchanged."

His look of disgust jerked me back in shock, but it soon morphed into anger. I didn't care that he was right. My own weakness in giving into my baser animalistic desires with Donovan was overshadowed by the fact that my best friend was acting like Donovan and I were never going to touch once bonded.

Not even I could deny how explosive we were when in the same space. That didn't mean I wouldn't still fight him at every turn and make his decision to trap me in a bonded match haunt him for the rest of his miserable existence.

"He was pissed," I answered bluntly.

Syr scoffed. "Sure he was."

Anger rose up in me, hot and volatile. I threw the door open and stormed across the street, barely missing a black car that sped by. My blood rushed in my ears, fists clenched at my sides as my wolf nature began to fill my veins, trying to force my beast form.

I'd nearly made it to the edge of town when a strong hand spun me around. Syr yanked me to him as his mouth came down on mine in a searing kiss. My body locked up with shock, but like a purring cat, I leaned into him, returning the press of my lips.

Then sense crashed into me and I stepped back, missing his heat and the feel of him instantly.

"Fuck," I mumbled, looking around for any sign of Donovan. For some reason, I told myself that since I couldn't sense him, he wasn't near. But we weren't bonded, which meant there was no way I'd be able to sense him if he were.

Syr's burning gaze tracked me as I paced back and forth like a caged animal, running a hand over my hair.

"Don't tie yourself to him," my friend said, though it sounded like a plea. "We can find a way to get those tracking devices without his help. He doesn't care for you, Dani. I've known you your whole life. He'll never know you like I do, and he certainly won't care to."

My mouth fell open and I stared at my best friend. "It's doesn't matter, Syr. It's not about a love match; it's purely a business transaction. We *need* those devices. I can't leave anyone's fate to chance. I need you to understand that, and I need you to accept it. Please." My words were tinged with desperation.

He looked torn between agreeing and arguing, knowing that what I said was true. But his desire was written plainly on his face. And my heart hurt.

For him and for myself.

I loved Syr, and clearly there had been attraction growing between us that I just hadn't let myself acknowledge.

Finally, he nodded, reaching out for me. I went to him, letting him pull me into his arms. "I'm sorry," he whispered.

I didn't speak—couldn't speak—with the lump rising in my throat.

"Let's get back before your mother decides to hunt us down," he suggested.

I chuckled, wiping the dampness under my eyes away before following him to his truck. As we drove back, I kept my mind on anything but my upcoming ceremony, though when we entered town, it became increasingly difficult not to notice that the center gazebo was cleared and at least a dozen people worked to prune and weed the flower beds on either side of the walkway. A task generally left to the pack's teens, but with the tying ceremony so close, my mother was likely insisting the entire settlement be picture perfect.

We coasted to a stop on the narrow dirt road outside my parents' house, and I jumped out. "I'm going to go see if Mom needs help with the hāngi," I told Syr, but I needn't have bothered. His steps were heavy on the wood of the porch as he followed me inside.

The smell of herbs and vegetables greeted us, and I breathed it in deeply. Several voices spoke low, followed by a feminine giggle. I cast a confused look over my shoulder at Syr whose jaw fixed tight.

All it took was the slightest inhale for me to detect two scents that I didn't want in my house, especially right now.

I stomped into the kitchen, prepared to cause a scene, finding a bandaged, bruised Autumn propped on a stool at the counter, stirring a bowl of something I couldn't see. It hurt to look at her and just how much damage I'd done. Her accelerated healing was aided by tinctures and herbs that were different than the ones going into the feast being prepared.

On the other side of the counter, Donovan kneaded dough, his shirt sleeves rolled up to show off his toned forearms. Both of them turned their gazes on me—Autumn rather gingerly—but I couldn't peel my attention from the scrap of frilly pink fabric the Dockhills alpha had tied around his waist.

My jaw dropped. "Is that a fucking apron?" I blurted out.

Mom looked up from her own work of tying herbs to the roast to gasp. "Daniella! What have I said about swearing in this house?"

"Sorry," I said without an ounce of remorse. "Is that a girl's apron?"

"I've been assured that it compliments my skin tone." Donovan replied with a smirk, knowing my eyes would lower yet again to the bronze skin of his arms. My entire body suffused with liquid fire remembering his rough, intoxicating kiss. Those hands on my neck. My waist. Which, of course, only had the arrogant prick's lips inching even higher. Out of the corner of my eye, I could see that Autumn bore the faintest hint of a smile as well, like she somehow knew what I was feeling.

Syr shifted closer until the heat of his body cloaked my back. *Fucking possessive males.*

I ground my teeth together. "Well, I was going to ask if you needed any help, but it looks like you have it well in hand," I said, spinning on my heel to make a quick escape, but was halted when my mother said, "There's plenty left to do, and you know it, Daniella Carvingwood. You too, Syracuse. Wash your hands and get to scrubbing the potatoes. Then I want you to get the pit fire started."

I heaved a sigh and did as she asked, feeling Syr unnaturally close. When we passed Donovan on our way to the sink, I heard the faintest rumbling chuckle.

Too bad I couldn't damage *his* face. Glancing sidelong at Autumn had me cringing. She really was a mess. I needed to apologize, but I didn't want to do it in front of my mother and Donovan.

If my mother knew it was me who had hurt her so completely, she'd have my head. Once Syr and I started washing and stacking potatoes, the tense air dissipated. My mother continued to chatter about something, Donovan and Autumn adding in monosyllabic responses while I tuned them all out and focused on washing the entire fifty pounds of potatoes piled in baskets on the floor as fast as I could in order to get the fuck out.

What the hell was my mom playing at like we'd be one big happy family just because Donovan and I were meant to be tied? Nothing would ever excuse the fact that they'd sold me to him. Yes, it was for a worthy cause, but that just made Donovan more the villain.

Several times my mother tried to rope me into their conversation, but my unenthusiastic and minimalistic responses soon became too much of an annoyance and she gave up. Syr tried to meet my gaze, but it was better to just pretend no one else existed in the room.

Soon my hands were raw and red, but the potatoes were clean. I knew what to do, having helped prepare the feast enough times. I grabbed the bottle of oil, set it in one of the baskets along with unclaimed sprigs of rosemary and thyme before hoisting a basket into each arm and starting for the door. Syr slid past me in the hallway with his baskets, maneuvering the door open for me.

I muttered my thanks before following him to the edge of the town where the pit was dug and ready. Stones and logs lined the bottom and already smouldered. We dumped the potatoes around the edge before sprinkling oil over them and rubbing the herbs on top.

I covered the pit with the large, soaked leaves, sighing when it was done. There was still an insane amount of food to go into the pit which would have a better seal once it was filled, but that would require going back inside my house which seemed more than a little unbearable at the moment.

"Come on," Syr said gently, taking my hand in his and giving it a gentle squeeze. He knew just how much I didn't want to do that, but the alternative was suffering my mother's wrath on hāngi night.

I blew out a harsh breath before nodding. Even though I knew it was a bad idea, I didn't pull out of his grip until we were standing back in the kitchen and Donovan's piercing golden eyes landed on where I was joined to Syr. They narrowed before his gaze snapped up to meet mine, knocking the air from my lungs.

His expression had his unspoken threat written out just as plainly as if he'd held up a sign. *You belong to me, not him.*

I let myself release Syr, but he tightened his grip. Turning my head toward him, I gave him a pointed look that said, *Okay, you've made your statement, now let go.*

Finally, he moved his glare to Donovan, holding it for several moments before letting my hand go.

Forcing myself not to roll my eyes, I started toward the counter, grabbing tin pans filled to the brim with meat and veg, and carrying them out to the pit.

Before long, the day faded to the golden rays of sunset. Outside, kids ran around, laughing and squealing. Music began to play from the square, and slowly the strings of lights strung like webs from house to house flickered on.

I stood, freshly showered, my hair dried, and makeup done. Dressed in a gauzy black skirt, and a spaghetti-strap, sheer, black top with my black and gold bra on display, I felt powerful. Sexy.

Despite how provocative it was, my mother had barely looked at me, too flustered with preparations.

A knock sounded on the door just after my mother had left. I paused, almost certain I knew who it was.

My steps were not hurried, despite the two extra knocks that sounded more like the door would be banged open at any moment.

I pulled the door open with a less than pleased glower on my face. Even that was wiped from my face when I saw who stood there. Donovan and a guy I didn't recognize. He had a leather bag slung over one shoulder, sunglasses that covered his eyes even though night had fallen, and highlighted brown hair that was artfully tousled.

Donovan stood beside him with a dark expression, his arms folded across his chest.

"Can I help you?" I asked flatly.

"You're going to let us inside, Little Wolf," he answered in that deep, sinful voice of his.

I pursed my lips. "No. I don't think I will. I need to get to the festival."

"*After* our business is concluded," Donovan said menacingly.

I stared back at him, letting my own anger rise to the surface. But I knew I didn't hold any of the power here. Moving aside, I let them both pass and shut the door.

In the living room, the mystery guy dumped his bag. "Here?" he asked.

Donovan nodded, before turning to eye my bare arms.

I froze for a beat when I saw what the guy pulled from the bag. Rounding on Donovan I said, "You cannot be serious! I'm not getting a tattoo!"

Donovan gripped my biceps and steered me toward the couch. "It's part of the agreement, Little Wolf, and I'm not feeling much like being a *good guy*." He sneered the last words.

My pulse rushed through my ears as I glared daggers at Donovan. "I will claw your fucking eyes out if you make me do this," I snarled.

He folded his muscular arms over his chest, and smirked. "Fine. I will leave your tiny, isolated pack without a single hope in all the hells of protecting their people." He took a slow step closer. Then another. I could feel the heat radiating off him, and with it, his scent wrapped around me, pulling me toward him. But I refused.

"Word through the valley is," he purred, "the Silver Vipers raided through The Reaper's Spines, burning towns and plucking women and children from their homes." He was close, leaning in until our breaths entwined.

My rage lowered to a simmer in my chest. "What will my being tattooed prove?" I spat. Better to hide behind the venom in my voice than face the way my body reacted whenever he was near.

"Everyone will know you are mine and will be less likely to try to take you. It's as much a protection as it is a declaration of our alliance."

I glared up at Donovan, hating that his scheme made even the barest hint of sense. Even if I was inclined to believe that the bandits and traffickers were not going to check for tattoos before stealing women.

Turning away from him at last so I didn't do something stupid—like lean into him—I aimed my anger at the tattoo artist. "Where?" was my simple demand.

He shrugged. "Boss?"

We both looked at Donovan who took one of my balled fists, turning my arm so the inside of my forearm was facing up.

"Here," he said.

I snatched my arm back. "Are you insane? Put it on my back or something."

Donovan shook his head. "It needs to be where people can see it."

My teeth ground together. Dropping onto the couch unceremoniously, I handed the tattoo guy my right arm.

He got to work pulling things from his bag before placing an inked piece of paper over the skin of my forearm. When he removed it, I got a look at the design. I'd expected some grotesque display of manliness like barbed wire or something, but instead, there was the head of a wolf—one faced in both directions. And the different phases of the moon started above, ending below in an elegant, feminine way. Small, twisting wildflowers curved up the sides, making the whole thing look like a family crest.

It was beautiful.

I looked to Donovan who stared at me intently, gauging my reaction. The buzz of the gun started up, but I held Donovan's gaze when the first subtle scrape of the needle pierced my flesh.

Neither one of us seemed willing to look away first. And the initial, careful expression he wore turned to one of challenge. Daring me to look away. My lips curved. *I will not be cowed by you, Dickhills*, I said with my eyes.

As if he could hear my thoughts, his lips tugged up to one side. When a knock sounded at the door, both of our gazes swung to the hallway as though we could see right through the walls.

And then I felt Syr's presence. Panic flared in me. I looked down at my arm, seeing that the small design was only half done. The knock came again. I know he could sense me too, and likely could scent that Donovan was here with me.

Biting my bottom lip, I thought for a moment, then said, "Let him in."

Donovan lifted a single brow. "And why should I do that?"

The hammering at the door became more insistent. I gestured with my free hand in the direction of where my best friend stood, probably thinking the worst. "He's just going to stand out there beating the door down unless you let him in."

A muscle flexed in his jaw, but he left the living room, and a moment later I heard the door open. Donovan's deep, raspy voice, and then Syr's burst of anger.

"What? Move out of my fucking way, Donovan. Let me see her!"

I cringed, meeting the tattoo artist's gaze. He simply shook his head and continued his work.

Syr burst into the living room, stopping short at the sight of me. I gave him a reassuring smile only a split second before he whirled on Donovan and threw his fist into his face.

CHAPTER TWELVE

Dani

The dude with the needles had the forethought to get them far enough away that when I launched to my feet, he didn't stab me with them.

Donovan touched the blood trickling from his lip and growled low. The heat pouring off of him was the only indication that he was seconds away from freeing his wolf right in my living room.

Syr too. His eyes were dark and bottomless. An abyss of rage that threatened to consume him.

I threw myself between them, holding my arms out.

The one with the partial tattoo was closest to Syr. His gaze lowered to it, and a animalistic vibration shook his chest. He bared his teeth, revealing his elongated fangs.

"Syr, look at me," I demanded, stepping close enough to touch his chest. His heart thrashed beneath my palm.

It took a moment, but the wolf that was mostly in control looked up, meeting my gaze. "I agreed to this. It's for our people. Our pack. I have to keep them safe."

"He branded you." Syr's response was almost guttural.

I didn't have the words to talk him down, so I did the only thing I could do. "Go, Syr. I'll meet up with you as soon as I'm done. Please."

The moment his anger was replaced with cold indifference, I felt my heart crack. He flashed Donovan an unreadable look before he turned and stormed out of the house. The walls rattled when he slammed the door shut behind himself.

Closing my eyes for a moment, I breathed in a breath that was meant to ease my nerves, but it served only to split the chasm of my heart further apart.

"Sit down, Daniella," Donovan said in a voice far gentler than he had any right to use. I spun, shooting him a murderous expression before I went back to the couch and collapsed, letting the other male finish the tattoo.

Whether it was due to distraction or my accelerated healing, I barely registered the scraping of the needle. When it was done and the area was wiped, cleaned, and covered with a jelly-type substance, the male rose to pack away his things.

I stared only at the artwork on the rug, the colors blending together. Someone said something, but I didn't hear them. I got to my feet, glancing down at the ink that was now a permanent part of me.

Then I strode for the door.

"I'll be seeing you later, Little Wolf," Donovan called after me. I didn't look back; didn't answer.

My only concern was finding my best friend.

The party was in full swing. I kept myself tucked on the outskirts of the throng. Everyone danced, but the beat seemed to only be for those tied together. The ones who found the sensual rhythm and moved to it like it was an art form were the true mated pairs. For many minutes I followed each heady twist, grind, and touch, feeling nothing but envy. Their bodies seemed to only serve the other, and every second of it was intense.

Beautiful.

Sadness for my own fate crept in when the song ended and lips crashed together, a sea of lovers. The likelihood of having a true mate in my life was all but non-existent. Soon I'd be tied to a man who hated me, had marked me, and I could scarcely tolerate a single conversation with him.

"Why aren't you dancing?"

"Speak of the Devil," I drawled sarcastically.

Donovan laughed darkly. "I wish I could say I've never been called the Devil, but that would be a lie."

"Which is different than the rest of the shit that comes out of your mouth, how?" I quipped, tightening my arms under my chest when my nipples hardened for no damned reason.

A gentle touch ran up my spine, and it took me a moment to realize it was the tip of a knife he dragged the length of my back. I shivered.

"Believe or not, Little Wolf, I haven't lied to you." His voice was low as he whispered against my ear.

I scoffed, trying to act like I wasn't half as affected as I really was. But from the answering chuckle, I knew I'd failed.

"You lied to my family," I said with all seriousness.

The knife halted its ascent before leaving my body altogether. Still, I held fast, unable to predict his next move. "How did I lie to them?"

I swallowed hard. "You act like you're not the villain. You paste on this mask that paints you like you're just a regular guy, and not the man trapping their daughter into a baseless union. The asshole that forced his mark on my skin without my consent."

Donovan's lips curled in my hair before he breathed me in. "That's funny, I could have sworn you quite liked the design I chose for you." And fuck me, I did, but that wasn't the point. "Bargaining for their daughter as my mate is the most honest I've been in my entire life. If they can't see that I'm a villain based on the arrangement *that they agreed to*, then that's their fault." He straightened beside me, finally looking from me to watch the mixture of lovers and mates dancing. "But what does it make your parents, Daniella, that they would give you to me?"

I spun toward him, my lip curled. "You didn't give them much of a choice," I snarled.

Donovan's gaze crashed down on mine, and the intensity nearly stole my breath. "Should I ever have a daughter, I would never offer her up as collateral," he said plainly.

Before I could march away from him, or even blink, he pulled me onto the dance floor and spun me once before tugging my body against his. My breath left me in a whoosh, and before I could think, the beat overtook me.

I rolled my hips against him, swaying as he led our steps in a near salsa type dance. Every grasp of his hands on my hips, or slip up my bare thighs, had my head spinning. My eyes remained locked on his, feeling the golden depths pulling me in.

Anchoring me.

Drowning me.

He spun me away, letting our fingers barely separate. My back bumped against a solid chest, Syr's scent filling my senses. I tilted my head back to look at him.

He didn't smile, his dark gaze boring into mine.

Without thinking, I spun into him, and suddenly we were dancing too. The beat was entirely too sexual for the kind of dance best friends did, but my body had a mind of its own, my hands roving over his chest.

"Dani," he started, but I held a finger to his lips. All I wanted was to enjoy this moment without the reality of what was to come looming over me.

I dipped then ran my ass slowly up Syr's thighs, feeling the full bulging length straining against his jeans.

Shockingly, I realized I wasn't disgusted, but incredibly turned on.

I didn't move away.

My heart pounded, sweat beaded my skin and I leaned into my best friend, twirling my wrists as my arms snaked up before wrapping around the back of his neck.

"Fuck, Dani," Syr growled.

I smiled, swaying against him, my eyes closed.

Until my attention jerked to the man standing exactly where I'd left him, looking both heated, and ready to murder.

He marched forward, yanking me away from Syr by my biceps. "That was quite the show," he rasped near my ear, still pulling me away from the dancing groups. "But I don't share."

Glancing back at Syr, I shook my head when he advanced, telling him not to intervene. It looked like it took a great deal of effort to comply, but he did.

We were soon out of the throng of partygoers and thrust into the darkness of the forest. He spun me abruptly and my back collided with the rough bark of the tree.

"How should I punish that act of yours, Little Wolf?" he asked.

My heart stuttered, equal parts arousal and irritation winding through my veins. I glared at him in the dark, but his eyes shone bright—like twin flames. "You've already marked me. There's nothing left you could do that would hurt me," I snarled.

Donovan's answering cruel grin was my only warning before he attacked, pinning my arms over my head and his mouth coming down on mine. His tongue slipped in and warred with mine. I pushed into him, nipping his lip which earned me a husky groan.

One of his hands released my wrists, trailing his rough fingertips down the inside of my arm—so near his mark—then over the swell of my breast and down my belly. Heat licked through me, pooling between my thighs. His hand seemed to chase the sensation, toying with me while he drew closer and closer to my now throbbing clit.

"Your arousal smells so sweet, Little Wolf," he taunted.

With his lips on my neck, I panted, "If you want something, Dickhills, take it."

His answering growl rumbled in his chest, then my skirt was yanked up, revealing the black lace beneath. He palmed my pussy, finding the fabric damp. Donovan's smirk was so arrogant, I wanted to roll my eyes and make a quip about the tiny dick he must be hiding. Even though I'd felt the very solid, very impressive length against my hip.

He maneuvered the fabric aside with his thumb before grazing my clit. I hissed in a breath, then two of his fingers began to explore my slick folds. Another sarcastic remark reached my tongue, but before I could expel it, he shoved inside me.

He swallowed my gasp with his mouth. Pumping his fingers in and out of my pussy, he kissed me so hard I imagined our lips would be bruised by tomorrow. The need to cum overrode my senses and soon I was grinding on his hand. Every delicious brush of the heel of his palm on my little bundle of nerves drove me higher.

"Fuck this, I'm going to taste you," he bit out. But before I could find my release, he withdrew his fingers, then hoisted me up. My back scraped the tree, and no doubt tore my top.

Hooking his arms under my thighs, he tossed my legs over his shoulders like I was little more than a doll. Then his warm mouth was on my cunt, licking and spearing my entrance with his tongue.

Never had someone devoured me like this. It was messy, yet unbelievably hot. My head fell back, riding the tidal wave of pleasure.

It was violent and unstoppable.

My moans were muffled by his hand that shot up just in time. Unable to contain myself, my hips ground on his face, and he lapped it up.

When my high began to ebb, my body went slack, and he set me on my feet more gently than I'd have thought possible for him. He grinned at me like he'd won some great prize, and I straightened my skirt.

With my brain back where it belonged, I realized this was a mistake. I'd given Donovan far more than an inch. And I could see in his eyes he was coming to claim the rest of me whether I liked it or not.

CHAPTER THIRTEEN

Brax

Rain fell in heavy droplets, even through the thick canopy. Soaked through, I swiped the water off my face, and tried to make out the trail we'd been following. The scent had dissipated, and my irritation with the situation only grew.

Rogue whined at my side. We'd climbed for nearly ten hours straight and his limbs quaked.

Taking pity on the beast, I patted my leg. "Come, boy. We'll find a place to rest." He obeyed, trailing behind me until I found an area that was only slightly damp. With the light of day still coating the forest, we wouldn't need a fire. But food was a must.

Rogue curled up on the leaves without protest, laying his weary head on sodden paws. His dark eyes watched me woefully as I set out with my bow and arrow.

I stepped lightly through the forest. With the continued downpour of rain, the birds had settled in the trees to keep dry. Animals below foraged for insects. I waited, listening with my eyes shut. Their movements were a cacophony that drowned out the desperation growing in my chest. The auction would be soon, and the path of destruction delivered by The Silver Vipers was devastating the land.

Part of me thought to just leave Rogue back at the cabin. To finish what I'd started. But by the time I made it back up the mountains, I would have lost their trail completely. No. I'd have to take it slow. He was my only *whanau*. Family.

A fattened hare bounced near. My eyes slid open and I loosed the arrow nocked in my bow. It struck the creature's skull with an audible *thunk*.

The meat was still barely enough to feed Rogue, but I finished off the last of my dried meat for my own lunch. Soon I would need to fell another deer to dry and cure the meat to keep with me for times such as these.

When we were back on our feet, the scent of diesel and refuse was closer than before. Then I heard the rumble of an engine and voices. A truck pulled a small livestock trailer through the trees, mud spraying behind their tires. They gave pack lands a wide berth and stayed off the main roads where the towns' policemen could stop them.

It was almost ingenious. And exactly what I'd spent the past two months hunting down. Rogue trotted along beside me as I ran to keep the truck in my sights. I barely summoned my wolf to the surface before my skin stretched and my bones clacked—shifting and giving way to my beast.

I sprinted harder and Rogue fell behind with a huff. We'd done this enough for him to know to follow at a distance. He was too old to have much of a role now.

Dashing through the trees, I ran parallel with the truck. It slowed, the driver looking across the passenger side. He sensed my presence. I used his momentary distraction to leap in front of the vehicle.

The male jerked and braked, but the front corner of his hood impacted on a tree. A loud crunch brought the truck to a complete stop. I snarled as the passenger side door swung open. The blond, middle-aged shifter's head was bleeding, but when he lunged from the cab into his russet-colored wolf, the blood barely matted the fur atop his skull.

I attacked before his paws hit the dirt, sinking my teeth into his side. We went down in a tangled heap, but I clawed and tore at every bit of animal I could find. Shaking a chunk of fur and flesh free, bitter blood blanketed my tongue. He twisted, snapping his jaws in feral desperation. I was bigger and my kill count likely as large as the number of people these lowlifes had transported for The Silver Vipers.

The driver—a burly, bald man with tattoos that filled nearly every inch of his pasty skin—stumbled around the front of the truck just as I launched his companion right at him. They went down, the tire-iron the driver had held skidded through the old fallen needles. The wolf snarled, getting to its feet, but only inched forward. His wounds dripped crimson to the forest floor, each drop sounding like a leaky faucet.

The tattooed man went for his weapon, allowing me time to spring for the wolf once again. I toppled him to the side and clamped my teeth into his throat. With one clean, efficient movement, I ripped through tissue and sinew.

His blood was a hot spray coating my face and showering the rough tree trunks around us.

I barely had time to let his body go limp before the man shouted, "You'll pay for that, *dog*!" He charged at me with the iron held above his head.

I dove out of the way, feeling the rush of wind on my back paws as the heavy metal struck the earth. Dirt, sodden with blood, kicked up in both directions. A growl shook my chest and I sliced through the thick, inked forearm holding the weapon. He hissed in a breath, but he didn't release it.

Lifting it again, he smiled, rising to his feet.

Movement in the trees snagged my attention, but I couldn't look away. I backed up a step, knowing if he got his bulk on top of me, he'd be able to do immense damage. Swiping the tire iron left and right, he advanced.

I crouched low, preparing to lunge when a large form streaked out from behind a tree, hitting the tattooed guy from the side. Rogue went for his throat, but the male caught my companion under the jaw.

He gave a high-pitched whine, stumbling away. Red-hot anger seared through my veins and I took my turn, landing on the prick. I clawed his face, tearing through his eyes.

The metal rod collided with my ribs in a brutal crunch. Whatever air had been in my lungs vanished, replaced only with pain. Blinded by it, I struck for his throat, biting down hard when I met flesh.

His screams were gurgled. I bit down again, tearing away everything that separated his head from his body. Memories fueled my morbid rage. Recalling the terror of Esme's cries; the fire devouring my home.

The hands that clawed at me, trying to tear me off went limp before falling to the ground. My chest heaved as my vision returned to normal and I spied Rogue shakily getting to his feet. I let my blood-covered wolf melt away before going to my only friend.

"Hey, Rogue," I rasped. My throat was raw and ached.

He shook himself then looked up at me, his tongue lolling to one side in what I could only imagine was a pleased grin.

I patted the top of his head. "Well done." My own lips twitched in a partial smile.

A knocking reached my ears and I spun, finding that the sound seemed to come from the trailer. Rogue whined but started forward, sniffing apprehensively.

I grimaced at my naked state and then at the mangled, bloody corpse at my feet. The older wolf was probably more my size, but his own clothes had been shredded when he shifted.

I tugged up the torn, blood-stained jeans, wincing at every ache in my body and started for the trailer. Chains and padlocks hung from the door, and with one, hard yank that had my vision spotted with black dots, they snapped. I flung the doors open, my heart dropping at the sight of several dirty bodies that barely moved when the light poured in.

A young boy, maybe five or so, clung to a woman who sat up lethargically. Dazed eyes blinked at me, and in the corner, a girl began to cry.

"You're all free," I told them in what I hoped was a gentle voice.

The one holding her son said, "Thank you." Her voice was crackly, like she hadn't had water in days. She cleared her throat and tried again. "Where are we?"

I sighed, raking a hand through my hair. The beads and feathers were tangled together from the fight, but I wrestled a few strands free. "At the bottom of the Reaper's Spines, roughly an hour from the Badlands. Where are you from?"

The mother spoke again. "Ashbourne."

I inhaled sharply, then immediately regretted it. Coughs racked my body and each gasping breath brought with it an intense stabbing pain. They were miles from home. "Alright, let's get you all cleaned up and I'll find a bus service to Ashbourne. Okay?"

Several of the women nodded. I sniffed the air, pushing away the sweat and filth to ascertain they were all humans. Something else tinged their scents though and it took me a moment to place the acrid metallic smell.

Flunitrazepam. A sedative that kept humans compliant and quiet.

A snarl worked its way up my throat, though only the barest of sounds escaped. I swallowed it down and said, "I vow to ensure you all get home safely. No one is going to hurt you."

I let them come to me, climbing out in their dirty clothing with glassy eyes. My anger was a swooping bird of prey flying above me waiting to dive.

They climbed into the back of the truck, most of the women fawning over Rogue who lapped up their attention while we made the slow trek back into the mountains. I tried to keep the vehicle from rocking too much, but the uneven terrain made my ribs sing with pain. My cabin wasn't too far. I'd let them get cleaned up, refuel, and send them to Shadow Ridge Pack for anything they might need. The alpha, Axel, was an acquaintance, but one I trusted and respected.

The little boy, whose name I learned was August, brightened after raiding the snacks and bottles of water in the back of the cab. He bounced on his mother's lap, excitedly pointing at every animal we passed.

When his small hand landed on my bicep, I started.

"What's that mean?" His bright green eyes were on the whorls of dark ink bisecting my skin.

"They're the markings of my pack," I answered.

His eyes widened. "Are you a shifter?" he asked with awe.

I nodded. "Sure am."

August's mother pulled him back, scolding him softly. I knew she was uncomfortable about what I was. My kind were the ones abducting and selling females off, after all.

Clenching my jaw, I sent him a tight smile. "Some of us are defenders, August. I promise we're not all bad."

Though his mother's expression dissolved into the darkness of memories that played out behind her eyelids, August grinned widely.

"I'm gonna be a wolf when I grow up too," he announced proudly.

My grip on the steering wheel tightened. August might not grow up fearing my kind completely, but his mother and the other women would teach their children to believe we were all monsters.

And I couldn't think of a single thing to say that would wash that away their fear or their pain.

But I'd do everything in my power to end the ones that gave shifters a bad name.

CHAPTER FOURTEEN

Dani

I crossed the square, trying to ignore the pink flowers being carted around. In the heat of the near summer sun, I hoped they all wilted and died. Even if they were daisies, which were my favorite. Yellow, though. Not pink.

The town was swathed in tulle and lace. My chest tightened at the sight, forcing my limbs to move faster. The summons to meet at the town hall likely meant that Donovan's men had arrived.

And our tying ceremony would be tomorrow night.

I entered the building, relishing the cool blast of air-conditioned air. My skin was sticky with sweat, but that was more to do with binding myself to a guy I both hated, yet was potently attracted to, than it was the heat.

In the meeting room, my parents sat around the table, Donovan to my father's right, and three relatively attractive guys sitting across from him.

Leaving two seats empty.

Next to Donovan, of course.

His searing gaze tracked my steps, but I didn't bother looking directly at him. I already felt it everywhere. The memory of the scrape of his teeth over my neck made me shiver involuntarily.

"Daniella," my mother greeted.

I nodded once in her direction before meeting my father's stare. His expression was carefully blank, save for the slight twitch of his brow.

"Alpha," I nodded to him as well.

"Ah, so you are able to be submissive, Little Wolf." Donovan's soft words were ear splitting in the aching silence.

My face flamed, as did my anger. The smirks from the Dockhills guys made me want to imprint my fist into their smug faces.

"To no one but my father, Dickhills. Remember that," I snapped.

Donovan chuckled, but my father cleared his throat, bringing the room's attention back to him. "A demonstration, please, Donovan," my father said tightly. No doubt Donovan's comment had flared my father's own irritation.

The Dockhills alpha inclined his head before getting to his feet. He walked to the wall behind us to a large stack of boxes that I hadn't noticed before. Pulling something out of the first one, he strode back with whatever he'd picked up, secured in his palm.

When he dropped back into his chair, he opened his fist on the table. I felt myself leaning in to see what it was.

It was only the size of a thumbnail; black with a reflective surface that I guessed was a screen. Donovan's eyes landed on me.

"If I may, Daniella." His use of my name instead of "Little Wolf" always threw me—this time especially.

My mouth opened and closed—at a loss for words when my father spoke.

"Yes, proceed. She will need to wear one anyway. We're not taking any chances."

Donovan's jaw clenched, but he kept his gaze on mine as he pulled out a second device from his pocket. It was much bigger and looked a little terrifying.

"What's that for?" I asked when he grabbed my wrist and pulled it toward him. His thumb stroked my skin where my new, fully-healed tattoo was. It was a possessive gesture, but it did things to me that I would never admit aloud. The back of my hand rested on his jean-clad knee, and I smelled the fresh aftershave on Donovan and his newly smooth jaw. Like an insane person, I wondered how soft the skin would feel under my lips.

He slid the tiny black chip into the bigger, tube-like thing, and it made a soft whirring noise. I tried to pull my hand away, but he gripped me tighter, lining the tip of the tube to the inside of my forearm, just below the dark ink. Before I could swat it away, he clicked a button and I hissed.

The sudden bite of pain was wholly unexpected, but when he released my arm, the bead of crimson where the device had been, grew engorged until it began to slowly run over the moons and the two opposed wolves. I blinked at it, suddenly realizing my father was on his feet shouting something, and a bunch of other voices joined in.

Finally, Donovan rose to his feet as well. "Placing the device under the skin is the only way to be sure they won't confiscate the tracker. He pulled out his phone, tapping the screen a few times before turning it around for my father to see. "This is an offline app that pings a satellite so the lack of cell reception will never be an issue on either party's part.

He turned to me, not looking an ounce repentant for shooting a little tracking device under my skin without my consent. Although, after last night, I knew he harbored less than no care for my consent in any matter. Though there had been something in his eyes before he did it. Like a warning. Or maybe I was just imagining it. His gaze dipped to my forearm where the blood had dried, and his lips turned down in the slightest of frowns.

I got to my feet too, the rush of hot anger lancing through my veins. "Great, so if any predators besides you try to kidnap me, I'll be able to be located. Joy. Can I leave now?"

Donovan's gaze lazily lifted to mine, lips twitching. "There's a second part to this device." He took my other hand and placed it over the now fully healed wound. I jerked away, not trusting him to touch me. "Hold your finger over the device for five seconds. It will send out an alarm that you're in danger. It has to register your fingerprint, which will keep the alarm from being activated accidentally."

I swallowed hard, running my fingertip over the minute bulge, before pausing on it. *One. Two. Three. Four. Fi—*

A sharp shrieking tone came from Donovan's phone. Nearly

everyone in the room, myself included, clapped their hands over their ears. Donovan, however, was unfazed. After a moment, he silenced the alarm, a light of triumph in his gaze.

"Now I know you'll be safe." His words were low, meant only for me, but then he turned to address my father again, who still looked ready to leap over the table and strangle him. I kind of wish he would. "As promised, I have supplied enough for your entire pack and then some, for the future generations of wolves. I'll have Gerard set up the program you need, and he'll explain how to register each chip to your program. Your mate and second beta should have it also, in case of emergencies."

My mother spoke up then. "Is the device detectable? What if they were to cut it out?"

Donovan's megawatt smile turned on, but the brilliance of it was lost on my mother, whose lips were pressed tight. "That's an excellent question. The device is currently adapting to Dani's body temp, her casual heartrate, and it's keeping a log of it. When that changes, there is another alarm that will sound. Her heartrate would have to spike rapidly for it to trigger, but it's more of a warning.

"If the device is cut out, the temperature differential will also trigger the alarm and since her heartrate will no longer be detected, it will flash with the message that the device was removed, sending her last recorded location for retrieval."

Seeming satisfied, my mother nodded.

"Well, thank you, Donovan, I'm sure this technology will go above and beyond what we need to help end these abductions," my father said gruffly.

The alpha beside me nodded. He turned to go and my mother cleared her throat, stopping him.

"We hope that you will be able to join us this evening for a private family dinner. It'll be our last chance before the ceremony tomorrow."

A bolt of panic seized me. I was trying my hardest not to remember the ceremony tomorrow, but it was getting impossible. Especially when the whole town was drenched in so much gaudy décor.

He glanced over his shoulder, flicking a smirk my way. No doubt he could smell the tsunami of fear and dread I was sure to drown in. "I wouldn't miss it." Then he marched out, two of his cronies trailing him, while the other engaged my father, going over the details of the trackers.

I looked to my mother who gracefully slid around the table to my side. Her smile was sympathetic. "Should we see if there's anything left to decorate?" she asked.

A lump rose in my throat, making my next words difficult to get out. "Oh, I don't think they missed a single inch. It's all so...pink." I wrinkled my nose.

My mother laughed, steering me toward the door. "If you had it your way, everything would be black leather and death metal."

That still sounded gaudy, but at least it would be slightly more palatable than pink everywhere. "Yellow would have been nice. For the daisies, I mean."

My mother's sapphire blue eyes twinkled thoughtfully. "I might be able to arrange that."

My shoulders relaxed a fraction. "Thank you."

She squeezed me to her, grinning as we stepped out into the square. "Attention, everyone! A slight adjustment." Faces all around lifted to us. "Scratch the pink where possible, we're going with yellow."

Some sighs of frustration rang out, and I felt terrible that everyone had gone through so much trouble to decorate everything, only for me to change it at the last second.

I groaned. "Maybe just leave the pink, Mom. I feel bad about making more work for them."

"Nonsense," my mother chirped, heading toward Delilah, my mom's oldest friend and Syr's mother, who began to remove the pink daisies from the steel buckets, dropping them into a wicker basket. She smiled at our approach, looking the least bit irritated. "This is likely to be your only mating ceremony. I want it to at least be to your liking."

"There she is," Delilah crooned, throwing her arms open to embrace me. I let her, comforted by her cheerful demeanor. When she pulled back to examine me, she asked, "How are you feeling about the big day tomorrow?"

I had no doubt that my mother told her every detail, which meant she knew that I was not tying myself to Donovan out of any sort of affection for the alpha-hole.

Forcing a smile, I said, "I'll be better once I've had a few drinks."

She laughed, releasing me at last. I looked around the square, watching everyone transform the eye-searing pink into vibrant yellow, and my stomach churned.

"Have you tried on your dress to make sure the measurements are perfect?" Delilah asked, though she glanced to my mother for the answer when it was clear I had no idea what she was talking about.

Delilah was a seamstress and her eye for fashion was on point, so it made sense that my mother would have asked her to make the gown I was meant to wear for the ceremony, but I hadn't heard anything about it.

"I was just about to show it to her, actually," my mother said. The curl of her lips was not quite a smile, and I wondered if it was because she knew I'd refuse to wear anything special for Alpha Dickhills, or if it was because she didn't like it.

"Well go now," Delilah urged. "If it doesn't fit perfectly, bring it by my place tonight."

My mother nodded before pressing a gentle kiss to her friend's cheek. "Thank you, Lilah."

Delilah shooed us away, smiling. "I've got everything under control, you two go."

I didn't need any more encouragement to get moving. My body's urge to run won out, and I sprinted back to the house, knowing my mother wouldn't be far behind.

Throwing my bedroom door open, I spied the elegant gown lying on my bed. I frowned at it. The traditional Tying Ceremony color was pink, not red. When I'd left this morning, it hadn't been there, which meant my mother had laid it out while I was at my daily training session. Syr had been absent, but after last night, I wasn't surprised.

Taking a step toward the dress like it might lunge out and strike,

I observed the intricate details. It was beautiful, yet sexy. A triangular panel of sheer lace cut down the front to just below where my breasts would be. Slender, black straps adorned with jagged, wicked-looking crystals crisscrossed the lower abdomen. The crystals appeared to rain down the skirt, getting smaller and smaller. The pleated, gauzy fabric would fit loosely around my legs, while the rest would hug my curves.

It was perfect. Clearly Delilah had made it especially for me, infusing my personality into the dress. But now I knew why my mother had been reluctant to get me into the dress. It bordered on too sexy for a Tying Ceremony.

I heard her soft footfalls in the hallway before she stopped in my doorway. "Do you like it?"

Hesitantly, I nodded. "Such a pity that I'll be wearing it for such a terrible event."

My mother scoffed. "Oh, stop. I've seen the way you two look at each other."

"Like we want to rip each other's throats out?" I snapped a little too harshly.

But my mother just smirked as if she was in on a secret. "Attraction is without limits. You may hate him, especially with *how* he got you, but the fact that having you as his mate was incentive enough to hand over millions of dollars of technology, proves that he does not hate you. Besides, you two may very well fall in love."

I snorted. "I'd sooner die."

My mother's smile faltered. "Don't do anything foolish, my love. This isn't the end. It's a fresh beginning."

Unable to argue further with my mother, I plucked up the dress and headed for my bathroom. "I'll be out in a minute."

When I stepped out of the bathroom, only my beating heart and the light swish of fabric could be heard. Until my mother squealed so loud, I nearly came out of my skin.

"Oh for the love of Chaos! You look amazing!" She darted forward, inspecting every inch, and though the dress was revealing and completely backless, Mom couldn't stop smiling. "Wow, Lilah really did a fantastic job, didn't she?" Her eyes lifted to me, seeming to expect an answer.

I nodded and meant it. "It's stunning."

"Go look in the full-length mirror," she shuffled me towards my closet. "I have to go start dinner since we're having a special guest tonight."

I caught her parting wink in the mirror before my gaze slowly swept down my body. The dress was breath-taking. The sheer panel in the middle, crossed with the jeweled straps was badass.

A slit rose up one thigh, and I had the wicked urge to wear a holstered blade there for all to see. My lips curled into a grin.

Without warning, a knock came at my window. Whipping around, my heart shot up in my throat. I half expected it to be Donovan, and a mixture of emotions swirled through me when I saw that it was Syr.

Rushing toward the window, I twisted the lock, and pulled the window open. "What are you doing here?" I asked.

Syr climbed into my room, taking in the dress with eyes that flashed silver. "Is that what you're wearing tomorrow?" His voice was raspy.

I nodded. "Your mom made it."

"Yeah, I think I saw it around her place once or twice. I should have guessed it was for you."

My stomach somersaulted. "Are you okay?" I asked.

He shrugged. "I just came to see if you wanted to talk after…" His words trailed off, but I knew what he meant.

My cheeks heated. That dance had been…intense.

"It was…a dance," I started, "and it was great. But it's not like anything has changed. I'm still tying myself to Donovan tomorrow." The familiar lump that kept surfacing chose that moment to appear, nearly choking off my words.

Syr's jaw clenched. The anger and betrayal radiating from him was so potent, it made my heart fall into my toes.

"Syr…" I reached out for him, but he moved away, backing toward the window. My chest heaved as my breathing turned ragged. "Syr, please. Stay with me. Stay for dinner…stay the night. Please."

He paused, searching my face. I know he could read my desperation. The desire to not lose him just yet. But it was just delaying the inevitable. By tomorrow night, I'd be tied to Donovan, and my best friend would be lost to me forever.

"I don't want to be around him." My shoulders sagged at his response, but then he added, "I'll be back after he's gone."

A spark of hope flared deep inside the tattered remains of my heart, and I smiled. "I'll leave the window unlocked."

CHAPTER FIFTEEN

Brax

My ribs weren't completely healed when I decided to venture back out. Rogue had attempted to herd me back to the cabin for the first few hours, circling my legs and nudging me back. But when I continued on, he fell into step beside me, realizing it was better to be by my side than to waste his efforts encouraging me to lay back down.

I patted his head, pausing to feed him some of the dried meat I had stored in the cabin. "It's alright, Rogue. We just don't have much time."

He ate his small meal before happily wagging his tail anew. The circular gap of his left ear stood out to me, turning my insides. Rogue's decade of service had earned him his own injuries; including a bullet that barely missed his skull entirely.

I scratched behind his ear, and then we started again, pausing only to drink what little water I carried in my pack.

It took less than a day to hear the rumble of engines. My veins turned to ice and I froze.

"Rogue, hide!" I commanded. Without looking back, I tore through the trees, flying over craggy rock. My blood sang with vengeance.

I sent my vow to the stars above. To any of the gods that deigned to listen. *Tonight, I will avenge you, Esme*. I squeezed the locket that slapped against my leg within my pocket.

All fear and self-preservation fled with a blinding need to make them all bleed as I raced toward them. My blades were out before the first flash of silver.

At least two dozen motorcycles blazed down the dirt path—the only slightly even terrain up in The Reaper's Spines. I let the first knife fly, then another. Both hit their marks, knocking the first two riders from their steely beasts.

The domino effect unleashed chaos. Bullets shrieked through the air near me. I danced between trees, making their target a tricky one.

My senses guided me as I sent blade after blade tearing through flesh and bone. Then the chase began. Some on foot, others on their motorcycles. I kept to the rockiest, steepest decline, sprinting down the mountain and ensuring few could follow.

But heavy footfalls and shouts chased me.

The thrum of my pulse was a steady beating drum. I was down to my last three weapons, not including my bow which wouldn't be any use at close range.

They grew closer as I ducked behind a tree, letting the first heavily tattooed man run past. I sank steel in the back of his neck, and he dropped, tumbling end over end down the rocky cliffside.

"Come on out, Lone Wolf. We hear you've been causing all sorts of trouble for us," a slimy voice said from maybe fifteen feet away.

I counted his slow steps, listening to the others fanning out around me. My breathing picked up speed. They were locking me in.

A soft whistle penetrated the near silence. The impact of an arrow through my shoulder sent me to my hands and knees. I snarled at the tip painted with dark blood protruding from above my pec.

Snapping it off, I got to my feet, reached behind, and grasped the long, slender rod. Then I yanked. My roar was drowned out by the dozen or so men who sprung into action.

I used the arrow to deflect blades, then punched the blunt tip into a taller man's gut. Their faces all blended together—marked with so much ink they almost appeared to be the same ghost split into different bodies.

I pulled my axe free from my back and lunged, swinging it with the practiced movements that severed muscle and tendon. Blood was a gruesome fountain of arcs shooting in every direction.

A boom sounded, and the pain that exploded through my abdomen and back sent me crumpling to the ground.

My axe fell away, and I felt the silver infecting my skin, penetrating my blood stream. A piece of it must have been lodged inside me. Fists and boots rained down on me, but my wolf wouldn't respond to the call.

I felt myself slipping away, the edges of my vision hazy.

What felt like moments or maybe hours later, I blinked, and the men were gone.

My entire body was an interconnected web of sheer agony, but I couldn't get myself to focus long enough to see the sky above. A high-pitched keening sound had my eyes jerking open again. Rogue stood over me.

"Hey, Old Friend," I wheezed. Coughed. Tasted the coppery tang of blood, wheezed again, hearing the rattle of my breathing and winced.

There was too much damage. I'd lost too much blood.

My spirit seemed to cry out for another, and Rogue attempted to nudge himself under my head, ever so gently. *Get up*, he seemed to say.

I groaned, rolling until my upper body was draped over his back. Pain shot through me like bolts of lightning. His weak body trembled, but he began to move.

"To the cabin, Rogue," I think I said.

Then it all faded to nothing.

Except a gleaming silver light reflected over a still pool of water. And a girl with midnight hair who turned to take me in.

She wasn't mad this time.

"Daniella," I breathed.

Then even she faded away too.

CHAPTER SIXTEEN

Dani

When the doorbell rang, I was helping my dad fry the potatoes and onions. His tense body language was plenty for me to read, but his scent reeked of aggression.

Mom opened the door, and Donovan's silky voice emanated from the foyer. Dad audibly ground his teeth together, while I stiffened. Was I ready for this? The four of us trying to pretend like we were some happy family? A smitten couple spending their last night with the female's parents…it was all too cliché for me.

Dad stabbed a steak hard enough to bend the fork, and I jumped. Mom and the overwhelming presence at the entryway paused.

I peered sidelong at my dad because that was preferable to gazing at Donovan. There was a sort of hostility between the two of them that didn't seem to just be about my upcoming ceremony with Dickhills.

Thank the Goddess our customs weren't like that of the humans, where females took their partner's name. I'd sooner kill myself than become Daniella Dockhills.

"Uh, here, I'll take that, Donovan, it was really sweet of you to bring dessert. We've been so focused on getting everything ready for tomorrow we didn't even think of making anything." Mom took the wrapped pie plate he extended towards her, smiling his irritatingly charming smile.

I opened my mouth, about to gesture to the silk pie Mom had made, when she cut me a silencing look.

The smell of lemons wafted toward me and my mouth watered instantly. Leveling Donovan with a glare, I asked with all the fake sweetness I could muster, "Did you seriously make lemon meringue pie?"

He speared me with those golden eyes, smirking. "Yep."

I smiled tightly. "Wonderful. I'll inform Betty Crocker she's been replaced."

Mom laughed loudly and Donovan chuckled.

"I'll take that as a compliment," he answered.

Dad turned from the stove with a plate heaped with rosemary butter steaks. "Let's eat before they get cold," he announced gruffly, cutting off my response.

I blinked, pulling the sizzling potatoes from the pan and into the bowl with the rest before killing the burner. Hugging the warm dish to my front, I made my way to the table with the others, taking my seat at the rectangular table across from Mom, but next to Dad. It was where I always sat.

But when Dad cleared his throat, indicating for me to scoot down, my hackles raised. It was tradition that the next in command in the room sat at Dad's right hand. As beta to the Carvingwood Pack, it was my seat. But with Donovan here, a fellow alpha, it was his seat to take.

Gritting my teeth, I said, "Fine," before scooting the chair back with a harsh groan and taking the next chair down.

My blood felt like lava in my veins and for several minutes, I couldn't look anywhere but at the pitcher of ice water on the table. Beads of condensation ran lazily down its sides, soaking into the fabric tablecloth.

I could feel Donovan's heat. His scent mixing with the delicious food on the table I no longer had an appetite for.

But I had to get through this dinner.

"Daniella, your mother asked you a question." My dad's terse voice finally lifted me from my internal raging.

"What?" I asked, my gaze lifting. It shifted from Dad—who sat tall and proud in his seat, to my Mother who sipped water from her crystal glass.

"I asked if you were packed yet," she repeated.

A scoff escaped me before I could stop it. She knew full well I wasn't packed. Dad's grip on the fork in his hand became so tight, his knuckles whitened.

I cleared my throat and shook my head. "Since I won't be able to carry much on the journey, I'll only bring a bag of necessities."

"Actually," Donovan started, but I refused to look at him, "the truck that we carried the devices in is now empty, so there will be plenty of room for anything you'd like to bring."

"What's the point?" I muttered under my breath.

My father stabbed a steak before slapping it onto his plate.

Donovan inhaled a deep breath—like that would prevent him from trying to strangle me. "Your comfort is the point, Little Wolf."

I tried not to laugh at that. No, I really did try. But it burst out of me all at once. A stream of hysterical laughter that I couldn't control. Donovan spooned potatoes onto his plate while both of my parents stared at me like I'd lost my mind.

Finally, I got myself under control, wiping the tears that clung to my lashes away. "Could you pass the green beans?" I asked my dad with barely contained amusement.

Donovan shook his head, but ate in silence.

My dad's eyes narrowed on me as he lifted the casserole dish. Why he was mad at me suddenly, I didn't know.

"So, Donovan, can we expect a visit every once in a while?" I didn't miss the sadness tinged in my mother's voice, and neither did Donovan, because he paused with a forkful of steak near his mouth.

Setting the utensil down, I braced myself for his rejection. My father seemed to as well if his stiff posture was any indication.

"Perhaps every few years," Donovan answered. "And you would be welcome in Dockhills too, Angel."

My angry retort was cut off when a bang sounded from the head of the table. Dad's red face had me bracing for a fight. "You will not keep our daughter from us, Alpha Donovan, and that is final!"

Donovan took a sip from his glass, unaffected by my father's rage. The wolf inside me wanted to growl at the man that dared defy my alpha, but I watched him, my knife in hand. Maybe if I stabbed the bastard this nightmare would end. "Actually, Alpha Evan," he said, flicking his gaze from me, to my father. "I can do with Daniella whatever I please because she will be mine in less than twenty-four hours."

My father shot to his feet, body seeming to grow. The room was suddenly hotter—all primal wolf heat and dominance.

"Then our bargain is—" he began, but Donovan held up a hand to stop him.

"Don't forget what I said earlier." His tone was chilling. "If word should get out about your little secret, the Carvingwood Pack would fall into chaos, would it not?"

I blinked, confused. "What secret?" I demanded.

My mother's face paled, but my father simply shook with rage.

Before anyone could answer me, a heavy knock sounded at the front door. We all stilled, noting that none of us had heard anyone outside because we were so consumed with our argument. One I fully intended to resume as soon as I found out who the fuck was making such a racket at the door.

I stomped through the foyer and pulled the door open, my mother close on my heels. But the second it was opened, a dark shape in the form of a man fell into me, knocking me back as I grappled to accommodate the man's weight.

His scent was woodsy but plagued with the coppery tang of blood.

My mother's shout of alarm drew both alphas into the hall.

Behind the man, reaching for him as though she meant to catch him, was Faith, our resident healer.

"Found him in the woods, injured badly. He's a lone wolf, I think," she rushed to say in her thick accent.

Just then the man's face turned, his nose brushing the column of my neck. Then I heard him inhale. Unable to control it, I shivered before glancing down at him. With his profile in view, I could tell he was handsome. Feathers and beads were woven into the long, coarse strands of his dark hair. He had rich brown skin, but his eyes were closed.

"Why did you bring him here?" I asked Faith.

She wrung her hands together, looking nervous. Faith was a short, plump woman from far off lands. Gifted as she was, everyone thought her a bit odd. I didn't, however. She was always good to me, patching up mine and Syr's injuries when we needed it. Her beliefs were different than most, but I respected them all the same. "He woke up a bit when I had him at mine. Went wild, thrashing about an' all. He's such a big man, I could'na keep him down long enough to tend all his wounds, but he came straight here, so I thought maybe he knew ya."

"Thank you, Faith," my mother said. "Would you mind coming in? We'll see if we can get him to make any sense, but I'd still feel better if you could look at him some more."

"Sure thing," Faith said.

Donovan and my father came on either side of me, trying to lift the unconscious man from my lap.

As they shifted him, I heard the faintest mumble, just a single word, but it froze me in place.

"Daniella."

Somehow, he was familiar, drawing forth a memory that slipped away before I could grasp it. Donovan must have heard him too because he jerked, suddenly.

I scrambled back, letting the men carry him into the living room. Never had I been so thankful for an intruder, even if I had no idea who he was.

They hoisted him onto the couch, and I was able to get a better look at his striking face. If I had to guess, I'd say he originated somewhere far north. My mother and Faith got to work cleaning up the multiple cuts still oozing blood, but the worst of it looked as though it was coming from his abdomen.

Without really knowing what I was doing, I reached out, carefully prying the guy's lightweight linen shirt away from his skin, sticky with blood. The garment was most likely a brownish color at some point, but now was stained dark and smeared with mud and leaves.

Before I could get the fabric up high enough, Donovan grabbed my hand.

I snapped my gaze toward him, opening my mouth to tell him to let me fucking go before I kicked his balls into his throat, but he surprised me with the calm in his eyes.

"He'll need stitches. Do you have a needle and thread?" he asked.

I stared at him for a moment, warring with my need to dismiss him like I always did, and help the man bleeding out on my couch.

“Uh, Mom has a sewing box in the hall.” Getting to my feet a little unsteadily, I headed for the hallway.

Thankfully the box was right where I thought it would be and I hurried back with it, stopping dead at the threshold.

The man’s shirt was cut open, revealing a hint of hard-earned abs beneath dark crimson that both Mom and Faith mopped up gingerly. Donovan’s penetrating gaze snapped up to mine and he extended his hand for the box I held.

“He had a bit o’ silver in ‘im that I was able to get out. Can’t tell if there’s any more though,” Faith said.

Remembering to breathe, I rushed forward and surrendered the box, then looking around for a way to make myself useful.

Dad come in the other way with a bottle of clear alcohol that Donovan snatched away without so much as a thank you. I dearly wanted to know what the source of the bad blood was. In the past four years when Donovan competed in the Pack Games, he’d interacted with my father on some level, and I never remembered a great deal of hatred on my father’s end.

Donovan, however, was always an asshole to everyone he met.

Which was why seeing him expertly stitch the massive hole in the guy’s abdomen without his usual swagger and arrogant smiles was just plain weird. The focus in his eyes, though, was downright intense.

I gathered the bowls with murky water and used cloths, taking them into the kitchen to dump and refresh. After replaying the man’s voice saying my name for the fifteenth time or so, it finally snapped into place.

The guy from my dream a week or so ago. Braxton.

With fresh supplies, I made my way back into the living room, wondering how in all the hells he had found me. Lone wolves were a rarity, for obvious reasons. And one wandering Carvingwood territory was beyond strange.

When I set the bowls on the coffee table, Donovan's attention swept over to me, but I ignored him, peering down at Braxton. They'd rolled him onto his back.

It was a bullet hole, wide and jagged—it looked like a small explosion had occurred.

And the hole on his shoulder was smaller, like that of an arrow.

"You're sure there was only one piece of silver?"

Faith glanced up at me and nodded. "When I found 'im he was practically dead from the poisoning. It was digging it out that made him go mental."

A strange silence passed through us. Mom glanced up at dad, then at me, before I met Donovan's gaze.

It wasn't humans that ravaged towns, gunning down those they couldn't make a profit on. There were two known groups that razed and terrorized: The Bone Crushers and The Silver Vipers.

Had they gotten close to Carvingwood? Were the neighboring towns untouched?

"Should we send out a border patrol?" I asked my dad, worry churning through my gut. "Ivywood and Shadow Ridge could have been hit. We need to—"

"You will do nothing but go to your room and get some rest. I will deal with the situation at hand." It stung a little when Dad used his alpha voice. My only choice was to back down and obey.

Two things I did not excel at.

Donovan stilled, needle hovering mid-stroke. He gave off almost as much heat as the wounded guy, making the room near stifling.

"Fine," I said with no shortage of irritation. Stomping to my room, I didn't dare look back at Donovan.

It would have made it too real.

I took a shower to rid myself of the stranger's blood.

My stomach rumbled just as I stepped out, wrapping a towel around myself. I wished I'd been able to eat a more substantial dinner but thinking about how one of the violent gangs of traffickers could be close quickly made my appetite vanish.

It wasn't long after I threw on a long, baggy T-shirt I'd stolen from Syr a few years back that I heard the front door close. I hurried to my window and peered down. Faith and Donovan walked together.

As if he could sense me, he paused, turning to look directly at me. I didn't cower or bother with embarrassment at getting caught spying. Instead, I flipped him the bird, earning a smirk.

Then he was gone.

I collapsed on my bed with a sigh, hoping that Syr would still come. When an hour went by and the house was quiet, I snuggled beneath my sheets. Distantly, I heard the mournful howl that didn't belong to any wolf. *Must be a stray dog*, I considered. Likely one of the council members would go put it out of its misery. My thoughts shifted to what tomorrow would bring, making it difficult for sleep to consume me, but eventually it did.

I barely heard the soft groaning of my window sliding open sometime deep in the night. My eyelids were too heavy to open fully, but Syr's arms, warmth, and scent wrapped around me like a blanket. And despite the questions I knew he wanted to ask—like who the extra male in the house was—we tangled together just like we had when we were kids.

CHAPTER SEVENTEEN

Dani

I jolted awake suddenly. Whatever dream I'd been having dissipated from my mind instantly, though my heart still pounded. Instinct had me reaching for Syr, but the sheets beside me were cool.

Empty.

My heart sank as I looked around the room for his shoes, or any hint that he was still here. Early morning sun peered into the room through the window. It brushed the delicate red tulle that pooled on the ground from the gown hanging on my closet door. I swallowed hard, knowing what today would bring. But Syr was truly gone.

I glanced at the clock beside my bed, seeing that it was a few minutes past six. It was a wonder that my mother wasn't already in my room shoving me into the dress.

Kicking my legs over the side of the bed, I got to my feet and stretched. As I rubbed my eyes, trying to mentally prepare myself for tonight, a faint crash sounded. Recalling that there was a strange man in the house, I pulled my door open and rushed into the living room.

The stack of blankets folded at the end of the couch looked like the person who'd done so, hadn't folded anything in a long time. Or maybe ever.

Dishes clattered in the kitchen. I followed the sound, finding the big, burly man with dark skin and even darker hair. His shirt was absent, leaving behind the most tantalizing view of the man's muscular back. Standing at the sink, he scrubbed the dishes piled there, albeit clumsily.

He must have registered that I was there because he whirled, the sudsy pan slipping from his grasp and sloshing back into the sink filled with water and bubbles. His eyes were the deepest, darkest blue I'd ever seen. And they locked on me, pinning me in place.

"You're Braxton, right?" I blurted out. Not, *Hey, you feeling better?* Or, *My, your abs sure are perfect.*

Okay, scratch that last one. But seriously, his physique was mouth-watering. Minus the old, silvery scars and the stitched wound on his stomach that was now an angry red circle.

The man didn't seem as though he'd heard me, staring at me like he wasn't sure I was human or ghost.

"Daniella," he breathed.

My brows pinched together. "Yeah."

He cocked his head to the side. "You remember me?"

For some reason, a swell of warmth filled my chest at the relief in his tone. I bit my bottom lip before nodding. "The dream?"

Braxton smiled, revealing perfectly white teeth.

"How did you find me?" I asked, instantly feeling like a jerk for sounding so skeptical.

The stranger's eyes slid down my body like cold honey—slow and sweet. "I sensed you. Or maybe you led me to you. I'm not sure."

I blinked. "How is that possible? How were you able to crash my dreams?"

He scrubbed a hand over the back of his neck, and the muscles along his torso rippled with the action, drawing my gaze lower. I could tell the simple action pained him, but fuck me he looked good doing it.

Lowering his hand, he shrugged. "Something about you called to me, and I walked across the dreamscape to find you. There are legends of my people being able to enter other's dreams intentionally, using them to influence people to change their ways, or for mates to find one another."

The last part had my eyes wide. "Mates?"

Seeming to be searching for a feeling or anything between us that might indicate that we're mates, he paused, then nodded nonchalantly. Abruptly, he whirled back toward the sink and began the menial task of washing up yet again.

"Why are you doing the dishes?" I asked, stepping closer to him.

"It is my thanks for your hospitality last night. And for stitching my wound," he answered gruffly.

I folded my arms across my chest. "I didn't stitch your injury."

My words were spoken like an apology.

Glancing sidelong at me, his lips curled slightly at the corners. "Well, I thank you all the same for allowing me to rest here."

Nodding, I felt the need to add, "My parents mostly took care of you, and Don—my, uh…soul tied…is the one that stitched you."

I couldn't help but notice the way Brax's nostrils flared as he stilled. Turning to observe me—this time a little differently—he said, "You're bonded?" Then, to himself, he muttered, "That explains the stench."

My nose wrinkled. "Gods, no. Another pack alpha wrangled me into a soul tie. He's a total dick, but I'm doing it for my parents. Hey, the ceremony is tonight, if you want to come. There will be food and dancing and—"

"No." His harsh bark silenced me instantly. Then he shook his head, taking a deep breath. "My apologies, I shouldn't have shouted. I didn't realize you were…spoken for."

My cheeks burned, though I didn't know why. It's not like I'd intentionally concealed the arrangement between myself and Donovan, but the guy had sought me out based on a single, shared dream.

He finished scrubbing the pan, rinsed it, and set it aside to dry with the others. Then he wiped his hands and turned to face me again.

And again, I was nearly pummeled with the force of his beauty. Odd that I'd ever consider a male beautiful, but he was truly a sight to behold.

"Please thank your mother for me, but I must be going. Rogue will be howling somewhere in need of breakfast." He started for the door and my feet carried me after him before I had time to stop myself.

"Rogue?"

"My dog," he supplied, heading back into the living room to gather the cache of weapons stored near the couch. I wasn't sure where they'd come from, since I hadn't seen anyone removing weapons from him. It made sense though, given that he was a stranger in our home.

"Oh, that must have been the howling I heard last night."

Just as I said it, a sad yowling sound emanated from right outside the house. Brax rolled his eyes. "Yep, that's him."

He strode through the house and pulled open the front door.

I stood on my tip-toes, trying to peer over the beastly man, and spied a large, muddy brown dog sniffing along the row of flowerbeds across the path. Still having not detected that his owner stood less than twenty feet away, he sat back on his haunches and tilted his head back to let loose another pitiful cry.

"Rogue!" Brax called.

The dog's head snapped in our direction, and then the hound was sprinting toward the man with almost a frantic gait.

Brax waited, letting Rogue leap into his arms. The dog furiously licked Braxton's face, tail wagging so hard his entire body vibrated.

"That's enough, Rogue. There's someone I want you to meet." His deep timbre vibrated all the way into my bones, and the dog stilled, seeming to understand his master's meaning.

Brax set Rogue down, though his back end still swayed back

and forth, his mouth open and tongue lolling lazily to one side. If ever an animal looked as though it smiled, Rogue was the picture-perfect image of it.

Moving aside so Rogue's path to me was clear, the dog met my gaze. He sniffed the air curiously, then all at once bounded toward me.

Leaping onto his back legs, Rogue's big, heavy paws landed on my shoulders. I laughed, scratching the dog's back while his tongue lapped at my face, which only made me laugh harder.

"Rogue, sit," Brax ordered.

The dog cast him a sad look before reluctantly plopping himself down onto his rump. I clucked my tongue at Brax, scratching the big teddy bear behind the ears.

"Can you point me in the direction of the nearest town?" Brax asked.

For some reason, my heart ached at the thought of him leaving. Which was completely ridiculous because I didn't know this man—even if we were somehow able to connect in our dreams.

"Uh, yeah. Ivywood is a thirty-minute run from here. Longer if you walk. I could probably give you a ride—"

"You are not going anywhere, Daniella, you have a Tying Ceremony to prepare for." My mother's voice behind me caused Brax and I to whirl.

Her dark brown hair was tied up into an elegant knot at the top of her head, a silken, forest green robe wrapped around her slender body.

"There's nothing to do between now and tonight, Mom. I'd be

less than forty-five minutes." My protest was met with my mother's disapproving look, though she examined the man as though considering his injuries from last night.

"I don't require a ride," Brax said. "I'm healed now, thanks to your kindness." He directed the words at my mother, though his oceanic gaze came back to mine.

I couldn't help the small smile that curved my lips.

"Yes, well, it was our pleasure," my mother answered, not unkindly, though her eyes took in the dog sitting just inside her foyer, panting happily, and distaste creased her otherwise beautiful features.

My father appeared behind my mother, clasping her shoulder protectively. "I'd like to have a chat with you before you go, if you don't mind," the alpha said in his commanding way.

I could tell the tone prickled at Brax, but he quickly smoothed away the evidence and nodded. "Certainly."

My father held out the bag filled with weapons and the fur-lined shawl that Faith must have brought over after I went to bed. Before following my father out, Brax turned to me. I could tell there were a lot of things he wanted to say but couldn't.

"If you should ever need anything—shelter or whatever—my residence is in the northern Reaper's Spines. There's no one for many miles. It's a farm really, you can't miss it."

I nodded. "Thank you."

He dipped his head, though his gaze remained entangled with mine until he'd backed out onto the porch. Even after he spun, calling Rogue to his side, I watched them go, feeling an odd sense of foreboding.

My mother grabbed my arm, pulling me out of the way before the door slammed shut. "Come on. Time to primp. Everyone will be here shortly. Have you eaten?"

I bit back my dramatic sigh and let my mother push me into another shower. She lathered all sorts of scented soaps onto my skin before applying fragrant oils as well. People began to show up with boxes and my belongings were all unceremoniously dumped inside them.

My hair was brushed, curled, and pinned up on one side, letting it flow over my other shoulder.

Small finger foods were shoved at me all day long, but my stomach was too twisted to eat any of it. I kept glancing down at the ink on my forearm as though it were some sort of direct link to Donovan.

I kept my gaze on the window, watching the sun slowly descend toward the horizon, and knowing the end of my life was in a matter of minutes. As much as I wanted Syr to be here to help my nerves, I was certain that seeing him would make going through with the ceremony even more difficult.

At the last possible moment, my mother forced me into the dress that hugged my curves in the most delicious way, but I wanted to claw the damn thing off.

Everyone simpered and complimented me on the match to Donovan. Wearing a forced smile, I nodded, letting myself be led out of the house as the sun began to dip into the trees.

My mother wound her fingers through my own and squeezed,

offering me a sympathetic smile. "You look beautiful."

"Thanks." My voice was hoarse, and my stomach tried to turn itself inside out.

The flower petals lining the path from the porch down through the streets were a pale pink, and more fluttered down from above. A gentle drumming sounded in the distance, serving only to ratchet my nerves up.

Taking one step, then another, my courage grew. Before rounding the last bend, my mother let go of my arm, pressing a kiss to my temple. I pulled my shoulders back, inhaled…

And left my old life behind.

CHAPTER EIGHTEEN

Donovan

My heart thumped in time to the growing rhythm of the beat. Each one pulling Evan's beloved daughter closer to me—and out of his grasp.

The tension in the square was so thick—pregnant with excitement and anticipation. I drummed my fingers against my thigh like I usually did when my nerves got the best of me. Faster the drums pounded, and a gentle breeze swirled through the waiting bodies, cooling the humid night air.

Then the soft scratch of tulle reached my ears. Her scent mixed with a floral concoction drifted around the corner only a second before she did.

The ruby red dress hugging her delicious frame made my lips quirk to one side. Gasps came from those not expecting such a bold move. But I had expected it. The panel at her middle was lace, crisscrossed with studded leather straps, but still giving me a glimpse of smooth skin.

The raven black of her hair falling over one shoulder made her look even more the dangerous goddess she was. Shoulders back, chin high. The slit up one side of her dress allowing peeks of decadent, creamy thigh had me waiting for the hint of a thigh holster.

Ah, there it is. I smirked, and let my eyes roam back up my little wolf's body, locking onto her violet gaze. It seared into me with both contempt and fire that I knew burned for me the same way I did for her.

She marched bravely down the row, and those on the edges dipped their fingers into the shimmery golden dust that they brushed on her arms, her cheeks, her hands. I didn't understand the symbology of the act since the ceremony amongst my pack was much more…animalistic.

I supposed it could just be to elevate her further amongst her people. She didn't so much as blink until she was before me, and her father—who still seethed—greeted those gathered.

He spoke the usual lines about the history of the chaos, and how it didn't always pair two compatible souls together. I wanted to roll my eyes at that.

Since there hadn't been a Chaos in nine years, it was impossible to know if those that chose to soul tie were not actually meant to be true mates. And though I scoffed at the mere idea, part of me wondered if the way my wolf paid Daniella's such great notice, if she might not have been my mate under the moon of the Chaos.

It didn't matter anyway. This was all purely to punish the Carvingwood alpha for what he did to my father.

Yet, when I took Daniella's hands in mine, the jolt ran all the way up my arms, heating my blood. She glanced up at me from lowered lashes, and I found myself wanting to tilt her head back so I could see her stunning eyes better. I wanted to command her to look at me, just to have her attention.

But I held still as the ribbon was wrapped over our joined hands and tied.

"With the flame to seal this union, let it be known before all gathered here that none should come between wolf and mate." Evan's voice was booming, but his irritation was palpable. He'd just signed his daughter—his beta—over to me.

One of the women from the pack, Faith, I think, came forward with a thick stick lit with golden crackling flames burning at the end. She held it beneath out hands, and the ends caught fire, burning away so fast the singe of flame around my wrist was barely more than a dull ache.

Daniella stayed silent but whipped away from me as though she hadn't been prepared for the pain. Her skin was red, but with wolf healing, the both of us would only bear matching silver scars by morning. She wore my tattoo as well.

It was a pity I wouldn't be able to mark her the way mates did while I fucked her.

Applause rang out, a dull roar filled with cheers. It was customary for the bond to be sealed with a kiss.

I snaked an arm around her middle, pulling her flush against me. She glared up into my eyes, and I barely held back my smug grin long enough to press my lips to hers. For a moment she was stiff and unresponsive, clearly battling the urge to push me away. Then, whether unconsciously done or not, I felt her lift up on her tiptoes.

I used her surge of deepening arousal to part her lips with my tongue and she met my invasion with her own. Kissing her was like having wings—the two of us tangled in a lethal spiral toward the awaiting ground. We could no less pull away to save ourselves than we could draw breath.

We broke away before it became embarrassing, yet my chest rose and fell faster. She turned away to face the crowd, studiously avoiding my gaze but there was no way in all the hells I'd let her off that easily.

Before I could pull her back toward me, however, the audience converged offering pats on the back and congratulations. As much as I tried to keep her plastered to my side, I felt her being pulled away, and in a blink, she was out of my grasp.

I growled possessively, earning a few chuckles from the males around. As if they had any gods-damned idea why my blood churned with the urge to claim her. To push her back against a tree once again and fuck her in the wild way I knew she needed. My Little Wolf was no timid woman—in or out of bed.

Over the past few years, the rumors were easy to sort through. Those that coveted the fierce raven-haired beauty and lied about how they took her all night long. And the fewer that had managed to wrangle her into bed and were barely able to satisfy her but made her out to be a lioness that needed the teeth and claws capable of subduing her.

I knew better.

There would be no conquering Daniella Carvingwood. She needed a male that was equal to her.

And from this day forward, I would be that male.

Music blasted from speakers, everyone breaking away to dance. The bass was deep and shook the ground beneath my shoes as I started for the woman who stood with—surprise, surprise—Syr Milton.

His expression resembled a kicked pup, which I found almost laughable. She was tied to *me*, and lover boy was only just realizing he'd waited too fucking long to make his move. I started for her with swift movements, knowing my presence would be announced before I reached them.

She glanced over at me just as I'd been expecting, the look of exasperation on her face morphing quickly to the usual agitation she wore around me. I liked her glares and craved her feisty responses more than was probably healthy.

I draped an arm over her shoulders like it was the most natural thing in the world, my fingers automatically caressing the smooth heat of her skin.

"Ah, lap dog. What are you going to do without Dani here to command you?" I teased.

Dani jerked, but I tightened my arm around her. A rumble of anger vibrated her slim frame, but I ignored it.

"Fuck you, Donovan," Syr snarled, stepping closer. Good. I was sick of seeing the bastard backing down like a bitch. "She's never going to belong to you the way she's *always* belonged to me. Didn't you smell me on her? *I* was the one who warmed her bed last night. Not you."

The leash I kept on my rage was a single cord away from snapping. Without meaning to, my fingertips dug into Dani's shoulder, and she struggled to get free. I had no doubt with a well-placed kick she'd find a way to get away from me, but she didn't.

Though I made an unconscious move to scent the air, she didn't reek of her chew toy like she usually did. Maybe that was why she smelled like an overpowering bouquet of flowers. To hide the fact that his odor had been on her.

"Syr," Dani said in a reproachful tone before I had time to snap at the man whose body expanded—his wolf trying to break free. Wolf or man, I'd put the asshole in his place.

"The only thing that matters is that you lost your chance," I told Milton. "She's mine now, and there's nothing you can do to change that."

He launched forward, preparing to swing. I pushed Dani away to keep her from getting stuck in the middle. His clumsy punch was easily blocked, and my own fist impacted under his chin, snapping his jaw together.

My Little Wolf pushed her way between the two of us, shoving us apart a few steps. She was strong for such a slender female, I'd give her that. But I let her move me, and I guessed the tank of a man who was her best friend allowed himself to be set back by her as well. Though, from the limited experience I had with the two of him, if she said to stick his head under water and count to a million, he'd do it with a smile on his face.

"Enough you two," she hissed.

Around us, the throng watched on with curiosity and confusion. My body thrummed with the urge to get Daniella alone. Syr shook his head, a smirk pulling at his lips as he took the hand she kept on his chest and pressed his lips to her palm.

A growl echoed low in my throat.

"Dance with me," he all but demanded, staring down at Dani with an expression I couldn't read.

"She's not going anywhere with you, mutt," I snarled. Pulling my soul tied away from the male who was two seconds from having his head ripped off, I began to march away. She made a disgusted noise, trying to dislodge my grip, but I was too fucking far gone.

"Get your hands off me, you brute!"

I ignored her, my heart thundering in my ears. My wolf was tearing at the threshold of my slipping control. If I didn't bend her perfect ass over, I was going to murder every male in the vicinity.

"Did you fuck him?" I asked in a voice that was only partly man. The rasp and growl of my beast made the words harsher.

She didn't flinch. Instead, she scoffed.

Like I was being ridiculous.

"What would it matter if I did?" she asked with all the venom of a viper.

Whipping her so close our breaths mingled, I spoke with well-practiced alpha control that she had no choice but to yield to. "Did. You. Fuck. Him?"

Her teeth audibly ground together. "No dickwad, I didn't."

Satisfied, I continued to yank her along, moving toward the trees.

We barely made it out of view when I had the top of her dress fisted in my hands, yanking it open in one swift movement. She gasped when the cooler air stirred over the pale pink buds of her hardening nipples. I took in her mouthwatering tits while my chest heaved with ragged breaths.

The need to claim her was pulling me deeper into insanity.

My mouth crashed down on hers, and she kissed me back with brutal force. She pushed my jacket down my arms, nails raking into my back with only my formal white shirt separating my skin from her.

But I wanted to feel them. Wanted to feel her rage, her wrath. Nipping her smooth flesh, I ran my tongue over her jaw, down her neck, drawing moans from her devilish lips.

It was the distraction of her body against mine, the tantalizing realization that I owned her now the way she'd owned my thoughts for years, that kept me from immediately hearing the rumble of engines drawing closer.

I was so fucking caught up in her that I didn't register the threat until Alpha Evan bellowed to take cover.

The screams began not long after, followed by gunshots. I tried to push Dani deeper into the forest with the command to stay hidden, but of course she didn't listen. Launching into wolf form, she sprinted back into the town center, heading straight for the gang that had wreaked havoc on the whole of Chaos Valley for years.

I chased after her, seeking out my own pack members that were somewhere in the melee. Using my alpha link, I felt for each of their presences, ordering them to stand and fight, though I needn't have bothered. Every one of my wolves were fighters.

Daniella was out of sight, but her scent wasn't far. I changed as well, leaping into the air right as a motorcycle tore down the main path. The man riding it had a tribal ink on his temples and chin, and was pointing a pistol at the scattering citizens. There were several dozens of them, a much smaller number than the pack they infiltrated, but their weapons were filled with silver bullets—a fact I knew all too well. My body collided with one of the massive males riding the beastly machine, knocking him to the ground. I sank my teeth into flesh, the tang of blood rolling over my tongue.

My target's body expanded, changing to wolf beneath me. His massive paw impacted with the side of my head, jarring me. But I didn't relent, snarling, and snapping my teeth before closing on his furry throat.

He kicked and growled in vain when at last I tore his throat out. The spray of blood soaked my fur and I got to my feet. Like a nightmare, flames engulfed the gazebo, spreading over the dry grass. Houses burned and smoke churned to the sky.

Most of the pack remained in human form, dousing structures with water from buckets and barrels hoisted by four or five shifters.

Looking around, I tried to spot Daniella, but she was nowhere to be found. A clawing panic rose inside me so swiftly, my vision edged with red.

I let loose a howl that only she would understand.

A moment later, an answering snarl—muffled by the chaos—reached me. I let out a huffed breath of minute relief before charging deeper into the attack.

CHAPTER NINETEEN

Donovan

The fight was vicious. Shots rang out and wolves dropped. Large furry bodies, as well as limp human forms, were hauled over their thunderous bikes. I managed to decapitate a few, while narrowly avoiding the spray of silver fragments.

My second fought beside me until I caught sight of one of the monsters with a bandana wrapped around his head tugging what appeared to be an eleven or twelve-year-old girl out of a burning house, toward his steel chariot. I launched myself at him, knocking him to the ground and snarling at the girl to go. She fled, giving me the opportunity to sink my fangs into flesh.

The guy was huge and tossed me off as though I weighed nothing. I lunged again, only spying the flash of steel a millisecond before the blade was plunged into my side.

A beastly snarl erupted from my throat. I slashed the smirking grin from the asshole's heavily tattooed face.

He roared his fury, kicking me back. Pain sluiced my abdomen and my vision doubled. "You're lucky I don't skin you for my coat, mutt," he sneered.

Just as I stumbled forward, teeth bared, a high-pitched whine sounded behind me. Whirling around, I staggered to the left, seeing the vibrant silver wolf I recognized collapse. Blood matted her silver fur in several spots—far more obvious than any that coated my own.

A laugh came from the hulking man in my periphery. I let him back away, struck by the horror playing out only twenty feet in front of me. My limbs were like weighted noodles, but I forced myself to move anyway. A broad-shouldered, dark-skinned giant flung my Little Wolf over his shoulder, toting her away from me.

A howl clawed its way out of my throat—strangled by whatever coursed through my veins from the blade. Poison?

It didn't matter.

Nothing fucking mattered.

I had to get to her.

Where the fuck was her damned lap dog when you needed him?

As though my thoughts conjured the wolf, golden fur glinting in the light of flames that still raged all around, Syracuse Milton tore after the bike now speeding away.

With my fucking soul tied, naked and human once more.

Why the hell had she shifted? And why wasn't she fighting?

I had to hope she hadn't been shot with silver. Depending on the size, she wouldn't make it.

Her best friend sprinted after her like a beast possessed with a mating bond. The world spun so fast, I hit the ground, stomach roiling.

Fucking hell.

I felt my body changing without my consent.

Then it hit me.

The blade was made from silver.

Son of a bitch.

Almost as soon as the devils roared into Carvingwood, they left. All that was left behind was a smoking trail of scorched earth.

When I came to, lying on a cot with only the stars above me, I sat up.

Then winced, hand going to the bare flesh of my torso. Where stitches sewed my flesh together.

The faces of my men swam, but their worry was still visible in my semi-cohesive state.

"He lives," Daniel teased.

I felt a damp, fragrant poultice of herbs meant to draw out toxins clumped over the wound. I left it there, feeling another wave of nausea wash over me. Steadying myself for a moment, I ignored my pack, looking around for any hint that my Little Wolf had fought her way back to me. A few houses appeared to be charred but salvageable, while others were heaped piles of rubble beyond repair.

The sheet at my waist began to slip, and I clenched it in my fists, feeling the clawing, aching swell of wrath rising through me. She wasn't here. I couldn't scent her or feel her nearby. Still, I found myself scanning the dozens of cots set throughout the square with still bodies atop them. The healer woman passed from one to the next, slathering mixtures onto wounds and checking dressings.

If she noticed that I'd awoken, she didn't let on. Near her, was the brute of a man I'd stitched up myself. His dark eyes flicked to me before he began to make his way over, a massive dog at his side. I tugged the sheet around my middle and stood.

The stranger stopped before me and my companions, examining the six of us like he was trying to decide if we were friend or enemy. I couldn't help but feel a niggling sense of dread that Autumn was noticeably absent.

"Where is Daniella?" I asked to no one in particular.

The man instead, disregarded my question. "How are you feeling?"

My teeth ground together before I could answer. "Like knocking skulls together, where is she?"

"I heard the Vipers when I was leaving, so I came back," he said as though that were an explanation. "I made it just in time to help out but not fast enough to…"

My pulse sky-rocketed at the words left unspoken. They were heavy in the air. A snarl tore from me, and I turned to Ryan, my third in command.

"Get my phone and a set of clothes from the house over there." I pointed to the house at the edge of the square. The windows were blown out and the bottom was blackened from the heat of the flames, but otherwise the integrity of the structure appeared to have remained intact. Ryan nodded before jogging away.

Using my telepathic link to my beta, I called for Autumn. But suddenly I felt the distance straining our bond. "No," I muttered in disbelief. "Autumn!" I bellowed, causing several people nearby to jump.

Whirling on the men behind me, I silently demanded an answer. She wasn't dead because I'd have felt that. But I wanted them to say she ran south for backup. Or that she'd already begun tracking Dani.

Anything but the obvious, glaring truth.

They bowed their heads but kept quiet. The damning silence told me my second had been stolen as well.

"How the fuck could you let this happen?" I spat at them.

Daniel opened his mouth like he wanted to retort, but I bared my teeth and uttered a menacing growl that had them all shutting the fuck up.

"We need to leave. Now," I commanded.

They nodded, but the rogue spoke up. "How do you plan on finding her? I've been tracking the Vipers and the Bone Crushers for ten years. Their movements are erratic at best. They're ghosts."

"No one is fucking invincible," I snapped.

Just then, I spied Evan and his jolly band of ignorant dickheads. Among them was Syr.

Evan's gaze was on me, narrowing to a glare that I returned. Striding toward him through the rows of wounded wolves, I forced myself to take even, measured breaths so I didn't rip the guy's head off. The stranger trailed me with the near silent mutt at his heels.

We met in the middle with Evan's entourage fanned out around him. Their dislike of me was palpable. Especially Syr's.

"How long have they been gone?" I asked through gritted teeth. "And better yet, why the fuck are you still here? I gave you the technology needed to track the assholes. Why are you wasting time?"

Someone put a hand on my shoulder that I shrugged off.

"I've sent a party to track her. They're moving south. I need to be here to oversee the damage control of my pack lands." The condescension in his voice had my nails lengthening, tearing into the sheet fisted at my hip. Then the bastard continued. "Interesting that my daughter has been in your care for less than a day and was snatched right from under your nose. And here you are, barking like a rabid dog instead of chasing her down yourself."

I took a measured step closer. "It was in *your* territory that the devils just waltzed through like it was an open invitation. It says more about your security measures than it does about my abilities to protect your daughter."

A muscle in his jaw ticked, and my satisfaction only managed to slightly abate my need to rip his throat out.

"*When* I get Dani back, she will promptly return to Dockhills with me." I let those words sink in, glancing lazily at Syr to make sure he got the message.

The curl of his lip told me he was as pleased by that as Evan.

Ryan's footsteps behind me had me turning to accept the stack of clothes and my phone. I switched it on, scanning the list of serial numbers until I found Dani's. After clicking on it, I handed it back to Ryan for him to hold the display out while I quickly dressed.

The map filled the screen, with her dot flashing red. I checked Autumn's next. Their locations were identical, which meant they were together.

My throat grew tight. They were almost outside of Chaos Valley, far from any known packs. With the glow of early morning beginning to light the horizon, I pulled on my boots and laced them, then stowed my phone into my back pocket.

To Ryan I asked, "My bike?"

He shook his head. "They torched it."

I pulled in a calming breath to stop my wolf from tearing through a fresh set of clothes. "We'll never catch them on foot."

"I have my truck," Syr offered begrudgingly.

I turned to face him. "Fine. I'll need to use it."

His features hardened. "Either I come with you, or you find someone else's vehicle to commandeer."

What was left of my patience was fraying fast. But time was running out. "Let's go then."

"I, too, will journey with you," said the feather-haired rogue.

"I don't have fucking time for this. We need to move. Now." I started for the hidden lot, not caring who followed.

To my pack, I issued a silent command for them to pack up Dani's belongings and what little I'd brought with and tote it back by whatever means possible.

As I reached the truck, throwing the driver's side door open, I heard Syr ask the stranger his name.

"Brax," he answered, hopping into the back of the truck with the dog without any sort of explanation for who the fuck he was and why he wanted to come on a rescue mission. I couldn't help but wonder if this man had somehow led the Vipers here. If so, there would be hell to pay.

But I recalled the way he'd made his way to Dani and uttered her name like a prayer. There was a connection there, and I intended to pry it out of the rogue.

The second Milton was in the seat next to me, I had the engine roaring to life and began speeding out of Carvingwood territory.

I prayed to the moon goddess for the first time in my thirty-one years on this planet. Prayed that Dani and Autumn would be unharmed when we made it there.

Because I *would* get to them.

And I'd raze the whole fucking valley if a single scratch marred my wolves. Those bastards would pay for taking what was mine.

CHAPTER TWENTY

Dani

Pain lanced through my skull, but my eyelids were too heavy to lift. The floor beneath me rocked and jolted, making me groan.

Every muscle and tendon was bruised, I was sure of it.

Jeering laughter sounded from somewhere, but it was muffled.

What the—

The ceremony replayed in my head, followed by the attack. I remembered the gunshots. Feeling the explosion of pain in my shoulder. The throbbing began anew and still I tried to recall it all. It came in bursts and flashes until my eyes flew open. My body was too heavy, too tired to move. I couldn't feel my hands, but I could tell that one was stretched out above my head. Slowly, I managed to roll my wrist, feeling the coarse bite of thin plastic and blanched.

I was tied to something.

It was dark, wherever I was. I tried to let my eyes adjust, cataloguing the smooth feel of vinyl or leather beneath me. Sweat dampened the fabric clinging to my skin.

Who dressed me?

Little by little, I managed to crane my neck to look around. My enhanced vision didn't seem to be working, but little details became visible. Like the fact that I was on a seat cushion, my legs dangling off the edge. They were bare, but the shirt I was in draped down mid-thigh.

There seemed to be at least a dozen other presences near. Someone cried softly, and whispered words that I guessed were meant to be comforting, but the language was unfamiliar.

The space was quite large, and given the fact that it moved and jolted—an engine rumbling not far off—I guessed I was trapped in an RV.

A chill swept over me, and I shivered suddenly.

"Dani?" a feminine voice croaked.

It took me a minute to place the voice. Then I gasped. "Autumn? They got you too?"

"Yeah," she rasped.

"Why am I so cold?" I asked. A bead of sweat ran down my temple, into my matted hair. I tried to lift my head to find where Autumn was being held, but couldn't.

"The silver. They shot us with silver." She was winded, and I understood the sentiment.

My eyelids drooped.

NO. Fuck. Stay awake, I ordered myself. Being shot with silver almost certainly meant death, but it wasn't always instant if the amount was small enough. It acted as a poison.

But from the searing, burning pain in my shoulder, I wondered if the silver was still inside my body.

"Where were you shot?" I asked her, trying if nothing else to keep her awake.

"Leg, I think." Her answer was slurred.

"You have a tracker, right?"

A pause.

"Autumn?" I called.

"Yeah," she said at last. "I have a tracker."

I gave a shallow nod, then realized she couldn't see it. "How long have we been out do you think?"

I heard her give a pained moan before she said, "Sun is coming up."

Glancing around, I noticed fabric curtains blocking the dim glow of morning light and my stomach dropped.

All night. We'd been traveling all night.

Why hadn't my dad come for me? Why hadn't Syr? Or even Donovan. He had two reasons to hunt us down. Yet he hadn't.

The idea that he was wounded or even dead had my stomach rolling with another wave of nausea.

"They'll come for us," I said aloud. "They have to know where we are."

Autumn gave a non-committal grunt of acknowledgement.

Just then, the vehicle slowed, and the movement ceased. My

heart lodged up in my throat and I tried tugging my arm down. The zip-tie bit into my skin, but I ignored the pain, struggling harder.

The door to the RV was thrown open, and light poured in, making my eyes squeeze shut for a moment. Boots thundered into the capsule and I forced my eyes open.

The man that entered held a flashlight in one hand and some sort of glowing wand in the other. It looked like the kind of device used at an airport to scan someone for weapons.

He was tall, bald, and built like a shorter version of the Hulk. Tattoos decorated his arms, his neck and up the back of his head. He looked as mean and ugly as one would expect from a kidnapper.

He wasn't the man that shot me and tossed me onto his bike, however. I'd never forget the eyes that glittered with the fires of demons.

My efforts to break free were fruitless, and eventually I went limp, choosing to glare at the intruder instead.

Like that would do any fucking good.

I tried to call up my wolf, but the shift to my other form felt blocked somehow.

The guy looked around, and I saw the stirring of females ranging from maybe eleven or twelve to mid-thirties. My stomach churned and I felt certain I'd vomit.

"Didn't think you'd be heard, didya?" He smirked. "You lot were scanned before you made it in here, but Imma do it again. Just to be sure."

Fuck. They know about the trackers?

Then he waved the wand over the first girl. One that was far too young, her face stained with bruises and tears.

My rage stirred and I tried to twist myself free yet again, moving in a way that wouldn't be blatantly obvious. Down the center of the RV, he carefully moved the device over each female, leering at them as he went.

Finally, he made his way close to me, bending down to scan the girl at my feet who I confirmed was Autumn by the flash of reddish hair.

The wand made a high-pitched static sound that had almost everyone cringing. My wolf stirred beneath my skin. Just a hint to let me know she was there.

Autumn kicked the man who grinned like he'd won the jackpot. He easily dodged her sluggish attack, barking a laugh. "Well shit. How did you make it on the van without getting scanned, sweetheart?"

"Fuck you," she spat, though the words were a jumbled mess that was hardly coherent.

I tugged harder, knowing the band was slicing into my skin. The slow trickle of blood running down my forearm would be a dead giveaway.

A second guy peered in. "You found one?" he asked incredulously. The man was older with sparse brown hair and deep creases at the corners of his eyes. He was old enough to be my grandfather.

"Yep," the first answered smugly as he straddled Autumn's legs. I couldn't hear the rest of what he said because when he pulled out a knife, she started to howl and scream, bucking with renewed vigor. But it wasn't enough.

The silver had made me desperately, humanly weak. If I'd been at full strength, a quick shift would have snapped the zip tie with no problem.

Her desperation fueled my attempt to escape. I could feel my hand starting to slip through the binding, and continued to twist myself free.

The second guy marched in as pandemonium began. All the girls cried and screamed.

On his way past, he slapped the young girl who tried to throw herself at his feet. The crack of his hand against her cheek silenced the caravan instantly.

"That's enough out of you bitches. If you think you're going to cause trouble, we'll give you a second dose of silver. Eh? That'll shut you up."

Storming over to help the guy who wrestled Autumn's arm out, he waved the wand over her pale flesh.

The crackling static sounded again. Too loud and too shrill to make me do anything but grind my teeth.

Then the tip of the knife pressed to her skin. She shrieked—the wild animal side of her taking over and fighting for survival.

I felt it too. And as my hand slipped free, I launched myself to my feet. Everything swam and spun, but I lunged for the men, tackling the first to the ground and prying the dagger from his hands.

My entire body jerked with lightning rods of pain jolting through every nerve ending. My muscles locked up, and the man tossed me off.

I realized all too late that the second guy had a fucking taser. It wasn't until the prongs released my skin that I understood what had happened. I just laid on the floor, spasming and tried not to throw up.

Dark spots danced at the edges of my vision and through bleary eyes I saw the nasty, greasy man hold the wand over me. It gave off that same traitorous scream, and then I was hoisted back onto the leather-padded seat.

I tried and failed to stay conscious.

Only when Autumn's screams echoed through the small space did I open my eyes. The tip of a knife pressed against my forearm, beneath Donovan's ink.

"Well, well. Two of Dockhills' bitches. What an honor." He grinned wide, and feral. "You lot are slippery."

The first slice cut through the haze of impending unconsciousness. Burning pain followed the blade and I was forced to watch as the guy pulled out the small black object that had, until this point, been keeping me alive.

He handed it to a third guy who had entered at some point—this one younger with the stance of a brain-washed soldier.

"Bury these," he commanded.

My panic was drowned out by the crushing wave of nausea. Tilting my head as far as I could, I vomited the contents of my stomach over the edge of the seat. Distantly, I hoped I hadn't just puked on some poor girl who was unable to move away.

The men left, and soon the RV was moving again. This time faster if the hard bumps and intense rocking were any indication.

They were trying to outrun the only thing that might have saved us.

I guess it's up to me to get myself out of this, I thought. But darkness crept in on silent wings and smothered my fight, forcing me to succumb to the blood loss and poison churning through my body.

CHAPTER TWENTY-ONE

Brax

The alarm blaring from the device in the Alpha's pocket inside the cab made him swear loudly, slamming his hand against the wheel.

"What?" the one called Syracuse asked, alarmed.

"Their fucking trackers were cut out!"

My blood ran cold. I didn't know any more than the fact that Daniella had some sort of tracking device we were following. I'd asked a handful of questions and gotten even fewer responses.

Rogue whined beside me, somehow seeming to understand the gravity of the situation. Or perhaps he simply sensed my distress.

Before Donovan decided to pummel the entire vehicle, I stuck my head inside the cab. "I might have a way of tracking her."

Syracuse glanced at me. "How?"

"It would require my falling asleep, and of course, she'd also have to be asleep in order for it to work."

Donovan scoffed. "What the fuck are you talking about, you crazy vagabond?"

I ignored his attempted jab. To wolves, not belonging to a pack somehow meant that you were unstable. Of course, it couldn't just mean that pack life didn't suit us. I didn't plan on divulging my past with him now, or ever, so I let it go.

"I can connect with Daniella through dreams, no matter the distance. It's how I knew where she was and was able to find her—though that was unconsciously done. I was simply trying to track the despicable creatures wreaking havoc on Chaos Valley."

"What, you can sense her location when you're asleep?" Syracuse asked.

"I can communicate with her. It's called dream walking. I enter her dreamscapes. It was the location of her dreams that told me where she was. If I were to enter her dreams, she could tell me where she is, or I could simply try to get a read on it myself."

"And if she has no idea where she is?" Donovan asked with more than a little malice.

I shrugged. "That's the best we've got, right?"

The cab was silent for a moment. Then Syr asked, "Why her? I mean, you came out of the mountains, right? How could you have forged a connection with her over such a distance?"

Donovan tensed, unable to hide that he was listening for the answer as well.

I slowly shook my head. "I don't know. There were stories among my people that told tales of dream walkers, but I never found out how it worked. And Daniella was the first person's dreams I'd ever been able to access."

"What do you need to be able to try it?" Syr asked. Clearly, he was the more level-headed of the two.

"Your seat, actually," I said with a smile that was all teeth.

"I'm not stopping this damn truck," Donovan shot back.

Syr eyed the back window and pulled it open further. "I haven't had to climb through there since I was seventeen," he grumbled.

Turning, he began to maneuver himself through it. I gave him a wide berth, knowing if he could fit through it, that I would be able to as well. He was stacked with muscle for one so young, and had to angle his shoulders out. Then he pulled himself out, into the bed of the truck.

I patted the top of Rogue's head. "Stay, old boy," I rumbled. The dog cocked his head to the side, but didn't make a fuss as I went feet first through the window, dropping onto the seat in one swift motion.

Donovan's knuckles were white on the steering wheel. We were eating up open road much faster than the gangs would have, since they'd have been confined to the forest paths. Soon we'd be forced into the woods as well.

"I don't have a freaking pillow for you, so that's going to have to be good enough." His tone was harsh and biting, but I paid him no mind. It was clear he was worried for the two girls, but part of me suspected a deeper attachment to Daniella that he wouldn't admit aloud.

Resting my head against the window I shut my eyes.

It took several minutes of listening to the engine's purr for sleep to take me. But the switch was seamless.

I sought out Dani's dreamscape, pushing my awareness all around until I found her. In an instant, I was standing before her.

She was bound to a chair with men circling her. They each had knives that dripped blood. Fury shone in the girl's vibrant purple eyes—not fear as one might expect. She caught sight of me, and her brows furrowed.

The men that leered at her finally sensed my presence looked up to find me standing there. I attacked first, drawing my blades and slicing through flesh that felt oddly realistic. But they fell too fast and too easy, reminding me that the blood they wore was not really hers.

But as a projection of her subconscious, I couldn't ignore the possibility that she was truly hurt.

I pulled the cloth covering her mouth down, allowing her to speak.

"I was about to do it myself," she said by way of greeting. Her hands came free, and she showed me, as though proving her point.

"I'm certain you had it under control, but that's not why I'm here," I said.

She swore. "This is a dream, isn't it?"

I nodded. "We need to know where you are. Your tracker was deactivated."

"I know," she snarled. "The assholes cut them out."

I tried to ignore the way my hackles rose at that statement.

"Have they done anything else?" My voice was lower and vibrated with barely leashed rage.

She waved my concern away. "I'll tell you later. I'm in an RV somewhere, that's all I know. I'm—"

The edges of the dream began to blur, and the chair that was behind her vanished.

"I'm waking up," she said, her eyes suddenly wide with panic. "Can you come back later? We must be stopping."

"I'll come for you I swear it." I reached out for her, the desire to take her in my arms undeniable.

But my hands passed through her, and then she was gone.

I jolted awake, breathing heavily.

"Well?" Donovan asked impatiently.

"She's in an RV. That's all I know."

He shut his eyes for a second, seeming to try to reign in his anger. "They'll have veered away from their original destination knowing they've found the trackers. The only hope we have is to intercept them."

I nodded. "I promised her I'd return to her soon. Best wait until nightfall though. By then they might be wherever they were attempting to take the girls."

"How did she look?" Syracuse asked.

"She was wounded," I answered. If anything, the truth would spur us on faster. And from the way the needle on the speedometer continued to rise, I knew I'd guessed correctly.

We soon ran out of road and had to slow to navigate over roots and through narrow spaces. Every so often we'd stop and scent the air for any hint of life that had passed through.

We got lucky, spotting a whole slew of tire tracks that we followed.

I wanted to believe we were getting close, but something told me she was farther away than ever.

CHAPTER TWENTY-TWO

Dani

Braxton's presence riled me. He'd said "we" which made me wonder who all was looking for us. Either way, I just needed to stay alive until then.

The fever made my body damp with sweat, yet my teeth chattered. I was retied, but this time with both hands. Apparently, they hadn't needed to fully tie a girl up before.

Good, I'll make them think me weak.

The RV slowed to a stop, and then the ugly faces from before appeared in the doorway. One by one we were blindfolded and carried out. Most of the women didn't struggle, and barring a few, who cried or muttered curse words, they were unconscious.

I pretended to be asleep when they slipped the foul-smelling cloth bag over my head and tossed me over someone's shoulder.

Lifting my head slightly, I peered at the ground through the only opening in the bag. But the sounds of birds and chirping insects in the distance told me we were near the forest.

Boots sounded on wood, and I saw the steps myself, counting four of them. The door was already open when the brute carried me inside what I assumed was a house. We wound through a hall, that led to another door.

Then we were descending steps. I counted those too, trying to memorize the layout of the house.

Finally, I was tossed onto a hard floor covered only by a few thin blankets, the air knocked from my lungs. My head hit something soft, but still it throbbed.

I had to get the silver out of my shoulder, or I was going to die.

The bag was torn off my head, but the room was as dark as I expected. Only a single light illuminated the large space. Bars divided us all. Dozens upon dozens of cells.

I blinked up at the man grinning down at me, his obnoxiously white teeth a show of dominance. It was tattoo-head from before. The way he was looking at me made me want to rip his dick off and shove it down his throat.

"I'll be back for you myself," he promised.

"Can't. Wait." I replied and meaning it. When the douchebag came back, I'd tear him limb from limb.

He narrowed his eyes, raking his gaze down me in an assessing way. "You'll fetch a high price, no doubt about that. But we'll have to do something about that fight of yours. Maybe a few sessions with a whip will straighten you out."

I huffed a laugh. "My death will be the only thing that drains the fight from my body."

His lips curled at one side. "We'll see."

With that, he spun, slamming the door on my cage shut. Gazing down, I looked at my blood-stained forearm. The tattoo was mostly untouched—a red, raised scar slicing through one of the moons where my tracker had been removed.

I spied the silvery ribbon marking from the tying ceremony and my heart squeezed painfully.

My head lolled to one side, and I saw Autumn in the cell next to me. Her back was to me, and she laid there, unmoving.

Unable to walk, I crawled to the bars the separated us and whispered, "Psst! Autumn."

I reached through the bars and brushed my hand over her back. She shivered, but still didn't respond. Her skin was hot, even to my touch and I knew I was feverish. I scanned her legs, not sure if I'd find was I was looking for. She wore actual clothes since she likely hadn't shifted during the raid on my pack.

But I managed to find the ripped fabric and pulled it aside as best I could. The skin around the wound was a deep purple and oozed pus and blood. It smelled even worse than it looked.

But I couldn't fish the shard of silver from her leg with my fingers. For one, it was too tiny, and of course, I couldn't touch it without it burning my skin.

I turned, looking around for something to use, but besides a steel toilet, a blanket and pillow, I was out of luck.

There was nothing to do but wait. Surely they'd provide

a toothbrush or utensils. Why they hadn't removed the silver themselves, I didn't know. Did they plan to sell us as dying cattle?

But if someone were willing to purchase another person, they probably wouldn't mind a little silver poisoning.

It kept us compliant and defenseless.

I tried to rouse Autumn again, but to no avail. The large space soon filled with cries and the stupid few who threw their drugged bodies against the bars as though they could do anything to them.

But even the foolishly brave soon grew silent. Not long after, a door was flung open at the top of the staircase, letting a little extra light bleed into the dank basement. Heavy footsteps followed, then Tattoo Head was back with few boxes of what looked to be protein bars. He tossed one into each cell, and I smiled when I saw the foil wrapper, scurrying towards it.

I didn't have time to care if the food was poisoned, but a quick sniff told me it was probably safe before I shoved it into my mouth and chewed greedily. It was like chewing sand, however, with how dry my mouth was.

I'd kill for some water.

No sooner had I thought it did the biker dude return with bottles of water.

"Don't drink them all in one go," he sneered with a cruel grin. "You'll only get one a day."

When he paused outside my cell, I couldn't help but glare up at the asshole.

"However," he continued for all to hear, but his eyes stayed glued on me, "if you're a good girl and you please us, there might just be some extra food and drink."

My blood boiled at the implication. Some might be willing to play the part of skank toy, but I was not one of them.

Lunging for the bars with the little strength I had in reserves, I collided with the cell door. The loud clang echoed in the space, beginning a girl's whimpering cries once again.

He flashed his teeth, barking a laugh. "I'm coming for you, Darkness."

Darkness? Because of my black hair? How original.

I bared my teeth, and a low growl shook in my chest, letting him know exactly what I thought of that idea.

Like lightning, his hand shot out, clutching me around the throat. He yanked me closer, still grinning like a feral cat. If my knees didn't shake just from the effort of being upright, I'd have gouged his eyes out. But as it was, he held me on my tip toes, and it was all I could do not to crumble to the floor.

"Bitches like you get tied down so we can all take turns fucking you. You'll be nice and broken in when you get your master."

The edges of my vision tinged red. I would spill this asshole's blood. Once I got this shard of silver out of my shoulder, I'd heal up and be back at full strength. And the first thing I planned to do was rip this guy's throat out.

"Bitches like me will be your end, you piece of shit," I snarled. His fingers tightened but still I managed to rasp, "When I get out of here, I'll make your last breaths a living hell. You'll fucking wish you were dead."

He launched me back and I hit the opposite wall, the air

painfully jarred from my lungs. I gasped and wheezed, desperately trying to fill them. He stormed away while I coughed and shakily sat back on my knees.

Eyeing the wrapper I'd left on the makeshift bed, I grabbed it, beginning to roll it to a small, bent point until it resembled a miniature tea spoon. It took several attempts thanks to my shaking hands. Sweat beaded my forehead when I scooted towards Autumn's cell.

"Autumn," I whispered, reaching through the bars to try to stir her.

Her skin was dangerously hot and I swallowed down my worry for the girl I'd never felt anything but resentment for.

"This might hurt a lot, but it's going to help," I told the girl. Then I shakily inserted the tiny device attempting to scoop the silver from her leg. For a moment nothing happened, though the wound bubbled and bled. Fortunately, I'd seen enough blood and vicious wounds in my twenty-two years not to be permanently scarred, but there was no denying that silver-poisoning was the worst.

My stomach turned, but I forced myself to focus on getting it out.

Her body suddenly began to convulse, and I drew back, horrified.

I checked to make sure she was still safely on her side and not in any danger of harming herself greatly, then carefully tried again.

This time when I drew the crimson-stained foil from her flesh, a tiny sliver of metal dropped to the floor.

I gusted a breath, and almost immediately, Autumn stopped seizing. But still, she didn't wake.

Swallowing hard, I wondered if I could do the same thing to myself. I went to scoot back to lay on the pathetic blankets provided when I noticed another torn scrap of her tactical trousers higher up—on her thigh.

My brows creased. Had she taken more than one piece of silver? That would explain why she was doing the worst of anyone in this hellhole.

Steeling myself, I began the process again, thankful when she didn't convulse this time. My vision swam, sweat running into my eyes and my arms growing weak. The one holding me upright shook violently, while the other—the injured one—ached from being stretched out to reach Autumn's upper leg.

Pain ricocheted up it suddenly and the forged utensil dropped as my arm gave out. I bit back my cry, and the exhaustion crashed down on me like a tidal wave. I huffed, gritting my teeth to try to stay conscious, but it was no use.

My body went slack, and my lids fluttered shut.

I stood in the middle of a darkened room, seeing only concrete beneath my feet. Taking a step, I heard the wet slap of my foot on the damp floor. The scent of blood coated the air so thick, it made my nose twitch.

Crouching, I ran a finger over the surface I stood on, and brought it to my nose. The coppery tang was an assault on my senses. My stomach turned and I rose to my feet, grimacing.

Something shifted in front of me, and I stilled. I had no weapon to defend myself, so I moved into a defensive stance.

Only for dim light to wash over a deeply bronzed chest. A faint clinking seemed to echo in the dank room. Dark hair came into view next, strands twisted with feathers and gems, which explained the sound.

Braxton's handsome face stared at me from less than ten feet away. Truly, he was far too beautiful. Like an ancient god made flesh. Somehow, I could smell his woodsmoke scent, even from our current distance.

Finally, his gaze tore from mine, looking around before he scented the air. Before I had time to speak, his attention snapped back to me.

"You're hurt." It wasn't a question.

"I was shot with silver and can't get it out myself. I'll be okay." Gesturing to the floor, I added, "That's not mine."

He nodded, seeming to have already worked that out. "Come here, let me try to extract it."

My voice seemed far away as I replied. "This is a dream. Whatever you do here, won't help me."

"I have to try." The intensity of his statement took me aback.

Then, I drifted closer to him, content to do just that—try. It's not like it could do any harm. Right?

I helped tug the baggy neckline of the T-shirt over to bare my shoulder, wincing as it gave a very real twinge.

He inspected the wound with gentle touches. Without warning his fingernail elongated to a wolf claw and he plunged it unto the tiny hole.

I gritted my teeth, trying to keep still. His eyelids fell shut, leaving me to fix my attention on the sharp lines of his jaw and cheekbones. The intrusion of his claw inside my shoulder felt all too real, so I moved on to counting the number of feathers in his hair. Eight. Interesting. I promptly moved onto the roughly carved beads made from black gemstones. There were three that were a dark purple and two that were an eerie green. In our previous encounters, I hadn't noticed so many of them. Or maybe I hadn't been paying attention. Braxton slowly twisted and maneuvered his half-transformed hand until his eyes flashed open.

Ever so slowly he withdrew his claw, and I caught the faint gleam of silver peeking through the crimson coating the small shard.

My shoulder still fucking hurt but already I could feel some of my former strength returning. The wolf within me stirred, and my natural healing began to kick in.

I exhaled a ragged breath. "Thank you," I whispered.

Brax's silver eyes were intense as he stared down at me. "We're coming for you. But in case we don't make it in time, run. If you can take some of those assholes down in the process, then so much the better. You'll be back at full strength soon."

A wicked smile curved my lips. "It would be my pleasure."

The relief that crossed his expression was alarming, but when he leaned down to rest his forehead against mine, I went rigid. It seemed like a too familiar gesture, but my wolf blood heated immediately.

He murmured something I couldn't understand, but before I could ask him to clarify, he smiled, pulling away. His form was hazy, his slow retreating steps making me ache to follow him out of this dream—away from the nightmare I was sure to wake up in. Everything began to shift, fading from my mind. The walls and the floor were magically void of blood.

"I'll see you soon," Brax promised.

I nodded, and then he was gone.

Blinking, I heard murmurs and whispers. My shoulder ached, forcing my eyes to fly open and my hand to yank the neckline of my shirt out of the way so I could see the wound. The skin was raw and red, but the small hole had closed.

I sat up, searching around me for the shard of silver, and found it when my hand accidentally landed on it.

I hissed in pain, the skin burning from the single touch. No wonder I'd been so sick.

"Hey," a voice said from the cell beside mine.

I whirled, finding Autumn sitting up. Though she was pale, she looked okay.

"Hey," I replied, scanning her, but her legs were folded to one side.

"I'm guessing you left me this?" She held up the poorly folded protein bar wrapper and I grimaced.

"I passed out before I could get the second piece. Do you have any more inside you?"

She shook her head. "I managed to get it out myself, thanks to you. I probably would have died with both fragments poisoning me for any longer."

I nodded my agreement.

After offering a small smile, she said tentatively, "You were muttering in your sleep. At one point you screamed."

That explained why nearly everyone was staring in her direction. "Has anyone been down lately for food or anything?"

Autumn shrugged. "No idea. I only woke when you screamed."

Oops.

Looking sheepish, I grumbled, "Sorry."

She shook her head, the matted auburn curls swaying side to side. "Don't sweat it."

I pulled my shoulders back and met her crystalline blue eyes head on. "I'm sorry about our sparring match. It was wrong for me to attack you the way I did."

Her gaze dropped to the floor for a moment before she slowly nodded. "Thanks. I mean, I know you were going through some shit, but it's still nice to hear."

It was my turn to give a hesitant smile that I hope conveyed my apologies. Truly, I'd almost killed her, and she hadn't deserved it.

Even if she was Donovan's second.

"So how are we getting out of here?" she asked with a lighter tone than before.

"Well, now that the silver is gone, we'll heal faster and regain our strength. If we can get all of the girls to help each other then we'll have the numbers needed—"

Autumn held up a hand suddenly and I frowned, snapping my mouth shut. Her eyes moved along the ceiling near the light.

I followed her gaze, catching the dull red flashing light and stilled. "They're recording us?" My whispered words were anything but quiet. Panic filled me. "Surely they saw my digging the bits of silver out of your leg and then you do it to yourself?"

"I made sure to angle my body, but they had to have seen what you were doing. The way you fell asleep gave them a perfect view."

My stomach dropped. They'd had audio devices inside the RV. It was stupid of my silver-poisoned mind not to consider that they'd have cameras hooked up down here.

"Why haven't they come yet, then?" I tried to make myself barely heard, but the men that captured us were undoubtedly shifters as well and would have no trouble hearing me if they really wanted to.

Her shrug was almost imperceptible. "We need to get everyone else to heal too though. We'll both have to whisper to the girls next to us and show them how to make one of those handy spoons."

I groaned. "I could barely see when I made that. Besides, I don't have another wrapper. Do you?"

Autumn nodded, handing me her empty foil packet. I took it and angled myself against the bars that separated us both, so my back was to the camera. No doubt they already knew I was no longer suffering from silver poison, but still I tried to look as though the bars themselves held me up while I slowly showed Autumn how to make the origami utensil so she could teach the girl to her left.

When she was able to replicate it, she crawled away, making the façade look all too convincing. I waited, listening to her telling the girl what to do. She was in her late twenties, with dull brown hair, matted with blood. She was completely naked for some reason, and it made my skin crawl.

I hadn't seen any of the girls completely naked.

The woman nodded, tears falling from red, puffy eyes before she set to work.

I took the wrapper back from Autumn and moved to my other cellmate. It was the little girl only thirteen or fourteen and my stomach turned violently.

"Hey," I whispered. She sat in the corner, hugging her knees to her chest with her head resting top them. Groggily, her head lifted.

My heart ached for the girl whose lips were tinged blue; eyes glazed over.

"What's your name, kiddo?" I asked.

Her lips parted then closed, then opened again. A look of confusion played across her slight features. "Kaylee."

"Did you eat, Kaylee?" I couldn't see the bar or the bottle of water, but her blankets were balled up across the small space.

She licked her lips, and I knew she hadn't. "When the guy came back and wanted to take me, I threw everything at him. He took the food and water." Her head tilted back to rest on the stone.

Gut twisting, I grimaced. "Okay, hold on." I turned and went for the remainder of my water. "Can you move?" I asked.

She nodded, unwrapping herself from the tight little ball she'd made of her limbs before crawling toward me. One leg dragged behind and my breath hitched.

"The silver is in that leg, isn't it?" I whispered when she was close enough.

She slurred a few sounds together, dropping onto her stomach in front of the bars. I stuck the bottle of water through the gap and held it out for her.

"I need you to drink this, okay? Small sips so you don't throw up."

"Kay," she answered. The word was spoken so softly I wondered if her heart was giving out. Just the thought had me reaching for her.

I felt for her pulse, and dread pooled in my stomach at how faint it was. Thankfully, she took the water, and lifted her head enough to take a drink.

"Am I gonna die?" she asked.

My chest officially felt like it was splitting in two. "No." I smoothed some of her blonde hair back from her face. "You're going to let me help you get the silver out of your leg, then you're going to heal and we're going to break out of here." I tried to speak quietly, but the firmness of my statement had her eyes flicking up to meet mine.

"Okay," she agreed.

CHAPTER TWENTY-THREE

Dani

With the instrument poised above the girl's leg, I swallowed hard.

"This is going to hurt," I admitted a split second before carefully sliding it in. She gritted her teeth but kept still. My eyes closed as I attempted to work off sensation alone. For the flimsy wrapper to catch against a piece of metal.

Around the room, all the women started to catch on to what we were doing and began to copy the process.

Whimpers punctuated the near silence, along with the occasional pained groan.

Just as I felt what I was looking for, the door at the top of the steps flew open and at least a dozen angry footsteps thundered down the stairs. I couldn't stop, I had to get the silver out.

Kaylee bucked from the pain, jarring my hand.

I swore. The piece was still in there, and the movement of it had her panting.

"I'm so sorry," I whispered.

The men funneled into the room, looking around. They didn't seem surprised by what we'd obviously been doing, though the big, burly one that had taken me tsked. A pistol hung from one hand as he looked around.

"You're all going to behave yourselves, or I'll put more holes in you. Got it?" he barked.

There was non-committal murmur that he took to be ascent. His eyes landed on me, and my stomach dropped.

"You're going to get cleaned up and shown to individual rooms before tomorrow night."

I didn't bother hiding what sinister meaning he'd cloaked in his words. Isolation was the last thing we needed around these bloodthirsty men.

"Time for your makeovers, ladies," the greasy-haired one sneered, breaking the big biker and I's glare off.

I blinked, comprehending the words. "What, you like to get us cleaned up before you rape us?" I quipped before I could catch myself.

The big guy stepped toward me, the muscles in his massive shoulders shifting like snakes. If he wasn't such a despicable creature, one might find his raw masculinity attractive.

His build was a little grotesque—not like Syr's. He was big and bulky, but he was tall enough to even it out. For the most part, this guy just looked like a giant.

"I'll take this one," biker guy rasped.

The rest of them spurred into action, throwing open cells and dragging the women from them.

When mine opened, I lunged forward, launching my foot into the guy's kneecap. Or I would have, but he anticipated that I'd attack and leapt back just in time before bending down and gripping me by the throat and lifting me to my feet.

"Cool it, Hellcat, or this is going to get a lot worse for you," he rumbled. I didn't struggle. Breaking out of this hold was easy but getting this close to him would only be allowed if he believed he was in control.

I spat in his face, but he didn't release me. Instead, his fingers tightened, and he leaned close. Before I could rear back and crush his nose with my forehead, I felt the kiss of cool metal against my neck.

Then the sizzling of my skin. Searing pain eating at my throat.

His dark eyes glittered with sick, twisted enjoyment. "Fight me and I'll slit your pretty throat. Got it?"

I didn't dare nod for fear of accidentally slicing my skin with the silver dagger. "Fine," I breathed.

Seeming satisfied with my response, he lowered the dagger. Hungrily, his gaze fixed on the ruined skin, watching as my wolf healing fought to repair the damage.

"Amazing, isn't it?" He licked his lips. "What something so simple as a silver blade dipped in wolfsbane can do?"

My lips parted on a sharp inhalation. "You fucking bastard."

He switched his grip on my neck from the front to the back as he steered me out of my cell. His low chuckle had my blood boiling, but I fought against the urge to kick his ass here and now. There were at least twenty other women that would need my help getting out of here alive.

We marched up the stairs and I heard the shrieks from the women before we stopped outside a large door.

"What the hell is in there?" I demanded.

The dude just smirked and shoved me toward the door, which slid open automatically with a barely audible hiss.

Barely warm water fell from tiny jets in the ceiling. It was a massive shower, I realized. There were the naked women who tried to cover themselves, and then there were other women with scars marring their faces. They wore bikinis which revealed even more deeply scarred skin.

I swallowed hard. It was those women—the ones too ruined to be sold, I guessed—that scrubbed the others, rubbing soaps into their hair and washing their grimy bodies.

One approached me, a girl about the same age as me with hair as dark as mine and brilliant blue eyes, though one was barely visible due to the wicked scarring that sliced right down her eyelid, continuing towards her cheek.

"Strip," she ordered.

"Yeah, I'm good," I said stubbornly, folding my arms over my chest to make a point.

She rolled her one good eye. "Just do it."

With a heavy sigh, I peeled the soaked T-shirt off my body, tossing it onto the wet floor against the tiled wall.

"Arms out," she said almost robotically. I wondered how many women she'd seen come through this place. How many she was forced to prep before they were auctioned off like cattle.

I did as she asked, feeling rankled by my own submission. She squirted a bottle of floral smelling soap onto a washcloth before studiously scrubbing my hands, my arms, and then my legs. When the cloth came too close to my lady bits for my liking, I issued a warning growl.

She shook her head. "Orders are orders, doll." When she moved up my torso, her eyes landed on the ugly patch of marred skin at my throat. "I see you managed to piss someone off."

I shrugged. "It's not like I'm going to not fight. They can't have my freedom."

She glanced around us with wide eyes, like what I'd just said was somehow dangerous. "You're an idiot," she whispered. "You don't want to end up like us." Straightening, she met my gaze, though she was marginally taller than me. "This is what fighting will get you," she hissed.

I pursed my lips. "How long have you been here?" I asked.

She shrugged. "There have been at least thirteen winters, I think. It's kind of hard to keep track when we never get to go outside for more than the occasional shift."

My gut clenched. They were suppressing their wolves. I couldn't imagine a greater pain that being forced not to shift whenever I wanted. "I'm sorry," I whispered.

The girl shook her head, wet black ponytail slapping from side to side. Without another word, she washed my hair and shaved me, though I insisted on shaving under my arms myself. The girl had relented easily enough, and by the end, I was grateful for another friendly face in this place.

The water shut off abruptly, and the servant girls walked away to begin passing out towels. I caught sight of Autumn, who tracked the girl I'd been speaking to with a look of fascination and sadness. When she made it back to me, I took the proffered towel, before asking, "What happens next?"

"Clothes, makeup, and then you'll go into a waiting room before the auction begins." She said the words with so little inflection, she might as well have been sleepwalking.

"What's your name?" I asked as those of us about to be led to our dooms were shuffled out of the steam-filled room and into another through a door at the back of the room. It was essentially a huge closet, but the dresses that hung from the racks still had price tags on them.

So, we were going to be expensively dressed chattel, if the first price tag I spotted was any indication.

The girl who stood beside me, rifling through the elegant and sexy gowns still hadn't answered my question. I thought she might not have heard me, or that she just wasn't going to answer when at last she said,

"Some of the girls call me Emmy."

I smiled at that. "Thank you. I'm Dani."

She returned the smile with one of her own, though I could tell it was broken from the years of abuse she'd suffered. Then her smile slipped. "I can't get attached." Her muttered words were more for herself than me, I guessed, but still she returned her full attention to the hundreds of available dresses before selecting one in blood red and held it out to me.

It was full length with a slit up on side, and sleeveless. Sexy and domineering. I couldn't help but admire the dress, but I hated what it represented. I hated the men that bought it. Or stole it, was more likely. I hated that I was soon to be paraded around like a peacock where some sick bastard would bid on me.

Not fucking likely, I told myself. *I'm not getting on that stage.* I couldn't let any of us get separated either. They sure as hell didn't deserve to be slaves.

As soon as I had an opening, it would be time to fuck shit up.

We were funneled into the adjacent room where dressing tables lined the walls. The women still in damp bikinis did our hair and makeup, but when Emmy tried to touch my hair, I waved her hands away.

"Don't bother," I murmured. "No one is going to see it."

Her brows creased. "There's an inspection before you're taken to your rooms."

I took the hair pins and ties and quickly wound two braids over the top of my head like a crown, securing it in place in minutes. Emmy's eyes widened.

"I'm good with braids," I offered. Eyeing the makeup, I grimaced. "Not so much with that."

The girl seemed to brighten slightly at being needed and sat beside me, getting to work on painting my face. When she was done, I was more than a little bit in awe of her skills.

Before I could tell her as much, a panel in the wall slid open and Tattoo Head marched in like he was going to war, another man behind him. "Line up!" he bellowed.

Emmy jumped to her feet so fast my brows creased. I watched her slim frame begin to shake, though she kept her chin up and expression hard, as I slowly got to my feet. I didn't have to wonder too much at what she and all the other women had endured. Their reaction to his presence was telling enough.

I leveled my burning hatred on the man, feeling my nails start to lengthen to claws. He was alone. If he got close enough, I could slash his throat before the others had time to intervene.

We formed a line across the room, each woman looking fierce and sexy. My eyes landed on little Kaylee and bile rose in my throat. She was dressed in a tiny sundress with hearts and rainbows.

Nausea churned through me at the realization that someone had wanted to play up the fact that she was way too fucking young to be here.

A rumbling started in my chest that drew the attention of the smirking man—Tattoo Head's crony. He started with me, looking me up and down.

"My boss said to give you this," he said. His smell intrigued me, making my lips curl with glee. Human.

Which meant slow.

Weak.

And then he drew a knife from his pocket. From the corner of my eye, I saw Tattoo Head lung for him. Rearing back to strike me with the dagger, I shifted back on one leg, and kicked the asshole as hard as I could in the chest.

He went flying and landed solidly on the carpet. I lunged on top of him, my claws at full length as I sliced him apart. Unable to stop, I tore out his gut. His throat.

The taste of his blood was everywhere, filling my mouth, my nostrils.

Hands gripped me, pulling me back. My pulse roared in my ears and I fought against the innate desire to shift fully.

My eyes lifted to find Tattoo Head gripping me to his chest. I pried myself from his grasp, thrashing until I was able to whirl on him. His grin was blatantly cruel.

The man tsked. "Naughty little wolf. You've gone and soiled your dress."

I tried to ignore the cooling blood on my face and limbs. How it soaked into the once glittering fabric. Straightening to my full height, I prepared myself for whatever demented attack was sure to come. "Who is your boss?" I demanded. "Who wanted me dead?"

"I warned you not to make a spectacle of yourself. Now it's too late." All traces of his grin were now gone. Which left only the devil standing before me, pretending to resemble a man. But I saw through that. He pulled another silver dagger from his jacket pocket—so similar to the one laying beside the dead man that I vaguely wondered if all of these criminals carried them.

"Kneel," he bit out.

I choked on my bitter laugh. Meeting his gaze with every ounce of contempt that rioted through my body, I snarled, "Fuck. You."

Whatever tether he'd kept on his anger snapped, and he roared as he leapt for me. I dove out of the way of the blade, feeling the ache of anticipation settle through my muscles. The recent disuse of them had me more than ready to take this bastard on.

"I'll have to keep you for myself after what I'm going to do to you." His voice was rough and grating.

I couldn't help but laugh as I barely dodged another wicked slice of his blade aimed directly for my face.

The women had fled to the surrounding walls, as far from the two of us as possible. I could sense Emmy watching, but it was Autumn's hard gaze that I saw.

Before I could warn her away, she surged into the ring with a wolfish growl. And then she transformed.

The jackass actually smiled at that, like two was a far better reward for his disgusting love of bloodshed.

I jumped toward the brute, blocking his arm, and pulling it back so hard I heard the pop of his joint dislocating. He howled, trying to pull himself free as I wrenched on the knife. But it wouldn't budge.

His other fist came flying for my head, but Autumn intercepted, her jaws clamping down on flesh. He flung her off as though batting away a fly. Then the door slid open and more grisly men flooded in.

They started pulling the girls away, leading them out while Autumn and I circled their leader. My skin itched, an odd longing to shift pulling at me.

"If you both don't follow them now, I'll make sure both of you bitches are filled with my pups every moment until the day you die."

I saw red.

My wolf tore free, and I roared my fury before launching at the asshole. Autumn lunged forward with me, each of us latching onto flesh.

I got the dislocated arm and twisted with his wrist between my teeth. He swatted Autumn off easily, sending her into the dressing tables which cracked and crumbled under her. I was so focused on her that I didn't have time to move when he kicked me square in the chest.

A loud crack in my ears had me wheezing as I fell to the floor.

The asshole chuckled above me and more men entered the room. My vision blurred but I could smell them. And when they effortless began to pull Autumn's prone form out of the room, I whined for her to wake up.

They came for me too, but I struggled to my paws, my ribs aching something fierce. At least one was broken, but in this form, I'd heal much faster than I would as a human. I bared my teeth at the four men surrounding me.

Their matching smirks seemed to have me pegged as a girl who was easily beaten by a few broken bones.

I snorted a laugh, which sounded more like a huff. Leaning back on my haunches I prepared to strike.

Tattoo Head lunged, and I rolled, my entire torso screaming in pain. Just as I prepared to strike, Autumn burst in still in wolf form. My heart soared seeing her alive and well.

We fought back to back, a flurry of claws and teeth tearing through fur and flesh. It was brutal—my wolf guiding me on pure instinct.

Only Tattoo Head was left, and Autumn and I circled him. His bloodied grin was haunting.

"You're tangling in a nest of vipers and you don't even know it," he said gruffly.

I wanted to ask him what that meant. Who they worked for.

But he lunged with his knife clutched in his fist. I knocked Autumn out of the way before the blade could sink into her back, and felt the silver slice into my back leg.

Pain had the room teetering. I stumbled to my feet, the room swaying. Then a prick came at the back of my neck. I craned my head around, and found Emmy with a small gun that had darts loaded in the top chamber.

I felt the sharp sting of betrayal, noting the remorse in her eyes before falling to the wooden floor where darkness consumed me.

CHAPTER TWENTY-FOUR

Dani

My eyes flew open as I gasped and flew upright. I looked around the room, trying to ignore the dizziness that overtook me. With a groan, I realized I was on a large, plush, queen-sized bed draped with a thick, golden brocade duvet. The drapes that hung from the four poster rails were pale pink.

A dressing table sat next to the bed, and a black, shimmery gown was draped over the back of the chair in front of it.

I rose to my feet, digging my toes into the soft beige carpet. As I approached the stunning table, I caught sight of my appearance in the mirror. I'd expected to be spotted with blood and gore from the fight last night, but my skin was smooth and free of grime.

And I wore soft, silky pajamas in a vibrant shade of teal. Which means someone had washed and dressed me without my consent.

My fists clenched, and I fully intended to take it out on the mirrors before me, when a knock sounded at the door.

It sounded light, and timid. Not the heavy hand of Tattoo Head.

"Yes?" I snapped.

The sound of a lock unclicking filled the silence, then the door creaked open slowly and Emmy, the servant, peered around the door. Her lip was split and swollen, and a yellowing bruise marred her cheek.

I folded my arms over my chest, though my heart squeezed painfully. The way her gaze fell to the floor for a moment told me they'd likely beaten her. For what, I didn't know.

With the door ajar, I heard the dull roar of cheers.

The auction.

My arms fell to my sides, and I leveled Emmy with a hard stare. "I need to get out of here. And so do you."

"I'm just here to help you dress," she said. I was surprised by the calm in her tone when her delicate frame, clothed in long sleeves and denim jeans, looked hunched and afraid.

I glared over my shoulder at the dress. "Are there any jeans here that would fit me?"

Emmy held my stare for a moment before nodding ever so slightly.

"Can you bring them to me?" I asked, feeling desperation sink its claws into me. Time was running out. A crowd was here, ready to bid.

"You can't run," she said, and the words came out sounding as dead and haunted as she looked. "They almost all try. No one gets out the door."

I scoffed. "Trust me, this will work."

Emmy eyed me wearily for a beat. Then she said, "What do you need?"

Less than an hour later, I was led into the hallway. Girls lined up with numbers pinned to their fronts. When I passed Kaylee who was mercifully in front of Autumn, I sent her a reassuring smile. She looked healthy. In fact, they all did, if a little tired. So they removed the silver after all.

With the two other servants facing away, I tripped on the front of my long dress. Autumn's hand shot out, steadying me, and I tucked the folded slip of paper into her palm. She froze, understanding dawning. I straightened, apologizing demurely before Emmy helped get me securely to the first spot in line. The two scarred servant girls rushed to Emmy, complaining that I was "much too pretty to go first." I had to tamp down on my rising nausea at that comment, while keeping my gaze fixed straight ahead.

We were led through hall after hall—all of them white with dark, wooden floors that could easily hide blood stains—and all guarded by men with guns. They assessed each of us as we passed, several making lewd gestures that made me want to take the blade strapped to my thigh and cram it into their eye socket. Finally, we reached a set of wide double doors, where Emmy paused.

I could hear an announcer winding up the crowd with promises of beauty as well as purity. My gaze automatically went to Kaylee. I hoped Autumn had assured her that we would get her out. That we would get them all out.

I had no idea if Braxton and the others were near, but I had to hope. My skin felt too tight and sweat beaded on the back of my neck. I wanted this to be done and over with. But more than that, I needed to free my wolf. I needed to run free.

The double doors opened just as my number was called, and Emmy nodded for me to take the stage. I sucked in a breath of cool evening air, the final dregs of sunlight sinking away into the inky pot of night.

One step onto a long, wooden platform that may have been a porch if it didn't look as though it had been designed to be an auction house stage. My breaths quickened, and despite the night bringing a cool breeze, I felt like I was suffocating from flames licking my insides.

I stopped in the middle of the stage, glaring out at the masses. There were at least a thousand males gathered below. My fingers itched to clutch the dagger at my thigh, but I had to wait for the perfect moment.

"This one is a real beauty, and feisty too, if you like such things. Trained and skilled in combat, this tight little bitch will satisfy even your darkest urges." The words boomed from all around me, yet sounded so far away.

I bared my teeth at the round of cheers that sounded. Sick bastards. You're not getting a single taste of this.

The bidding began, starting at two hundred thousand dollars.

My spine lengthened when the first male lifted his blood red paddle with the number seven on it. I latched onto him, and sucked in a sharp breath.

Braxton stared up at me with vibrant blue, shimmering eyes.

The bidding kept going so fast I didn't have time to track each bid, but when another hand went up, I instantly recognized Syr. He was on the opposite side, close to the stage.

My chest seized, and somehow my eyes knew where to go next.

Donovan stood toward the back, arms folded over his chest. We locked eyes for what felt like minutes, but then I heard, "One million dollars," and Donovan subtly lifted his paddle.

The three of them were there. Another quick scan and I saw Javier as well as at least a dozen Carvingwood wolves. But my dad was not among them. I couldn't sense him either.

Had he not come for me too?

The sharp rap of wood on wood ended my bidding, though I hadn't seen who won. Two of the heavily tattooed men approached me, preparing to grab me.

It was now or never.

I reached for my dagger between the folds of my skirt, gripping the handle like my only lifeline.

Then a loud bang shook the entire space; dirt, rock, and gore flying as screams erupted. What looked like grenades were being tossed into the mass of gathered people before erupting in a gruesome shower. My eardrums screamed in pain.

An uncontrollable ache grew within me, but I didn't have time to examine it. The two men lunged for me, and I drew the knife, slashing through a meaty bicep. I spun, sending my heel into the other guy's chin hard enough to hear the gurgle, feel the heat of crimson sliding down my ankle, between my toes. I jerked my stiletto free, ducking just in time to avoid a fist to the face.

I sent the blade flying right into my attacker's gut. The silver made the wound fizz and bubble while the man shrieked in pain. I didn't wait to see if he pulled the blade out before sprinting around him, back inside the hall.

The guards were trying to herd the women away from the attack, and I sprung into motion.

A gun lifted and I palmed the bottom of it, pointing the barrel up before twisting his arm. The crack of bone splintering had his grip loosening. I took aim and fired.

He went down in a spray of blood. Stepping over him, I released two more silver bullets that hit their target. More men were flooding in, but Autumn and several of the other girls had spurred into motion—Emmy included.

I called for the girls to follow me, though I had no fucking clue where I was going. Emmy appeared by my side just as a big dude in full body armor ran down the hall toward us. I lifted the gun and squeezed the trigger.

He staggered back a step before lifting his rifle. I put my arms out, trying to make myself as big of a target as I could. A snarl erupted from behind and the man whipped around just in time to see a massive golden wolf leap into the air.

He hit the guard, but before they even made contact with the solid wood floor, Syr had severed the man's head from his body.

I flashed my best friend a grateful smile, and then we were tearing through the mansion again. Emmy got us to the front door, which was already obliterated into a million shards on the floor.

I stopped to help shuffle the girls out.

Emmy stood just outside the door. "We're going to head for the forest. Meet us there!"

I nodded, spotting Kaylee limping at the back of the group. Tears streamed down her face. Blood soaked the hem of her pale pink dress, coating her shin as well.

I ran toward her, scooping her up into my arms. Emmy took her on the porch as the fight continued. I made sure Emmy and the others were far enough away before turning and launching myself back into the fray.

It didn't take me long before I spied Donovan's dark hair, mussed, and his golden eyes aflame. He held two blades—that I had a sinking suspicion were silver—while surrounded by at least four men. I'd seen him in combat situations before, but still his grace and speed were mesmerizing.

He stabbed two dudes through the chest at once, crisscrossed his blades and did it again with a successful backward kick under the jaw, dropping a fifth guy in the process.

It was a flurry of wolves and men. My eyes sought Syr and Braxton out, but I could only spy Braxton's wild mane of black hair. He held an axe in the air, chopping through man and wolf alike. There was something primal and wholly animalistic in the way he killed without mercy.

Justice rolled through the estate on an eerie fog that reached its spindly fingers around everyone as though to squeeze the life from those it deemed unworthy.

Darkness had finally enveloped the valley at last. And just as two men turned to charge me, an odd pulse tugged in my chest. My heart raced and internally, I wanted to howl. The men stopped. Looking around, I caught sight of Donovan, Brax, and Syr. All three of them were focused on me.

In fact, everyone paused as the clouds retracted away from a blood-red moon.

Whatever strange sensation had been building within me had grown to a crescendo. I gasped, feeling the bonds of my mate snap into place.

CHAPTER TWENTY-FIVE

Brax

I felt it like a cord suddenly pulled taut. My cock hardened painfully, and my inner wolf fought to claw free as my eyes landed back on the female it so desperately craved.

My mate.

How did I not see this? I wondered.

Our dream connection. My ability to locate her while only partially conscious. It all spelled a greater meaning that I'd turned a blind eye to.

Her violet eyes shone brighter; the breeze tossing her mane of raven waves over her shoulders.

Claim her.

Rogue whined softly beside me, but I barely heard it. My heart beat increased its tempo. All around, a frenzy began.

The Chaos was finally here.

Instinct rode me hard and suddenly I was moving. But the moment I did, panic flared in her eyes. She turned and ran.

Back inside the mansion.

I paused, noticing my two companions moving toward her as well.

But neither of them hesitated.

Syr was fastest in his golden wolf form, but Donovan raced after him with the speed of a man with a prize in sight.

I frowned, then doubled back, winding around the estate with Rogue jogging along beside me.

Her scent was stronger than ever, and it consumed me.

After all this time, I'd finally found my mate, and she'd run from me.

The girl was near twelve years my junior. She was a fighter; her grace unparalleled, but I was a hunter.

My sole purpose in this life was to avenge my sister, and now I had. We'd made sure every member of The Silver Vipers was dead. Now each step I took into the thickening forest drew me closer to my new goal: claim Daniella as my mate.

Just the thought of ravaging her amongst the trees made my cock twitch.

"Dani!" Syr called out through the deadly silent forest.

"Give it up, lap dog, she's not going to choose you," Donovan snarled.

I converged on the two, forcing them to stop, though they proceeded to argue. Loudly.

"What is going on?" I demanded, my chest heaving with ragged breaths.

They'd clearly stolen clothing and other items since Syracuse was clothed and they both carried linen backpacks.

Donovan bared his teeth like the alpha he was, but I was not one of his wolves. I didn't cower in the slightest.

"Lover boy here seems to think my soul tied is his mate. I felt the bond. She's mine." He growled the last part.

I cocked my head. "Interesting, since I too have felt the bond."

Both men gave looks of confusion and irritation.

"Of course my mate would be greedy enough to secure three bonds instead of one," Donovan grumbled.

I suppressed a smile, thinking that it was fitting for such a fiery woman.

"Well, she's known me the longest. If it hadn't been for you, we would have tied ourselves this year." Syr gestured toward Donovan, and though he wasn't the alpha of his own pack, his chest inflated.

He wasn't going to back down.

"She's not likely to choose any of us if we stand here bickering," I pointed out. "Goddess knows she's probably halfway into the Reaper's Spines by now."

Donovan squinted, eyeing the faint outline of distant peaks as though trying to assess if she had actually made it that far. I shook my head and began my hunt anew.

The breeze was nonexistent in the thick of the forest, but the moment we came to a clearing, her scent hit us with the force of a great waterfall. My mouth watered, and suddenly I was sprinting.

The other two raced for her, Donovan whooping like his prey had already been caught within a trap.

Surely, he knew it would never be so easy.

Syracuse called her name again, but I heard her faint pants for breath—the pounding of her heart.

My canines lengthened and I whirled to the left, lunging like the animal I was. I gripped her bare shoulders, hauling her to my chest.

She shrieked—not in fear, but in rage—before pounding her fists on my back. I crushed her to me, my dick straining to be free. Burying my nose into the crook of her neck, I inhaled deeply, and she froze.

Then with a rough grunt I slammed us into a tree, grinding my hips against hers. She whimpered, turning pliant for a moment where I'd foolishly thought she wanted to feel me against her.

Then she slashed wolf claws down my back, severing skin and muscle.

I roared my pain to the trees, stumbling back several steps. Hot blood streamed from the wounds, but I made no move to tend to them. My gaze was locked with Daniella's.

It was decided that never a creature looked more ready to deliver a kill than her at that moment.

Just as I opened my mouth to apologize for forcing myself on her, my two idiot companions burst from the surrounding trees.

Donovan had her by the throat, toes dangling over the roots in an instant. "Where the fuck did you think you were going, Little Wolf?" he crooned.

Syracuse looked ready to murder him, and my own wolf was pacing inside me, restless and eager to strike.

"Far away from you," she spat.

CHAPTER TWENTY-SIX

Dani

"Now why would you want to get away from your mates?" Donovan grinned like the smug bastard that he was.

I kept myself balanced on the tips of my toes, which kept his grasp on my air supply minimal.

The presence of all three males the Chaos had inexplicably mated me to were like warm, inviting fires on a frigid day. No matter how much I wanted to curl into them, I knew I would get burned.

I was not about to bow to any man for any reason. My goal was to be Alpha of Carvingwood.

Not a bitch that three arrogant—*sexy, delicious*—hot heads fucked and bred. I wasn't that girl.

Even if my pussy clenched at the mere sound of Donovan's voice.

Their combined scents had me wet as fuck, and I knew they could smell it. But this was simply the Chaos.

If I rejected the bonds, then everything would go back to normal.

But the idea of breaking something so sacred had my heart hurting for no reason. And then, of course, Syr's honey brown eyes captured my attention, and I sank into the comfort that he'd provided me since we were kids.

I loved Syr. Probably for longer than I realized.

But I couldn't forge a mate bond with him, and certainly not the other two. I didn't have to dwell on the idea to know that the three of them were meant to be a package deal. Years of friendship and bonding with Syr couldn't erase the claim my wolf was ready to stake on Donovan and Brax. They were all mine.

Which meant none of them could be.

My arm shot out, knocking Donovan's hold loose. I slid down the tree grasping it to hold myself steady. Panting slightly, I straightened, glaring at the men surrounding me.

"I don't want to be anyone's mate. Release me from the bonds or I will." My voice held firm and steady, but something inside my chest fractured just from speaking the words aloud.

Syr's expression morphed into one of horror. "Dani." He reached for me, but I stepped back, giving him a warning look. His hand fell and he sighed. "Please don't do this. You know we were meant to be together. This is perfect—"

"Like hell it is," Donovan interrupted through gritted teeth.

I ignored him, focusing on my best friend. "You know I love you, Syr. You're my best friend. But we can't do this. I intend to be alpha. And while you might be okay with being my second, I think one day it won't be enough for you. As my mate, you'll naturally attempt to top me, and I can't have that within the pack."

Donovan's sneer was cut short by my next words directed at him. "And I won't be your bitch. The devices were found. That makes the arrangement void. Once I get back to Carvingwood, I'll petition to dissolve our Soul Tie. We're done."

I didn't have a chance to address Braxton who looked on in silence before Donovan was in my face. His fingers brushed the wild, unkempt strands of darkness back from my face, breathing the words, "You wanna play this game? Then get ready, Little Wolf." He ran his thumb over my bottom lip as his lips curled into a slice of cruel amusement. "The rules just changed." The words ghosted across my cheek.

I shivered with equal parts desire and maddening rage.

Donovan Dockhills brought out the very worst in me. He was sin incarnate and made just to torment me with his smug grins. But damn if I didn't love to dance with devils.

Though I'd planned to use it for a different reason, I reached behind my back into the waistband of the jeans Emmy had allowed me to wear beneath the dress, and withdrew the miniature pistol I'd found in my sprint back through the manor. It was loaded with exploding silver pieces.

A real pity I'd have to put so many holes into such beautiful men.

I cocked the hammer back and aimed, receding into the forest with slow steps.

Donovan eyed the gun still smirking, but it no longer reached his eyes. Syr and Brax held their hands up in surrender—my best friend looking betrayed.

Truthfully, I didn't want to shoot any of them, but I knew they'd follow me. The Chaos would only grow stronger and our urges to fulfill the bonds would drive us all wild with need before long. I felt it so strongly already that the hand pointing the gun at my mates trembled slightly.

"I'm going back to Carvingwood to stake my claim as alpha," I announced.

Syr frowned. "You're going to challenge your father?"

My stomach clenched. He would see me as a traitor to our family name, but I didn't have a choice. There was unrest. And Carvingwood had endured too much trauma. It was time for new leadership. Unable to voice these things, I simply nodded.

Donovan barked a harsh laugh. "I came to Carvingwood to sow a single seed of discord. I never imagined it would grow into this." He looked far too pleased with himself.

I narrowed my eyes, refusing to give voice to my questions.

His eyes slid to the barrel of the gun as though he knew exactly what sat inside the chamber. "Poison," he said simply.

I lifted my brow. "Poison? Do you mean silver?"

His gaze rose to meet mine again. "I mean, it's the reason I despise your father. And it's the real reason I was able to demand you as payment. He didn't know I knew his secret, but once I made that clear, he was willing to give me everything. Even you."

My lip curled. "And what secret is that?"

His smile was a menacing flash of white, canines elongated. "You should ask him yourself when you get there. Haven't you always wondered why your father is undefeated against any and all challengers? Your father is a liar and he's loyal to no one but himself. Why do you think he didn't bother to come looking for you? He knew that you were about to be auctioned off, and he couldn't be bothered to leave Carvingwood for his own daughter."

I shook my head, but I couldn't deny how much his words had struck a chord within my chest. I'd expected him to come for me. To be here and exact revenge on those who'd harmed me. "He's alpha of the pack and Carvingwood has suffered enough. It's not as if he could leave."

Donovan's smile faded, leaving only disdain. "He sent his beta and a handful of wolves to fight in his stead instead of uniting the pack to bring death upon the whole of The Badlands. That's not strategy, that's cowardice."

That was all it took for me to pull the trigger.

I didn't wait to see the damage before turning and sprinting through the trees. Donovan's roar chased me.

"Run, Little Wolf!" His footsteps didn't sound far behind, but his staggering was clearly putting distance between us. "Run, if you think this makes feel like you have any chance of escaping! I will find you and when I do, I'm going to pin you down and fuck you like I should have done years ago!"

I increased my pace, feeling as though he and the other two were breathing down my neck. Panting, I didn't bother trying to navigate as the black, gauzy skirt of my dress snagged on twigs and roots. My senses told me I was heading in the general direction of Carvingwood territory, but all I wanted was space between me and the enraged alpha I'd shot.

The three tracking me eventually grew silent, and I allowed myself to walk. My legs screamed from the exertion, and my lungs protested each breath.

The ache deep within the muscle of my shoulder where the silver had been was sharper than before. I wasn't fully healed, and I felt it in every step up the steep incline. Several times I stumbled, but managed to catch myself on a near tree to keep from faceplanting into the damp leaves and mossy forest floor.

The night air was far cooler here—the damp air clinging to my skin. I wrapped my arms around myself to try to keep warm.

Exhaustion pressed in on me, but I knew I couldn't stop. The weak part of me questioned why I was even running from them. They were my *mates*. It wasn't as if they'd hurt me.

But then I recalled Donovan's treatment of me the past five years. And the fact that being their female instead of being Alpha made my insides twist into a million knots. It gave me the strength I needed to keep walking for several more hours, even when my eyelids felt like they were made of lead.

The soothing sounds of insects chirping and an owl hooting overhead told me that nothing too scary lurked ahead. It was peaceful.

Which was why my head bobbed as my eyes began to close.

I tripped over my feet, snapping me to attention. But by the time I realized my body was rapidly approaching the ground, it was too late. My hands shot out hitting the ground that snapped.

And gave way.

A scream tore from my throat as I fell.

And fell.

I landed on my back, all the air knocked from my lungs as I laid there, gasping, desperately trying to catch my breath.

Everything hurt.

Moaning, I struggled to roll over. Pushing myself up on my hands and knees, I gulped down icy breaths that stung with each heaving inhalation. The world swayed and I let my head drop, resting against the cool earth.

When my equilibrium righted itself, I moved gingerly to my feet, cursing the three males who had thought this a game. A fluttering sensation stirred in my chest, but I pushed it away, focusing on how I was going to get out of this.

I looked up at the surface which was a good fifteen feet higher than my head and grimaced. I'd have to shift back into my wolf form in order to jump out, but even then, it would be a challenge—especially with as sore as I was. The hole was too wide to do any zig-zag maneuvers.

Shivering, I lifted the dress over my head. Discarding it and then the jeans onto the floor of the pit, I called my wolf to the surface. The shift was more painful than usual, but desperate times and all that.

Panting, I crouched low, preparing to jump. My limbs shook, but I used as much energy as I could muster into propelling myself upward. I hit only midway and yelped, sinking my claws into dirt while frantically trying to claw my way out.

I fell back, barely managing to twist myself around and land on my paws. My legs gave out and I collapsed, breathing heavily.

After taking a moment to rest, I tried again, making it a little higher this time, but still not high enough. Landing on my back this time, I snarled, pain lancing through every inch of my body. I forced myself to my front and pushed back up to all fours, though my entire frame quaked.

Distantly, I heard voices and froze. My form dissolved back into my human body without my consent, and I had a sinking suspicion as to why. Scrambling for my clothes, I dressed in a rush, though the dregs of my strength only allowed me to sit on the ground with my back to the wall. My heart began to beat a frenzied rhythm and my nipples stiffened.

Fuck. They found me.

"I laid claim to her first, Milton, there's nothing more to discuss. She'll be returning to Dockhills with me as soon as I—" Donovan was cut off by Brax's husky voice.

"Shhh! I can sense her."

I tried to ignore the way my body alighted with that statement by slowing my breathing.

"So can I," Syr said, much closer than the other two had sounded.

"What's that?" Donovan demanded. They were practically on top of me now and I wished I could bury myself in the ground to keep from being found.

"One of my traps." Brax said it with a hint of confusion.

Yeah, well it's dark and I'm tired, I thought bitterly. *And you assholes chased me, so of course I fell into your stupid trap.*

Donovan's low chuckle was so close, my head snapped up.

And locked onto his stunning golden gaze.

He looked down at me with a lazy arrogance that had my hackles rising. "Well, well, Little Wolf. I have to admit, I thought you'd have gotten further than you did."

My only response was to flip him the middle finger.

He chuckled again, then Brax peered over the edge. "Are you injured?"

"Fuck off," I groaned.

Syr landed in front of me without warning.

"Great job, moron, now you're both stuck," Donovan called.

Syr ignored him, crouching in front of me to inspect my body for wounds.

"Get away," I snapped.

He stilled. "Dani?"

I could feel the pull of the mate bond so strongly I wanted to crawl to him, but I didn't have the strength to move. My eyes squeezed shut.

"Why you?" I whispered, pain etched into my voice.

He didn't move or breathe for several blissful moments. Then he said, "I think part of me knew you were always meant to be mine. It's why we were drawn to each other as kids. It's why I was going to ask you to tie yourself to me…before Alpha Dick showed up."

My eyes opened. "You were?"

He nodded with a small tilt of his lips. "I love you, Dani. I always have."

I shook my head. "Don't say that. I'm not right for you. I can't have a mate."

Syr's face hardened. "I've been in love with you since you were sixteen and I'm not going to keep quiet just so you can live in your stubborn little bubble where you deny yourself the one thing I know you want but thought you'd never have."

My heart stuttered to a stop. "Syr," I breathed.

Syr opened his mouth to respond when Donovan cut him off. "As cute as this is, there is a lot that needs to be discussed, and it's best if we do that somewhere else."

"My cabin is just over an hour north," Brax offered.

I groaned. "An hour?"

Syr continued to spear me with his intense stare, warming my blood. "How do we get out of here?" he asked, but didn't take his eyes off me.

"If neither of you were injured, you could easily scale the walls, but I can see she's already tried that. I have rope, we can easily pull Daniella out, but you might have to try to climb out." Syr nodded resolutely.

"Not very good traps if people can just climb out," Donovan muttered.

"They're not designed for innocents to accidentally fall into. They're meant to capture the prey I've wounded first," Brax shot back.

I sighed dramatically, breaking up the guys' pissing contest. "I'm good here. You guys just go. I'll catch up. Or not, whatever." The idea of sleeping in this cold, dank hole was better than going anywhere with Donovan.

The jackass snorted. "Not a chance, Little Wolf. You shot us, and then made us chase you. I'm not letting you out of my sight."

Cringing, I grumbled, "Apparently I need to work on my aim."

Brax laughed that time. The sound was deep and rich, and I couldn't help but crack a smile too. A moment later the end of a rope dropped, stopping near my head.

I eyed it like a deadly snake, then turned my attention back to Syr. "No chance that you could just kill me instead?"

He lifted a single brow by way of response, and I pursed my lips at his lack of humor. When I turned and grabbed the rope, I began to lift off the ground instantly. Every bit of my body shrieked at the effort required not to drop it, but my ascent back to ground level was far too quick. Suddenly I was held captive by Donovan's grip on my bicep.

"Lemme go, I can stand," I muttered. Or something like that. It might have come out a little garbled.

Donovan's smirk twisted. "Sorry, didn't catch that, Little Wolf."

I waved him off, not trusting myself to speak again.

Brax shot me a concerned look. "I should carry her back."

Donovan bared his teeth threateningly. "Like I'm letting you take off with her."

Brax rolled his eyes.

Just as concern began to churn within me from the grunting and weird noises in the pit, I leaned forward and saw Syr literally climbing up the side.

He pulled himself up over the edge and got to his feet, barely winded.

"Oh sure, make it look easy," I slurred, my head so heavy I had to rest it against Donovan, though every fiber of my being rebelled at the action.

Syr's lips quirked. "Give her to me," he demanded so alpha-like, I almost wanted to go to him.

"I can walk," I argued, trying to enunciate each syllable, which ended up just making me sound like I was drunk. Which would have been way more fun than standing around in a forest.

Donovan made a growling sound before sweeping me up in his arms. "Lead the way, dream walker."

The light rocking motion combined with the alphahole's delicious scent made my eyes fall closed. I wasn't sure when we made it there, or when I was laid on the world's softest mattress, but eventually I lost all sense of where I was and fell into the deepest sleep of my life.

I awoke feeling so warm it was almost uncomfortable. A yawn escaped me, and the firm arm draped over my waist gave me pause. It was familiar. But the chest steadily rising and falling beneath my cheek was not Syr.

My eyes snapped open and confirmed what I'd already suspected. I was laying partially on Donovan, while Syr was tucked against my back. A flash of horror shot through me. How had I ended up in bed with both of them?

All at once the memories from last night returned in a rush, highlighting the pulsing ache that began between my thighs.

I had three mates. And I was in bed with two of them. And I was only wearing a baggy T-shirt that smelled of Braxton, and jeans.

Who had taken the dress off me and why? The sensation of bare flesh at my back as well as the firm torso beneath me told me that the guys were at the very least, shirtless.

My legs were tangled with someone else's, adding to my horror.

Lifting my head slowly, I looked around the unfamiliar room. Dull blood-red moonlight creeped in from around the curtains drawn over the window beside us. The walls were a light wood paneling, and the only pieces of furniture I could make out were a dresser and the bed the three of us were curled up on.

This must be Brax's cabin, I thought to myself.

I lifted Syr's arm, attempting to extricate myself from the tangle of men, but Donovan stirred, mumbling, "Where do you think you're going?"

Syr clamped his arm over me tighter, pulling me flush against him, and *something hard* dug into my back. I sucked in a sharp breath.

My long since neglected lady-bits chose that moment to throb and suddenly Donovan yanked me out of Syr's hold, his body covering mine.

He growled low, eyes blazing like wildfire. The way he looked at me was wholly wolf. Predatory and dominant.

"What the hell, Dickhills?" I shoved Donovan's chest, but he didn't budge.

"Dude, get off her," Syr snapped, sounding far too awake.

For a moment Donovan looked ready to rip my best friend's

head off, but finally he blinked, and some of the mate bond craze left his eyes.

However, his rock-hard cock was still pressed against my apex, my desire likely soaking my jeans. "I don't think she wants me to," he said in that low, rough voice. My toes curls as he rocked against me ever so slowly, and I forgot how to breathe for several moments.

Until his arrogant smirk returned, and I pushed him again, this time managing to shove him off. He laughed, getting to his feet.

I sat up and glanced beside me. The look of pain on Syr's face told me I was right in moving.

"Where is Brax?" I asked, my voice sounding strange to my ears.

Just as I said it, I heard sounds deeper in the house, like pots and pans clanging together. I made a point of climbing over Syr, stopping on all fours over his lap to shoot Donovan a wink before climbing off the bed.

I heard Syr mutter a curse and I bit the inside of my lip guiltily. Perhaps using my best friend—who also wanted to fuck me, thanks to the mate bond—as a way of getting back at Donovan wasn't fair.

Just before I reached the closed door, it shot open, and Brax stood in the doorway, his pupils blown wide.

"What is going on in here?" he demanded. His chest was bare too, showing off all the dark skin covered in tattoos. I stared so long I barely heard Donovan answer.

"Nothing, we were just about to find you."

Rolling his shoulders back, every sinewy inch of muscle moved and flexed. Brax cleared his throat, finally dispelling me from my current fantasy of licking my way over his abs.

"How do you like your eggs?"

"Uhhh," I said, about to say something cheesy like "fertilized," but Syr answered for me.

"Over easy and drenched in hot sauce. I can't imagine you have any hot sauce out here though."

Brax quirked a brow. "Of course I do."

"Well, he's perfect," I quipped.

The other two men were glowering at me when I peeked over my shoulder.

Brax smiled in my direction, however, then gestured out the door. "I'm making breakfast."

I nodded. "Lead the way." Fortunately, I managed to get those three words out without tacking on anything embarrassing, because apparently this male scrambled my brains. And then I pointedly stared at the floor in front of me so I didn't think about what else he could do to my brain with his likely impressive—

"Okay, you've got to cut that shit out or we're all going to die," Syr said from behind me, and my cheeks heated. I took a small whiff of the air and smelled all three males' strong scents.

Oh fuck.

"Oh, well in that case, I'll try harder," I shot back as we entered the kitchen. The ceiling was pitched high above with exposed beams and a large pane of glass that would have invited the morning sun in to bathe the small space, if there'd been sunlight at all.

My jaw dropped. "Wow, this place is really beautiful," I said.

Brax nodded. "I built it right after I found Rogue as a pup." At the mention of the hound's name, he lumbered into the kitchen, nails clacking against the hard wood floor.

The dog bypassed his owner and headed straight for me, his tongue hanging to one side as he parked himself at my feet.

"Hey, Rogue," I cooed, kneeling to scratch behind his ears. He licked my face happily, his back-end swaying so hard with his wagging tail he almost looked like he was dancing.

"Unbelievable," Brax muttered. "Twelve years of companionship and you fall for the girl in ten minutes."

I shot him a glare that lacked any real heat while I scratched under the dog's chin. He leaned into my touch, nearly falling over. Giggling I said, "That's because I'm amazing. Dogs are great judges of character."

Brax smiled. "That you are." His softly spoken words made me pause. He turned suddenly, heading for the counter that had eggs, milk, and a massive pack of bacon laying out. "I'll give you a tour of the place after we eat."

I patted Rogue on the head before standing. "I can help."

Brax gestured to the potatoes sitting in the sink without looking away from his own work of frying bacon. "You can grate those."

Syr stepped forward to offer his assistance while I felt Donovan's presence behind me. When I turned to see why he just stood there, I got the brunt of his scowl.

"I'll be back," he muttered.

Despite my conflicted emotions where he was involved, each of his steps away from me tugged on my heart until the front door opened and shut.

CHAPTER TWENTY-SEVEN

Donovan

I needed to clear my head. The scene of domestic bliss I'd left behind was almost too much to handle.

Perhaps Braxton and Syracuse could handle sharing a mate, but I couldn't. I wouldn't. She was mine. I laid claim to her before any of them, and I didn't see why I should have to compete for her.

My tattoo was still on her skin, proving that she was every last bit mine.

But that thought only served to worsen my mood. I spied a pile of tree rounds and made my way over to it. The axe, wedged into the chopping stump, stood tall and beckoned me. With a huff, I yanked it free before grabbing a hunk of tree trunk, sliding it onto the stump.

Lifting the axe above my head, I pulled in a long, calming breath. And swung the tool down with all my strength. It sang through the air, slicing through the wet wood with a *thunk*. One half tumbled off the stump. I nudged the remaining piece into the center with the toe of my boot, then brought the axe down on it again.

My blood pumped through my veins, quieting the riot of chaotic thoughts in my mind. What I really wanted was to spar.

Especially with the raven-haired beauty who stubbornly refused to admit that I was her rightful mate. Though, begrudgingly, I could somewhat understand why whatever higher power deigned to pair her with three men instead of one, and had made Syracuse one of her mates.

He balanced her recklessness with his calm, steady presence. His love for her was the mushy shit you saw on TV. Braxton was a mystery to me, but I was the flame to her raging temper.

I could challenge her. We didn't have to be sweet or gentle with each other. It was a type of passion only we were versed in.

She needed someone rough. Someone who could handle the alpha in her without being submissive. Her and I would fuck with claws and teeth.

I could take her wolf on like no one else could.

She needed that.

And I would be it.

I just didn't want to admit that maybe she needed what Syracuse had to offer too. And who the fuck knew what Braxton brought to the table.

Swinging the axe down yet again, I halted at the sound of shrill screams far off in the distance.

A moment later, I heard Autumn's voice in my mind. *Donovan! Fucking hell, where are you?*

I dropped the axe, sprinting in the direction of my beta. Cursing myself for being so focused on the frustrating female inside the cabin, I hadn't thought of my second since I saw her guiding a group of females into the woods, away from the auction. After the Chaos began, I'd been consumed with Daniella.

It was so unlike me. My pack was everything, and I hadn't concerned myself with Autumn's wellbeing beyond ascertaining that she was alive.

I heard another scream, and Autumn called for me again.

Where are you? I asked through my alpha link.

In a fucking pit, of course. My mate is wounded.

Her mate? I shouldn't have been surprised. Few were exempt from the Chaos. But what that meant for my second who preferred only women, I didn't know.

I was within earshot before long, hearing soft sobs and soft comforting whispers. When I stepped out of the trees and into the small clearing, I froze.

Autumn's face was bruised. A wicked gash oozed fresh blood on her cheek. But she held a dark-haired girl, rocking her and murmuring against her matted curls. Autumn met my gaze, visible relief washing over her face. When a twig snapped beneath my boot, the girl she held whipped around, the distinct scent of fear wafting from her. She was clearly of Asian descent, a striking beauty though her eyes were red-rimmed, her face puffy.

"What's wrong with her?" I asked.

"She broke her leg when she fell in," Autumn said.

My brows creased, then understanding dawned on me. "She's human."

Autumn nodded, her expression torn with guilt and despair.

"Your mate is human," I repeated, trying to wrap my mind around that fact. It wasn't unusual, but that the Chaos selected for her a female as well as a human, was incredibly rare.

"What's her name?"

"*Her* name is Arya," the human spat. Disdain morphed her beautiful features, but I had to suppress the amusement that rose through me.

Small but feisty, I said to Autumn so her mate wouldn't hear.

One corner of her mouth tilted up slightly, but even Autumn looked tired and beaten. Had they run all night?

"My apologies, Arya. I thought you might be in too much pain to speak," I offered placatingly.

Arya sniffed angrily, burying her face in Autumn's shoulder again.

"What happened?" It was all I could think to ask. I'd assumed Autumn was leading the girls to Dockhills, but we were much farther north now.

She gingerly pinched the bridge of her nose. "We were followed by several men. I fought them off, allowing the girls time to escape. When the Chaos began, everything got crazy. I went for Arya instantly, but a male started to chase her too. He got to her first and was going to…" She swallowed hard, and rage rose up inside me.

"Anyway I killed him. But he was apparently her mate also. She's fucking human. He'd have killed her, and the bond wouldn't have taken properly even if she'd survived."

"Fuck," I said on a long breath.

Autumn nodded. "Now if you don't mind, we'd really like to get out of this damn hole."

I thought for a moment, trying to figure out how to get the human out. "Can you shift and climb out with her on your back?"

She shook her head. "I don't think I could shift if I wanted to."

I sighed. "If I drop in there and shift, Arya, could you hold onto me?"

The girl turned to look at me again, examining me like a predator capable of mauling her in a blink. Which is exactly what I was, but her terror was a complication that I didn't see any way around.

"He's a friend, Arya," Autumn said gently. "He can get you out."

"What about you?" she asked, new tears forming in her eyes.

"I'll carry her out as well," I offered.

Finally, Arya nodded.

I shed my clothes quickly, ignoring Arya's squeak of surprise. Then I donned my beast and leapt into the pit.

Autumn helped the human girl rise onto the leg that wasn't bent at an odd angle before lifting her in her arms and placing her on my back. The girl's slender frame shook but she wrapped her arms around my neck, holding on as best she could.

With only a huff for warning, I paced back a few steps, then raced for the wall. I put all my power and strength into that one leap, catching the very edge with my front paws. Clawing and straining, I managed to pull myself up.

The human's grip around my neck was almost unbearably tight for one so small and frail. I crouched low, indicating she could dismount. And she did.

With as much grace as a sack of potatoes tumbling off a shelf. She landed in a heap, gasping and crying once more.

The sound of paws slapping against cool morning earth reached my ears, and my body went rigid.

Then I smelled my mate—cinnamon and vanilla with a hint of leather. Spicy and sweet, like the rest of her. The irony wasn't lost on me.

"What the hell?" Daniella halted at the edge of the pit, eyes flaring brightly and tendrils of her dark hair curling around her face.

The draw towards her so was so strong, a growl tore from my throat even when I forced myself to focus on what I was doing.

Milton and Brax appeared behind my Little Wolf, both assessing the situation while trying to spot potential threats. I rolled my eyes. Like I'd ever let any harm come to her.

Well, besides the destruction of her father and dissolution of her pack…

"Autumn and…her mate fell prey to one of Braxton's super convenient holes," I supplied in wolf, gesturing with my nose for added effect. None of them were from my pack, or in wolf form which meant they may not have understood my growling noises.

Brax scowled, folding his arms over his still bare chest—did that guy own any shirts? But then he answered, "They were never a problem before."

Autumn scoffed, reminding me that she was still stuck below. I jumped over the side, landing gracefully on all fours.

She managed to climb onto my back slowly, wincing as she situated herself. I crouched low to the dirt floor, pulling as much strength as I could into my next spring.

With a rough exhale, I launched. My claws scraped roughly through dirt and stone. I scrambled up, snarling when I reached the top, hauling us both over the side. Autumn rolled off me onto her back and gave a crazed sort of laugh.

"Didn't think we were gonna make it there for a second," she murmured.

My limbs were on fire from the effort, and the transformation back to my human form drained me further. Without looking at the audience who rushed around the pit to check on my second and her human mate, I plucked up my clothes and dressed. By the end, my body trembled.

Braxton noted the strain and lifted Arya into his arms, gesturing to me. "Let's get back and eat." I nodded, starting back up the mountain while Daniella watched me. Arya fought Brax for several moments until Autumn calmed her with soothing words and gentle touches.

I noticed the confusion in Dani's gaze before her eyes flicked to mine. After only a beat of shared, silent communication did she look away. The moment her attention was elsewhere, I wanted it back on me.

Look at me, I willed.

But she trudged on at Syracuse's side. He bumped his shoulder against hers, drawing a small smile from her lips.

A tightness swelled in my chest. Never would she look at me like that. I would forever be a monster to her.

That's what you wanted, a bitter voice reminded me.

For the briefest of moments, I allowed myself the image of the four of us making this peculiar mate situation work. Syr would buy her roses and do sappy shit that made her smile. Brax, ever the protector, would squawk over her safety like a mother hen.

Before I could add myself to that equation, my rage kindled to the surface.

She was mine. Tomorrow, I'd take Daniella back to Carvingwood to ensure Evan's destruction, then I'd drag her to Dockhills, where I would keep her.

I pictured her belly swollen with my pups, and my blood heated.

Autumn, hobbling at my side, cast me a wary look. *What are you thinking?*

I flashed her my teeth in a cruel smile. *Tomorrow I'll be leaving for Carvingwood to hand Evan his demise.*

She nodded, expressionless. *I won't be joining you. Arya is not ready to live among our kind.*

My steps paused. *How long will you be away?*

She inhaled deeply before glancing at me. *I'm not sure.*

The uncertainty in her gaze made my jaw clench, but I forced myself to relax. *Your mate is important. Go and help her adjust. Your position as my right-hand is still yours when you return.*

Thank you, she answered.

When we arrived back at the cabin, exhaustion weighed on me, and though the smell of food wafted out to greet us, I paused in the doorway, behind the rest.

Daniella turned, noting my hesitation. "I'm going for a hunt," I said gruffly. Before anyone had time to protest, I spun for the door, slamming it shut behind me.

My wolf tore free despite the fatigue aching in my bones. I couldn't go back in that suffocating cabin with two other men who vied for her attention. Entertaining a big happy family was not going to happen.

Tomorrow I'd take her back to her territory and take what was rightfully mine—Evan's ruin. And by the end of the next night, I'd fuck her, mark her, and keep her forever.

CHAPTER TWENTY-EIGHT

Syr

Breakfast was uncomfortable as fuck. Everyone ate in silence. The Dockhills beta kept sending worried glances out into the living room area where her painfully-human mate lay. Asleep after her leg was reset by Brax.

I had to admit, I kinda liked the guy. He was quiet, but being the oldest of us, and a rogue, his knowledge of damn near everything was fascinating. I knew how to reset a bone, but only he had the forethought to check for any fractures that would cause the reset to be unsuccessful.

His ability to sense shifts in a person's energy was almost otherworldly. But Autumn insisted that she take Arya to a human doctor as soon as possible. Brax agreed and I offered to drive them in my truck, but there was no way to get it up the mountain to them.

Donovan's second had straightened her shoulders and declared that she'd carry Arya on her back to the next human town.

I could smell her worry like a thick cloud in the air. But it wasn't just her that worried. I felt Dani's too. Her brows creased while she helped clean up the kitchen. Brax met my gaze and I nodded once in agreement. Drifting to her side on autopilot, I rested a hand on her shoulder.

She nearly dropped the pan in her hand that she scrubbed vigorously, face whipping up to mine.

"What's wrong?" I asked. It didn't take a genius to know her worry was for Donovan, but I wasn't sure why. She still hated the guy and if he ran himself into a coma, surely she'd be content to leave his volatile ass here.

She shook her head.

I turned her fully to face me, forcing the scrub brush to plop into the soapy water. "What is it?" I let her see the openness in my expression. Whatever she said, I wouldn't mock.

With a slow sigh, her eyes flicked to the floor. "It's this whole situation. Why three mates?"

Braxton approached. "Because you are worth more than just one male. Perhaps we balance something in you, or you balance something in us. Whatever the reason, it's not a problem that rests on your shoulders alone." He stroked two fingers down her bicep, and instead of feeling my usual possessive rage toward Brax, gratitude rose within me. I nodded.

"What he said." I added a smirk for good measure. "Plus, you're a bit of a handful."

She slapped my chest playfully, grinning along with me. "Oh shut it, Milton."

I laughed, bumping her away from the sink. "I'll finish up if you want to go shower."

She nodded, but hesitated for a moment, and my breath caught. Was she going to suggest I shower with her? Or maybe ask Braxton to join her?

The atmosphere in the room changed, growing heavy and my cock twitched. Seeming to sense the shift, Dani's back straightened. Her gaze raked down me slowly, heat filling her violet eyes.

Biting her lip, she sucked in a sharp breath through her nose, then spun on her heel. Without a backward glance, she fled the kitchen as though demon dogs chased her.

Braxton gave a low chuckle. "We're in so much fucking trouble," he groaned.

I nodded, running a hand through my hair before directing my attention back to the sink. Scrubbing the dishes did nothing to ease my frustrations. My mind was clouded with images of Dani naked with bubbles running down her perfect body.

"Whoa, man," Braxton said after a few minutes. "Cool it over there."

I cleared my throat, but I didn't have it in me to feel shame. If we were all meant to share Dani, then sensing each other's lust for her would be a regular occurrence. "They call it the Chaos for a reason," I said through gritted teeth.

He was silent for several minutes, then threw the rag he wiped the table and countertops with down near the sink, hard. "I'm going to go chop some wood or something."

I made a face at his retreating form. "TMI, man."

His bark of laughter followed him out the door, until he was gone.

My gut twisted. I was alone in the house with Dani. Well—Autumn sat in the living room beside her mate, but she no doubt overheard everything. I finished the rest of the dishes in record time and made my way through the cabin toward the bathroom, hearing the water still running.

Slowly, I reached out for the handle, wanting to test to see if she'd locked it, when I heard Donovan and Brax talking outside. It was too muffled to make out much, other than Donovan being his usually prickly self.

I dropped my hand, my jaw clenching. Right as I turned away from the door, the water shut off.

Dammit, I'm too late.

The front door flung open, and Donovan marched inside like he owned the place, striding directly for the bathroom. I folded my arms over my chest, blocking his path. He rounded the corner, eyes flaring wide at the sight of me but didn't stop until we were nose to nose.

"Get the fuck out of my way, Milton."

I cocked my head to the side, eyeing him with disdain. How the universe thought that Donovan Dockhills was a suitable mate for Daniella, I didn't know. "Not happening."

His lip curled. "Daniella, get your shit. We're leaving," he called to the still closed door.

At his words, it flew open, and the fresh scent of her surged out, making my skin feel too tight. The urge to spin and pull her to me was fucking with every molecule of my being.

"Move, Syr, I've got this," she said to my back.

I didn't move right away. In part because I worried that my now rock-hard cock was going to burst through my jeans if I did. When I finally sidled out of the way, she leaned against the frame in nothing but a bra and panties with a cool calmness that spoke volumes of her self-control.

Donovan growled at the sight of her, and part of me understood the feral desire swirling around the three of us. Even her own arousal mingled in the air, heady and primal.

It carved away a bit more of my fraying self-control.

"Get. Fucking. Dressed," Donovan hissed. His eyes were aglow with golden flame. I braced myself, preparing to intercede if he tried to force himself on her.

Dani's lips quirked. "Why?" she purred. "Does it get you hot, Dickhills?"

I forced myself not to adjust my straining dick in my pants, but Donovan's ire turned to a wicked kind of playfulness that I'd never seen on him. And suddenly, I felt like I was an outsider in this exchange.

Swallowing the lump in my throat, I started to back away, but Dani grabbed my hand, stilling me.

Donovan's gaze snapped to the point of contact, boring into that simple touch as though he could melt me where I stood. An odd sense of satisfaction thrummed through me. She wanted me here with her.

Donovan flicked his gaze up to his tattoo on her forearm, then to her face. "We're going back to Carvingwood. Now."

"Why?" she snapped, folding her arms beneath her breasts which only managed to lift them and successfully draw my and Donovan's gaze to them. Though his was only a cursory glance.

"I have one last piece of business to conduct there before we head south."

She lifted a single brow. "I'm not going to Dockhills. My pack needs me. Besides, your oh-so-precious devices were worthless. That makes our deal void."

His teeth audibly ground together. "We're already bound. The only way around that is to petition a dissolution."

She lazily peeled herself off the doorframe and stepped closer to him. "Then that's exactly what I'll do," she whispered, before pushing between me and Donovan, then heading into the bedroom and slamming the door shut.

CHAPTER TWENTY-NINE

Dani

My need for clothes made my desperation to return to Carvingwood even greater. Dressed in the only items I could find that remotely fit me while what I brought dried on the line—which seemed impossible with nothing but an angry red moon in the sky—I marched back into the main sitting area. Autumn sat on the couch with Arya's head in her lap while she stroked her mate's hair in such an intimate gesture that I couldn't help but feel like I was intruding.

I could sense that all three of the men were outside, but I didn't particularly want to be around any of them, especially in the direct moonlight of the Chaos. A dull throbbing started in my temples, and I massaged them, standing at the window to try to glimpse at what the guys were doing.

Out of the corner of my eye, I saw Autumn gently extricate herself from underneath Arya. I turned fully to eye her, preparing myself for a verbal lashing about how her alpha is kind and generous, *blah, blah, blah…*

"Coffee?" she asked instead.

My mouth opened and then closed, then opened again before I managed, "Is there even any coffee in here?"

She started for the kitchen. "I scented some right after breakfast."

I followed her eagerly. "I'm surprised my caffeine addiction hadn't led me right to it," I said with a laugh.

Autumn was silent as she started opening and shutting cupboards.

Okay then. Apparently we weren't at the joking stage yet.

Finally, she pulled an old canister of coffee down, grimacing. "It might be a little stale."

I shrugged. "I'm sure I've had worse."

A small smile tugged at her lips. We got to work in silence finding the actual coffee machine beneath the sink, and filters shoved in a drawer that held bolts, screws, and matches inside.

I couldn't help but snort a laugh at how painfully bachelor-pad-esque this place was.

We both watched the coffee pot slowly fill with dark, bitter liquid, taking turns filling our cups before adding the powdered cream sitting on the countertop.

I took a sip, expecting it to taste like tar, but was pleasantly surprised. Autumn hummed with satisfaction as she drank deeply from her mug.

"You were really great back in those cells," I said at last.

She looked up, meeting my gaze. Slowly, she lowered her mug to the counter beside her and cleared her throat.

"You were too. If you hadn't saved my life..." Her words trailed off, and I nodded, feeling a weird tightness in my throat.

"Figured it was the least I could do after the sparring ring." I forced myself to hold her gaze and let her see the sincerity of my remorse. "It was never about you," I added. "Donovan gets under my skin like no one else and I reacted. Badly."

Autumn snorted. "A bit," she agreed. Then, smiling, she said, "You get under his skin too." She shrugged. "For whatever that's worth."

And just then, the front door opened, and all three men stepped inside the cabin. Their mixture of scents had me stiffening.

My breath caught, and I held it, not wanting to breathe them in. Not when my nipples hardened for no damn reason.

I turned toward the entryway, spying the three of them pulling off their boots. Syr was shirtless, the fabric tossed over one shoulder and leaving the rest of his exquisite form on display. I didn't know when I'd started to think of my best friend's body in such a blatantly sexual way, but I was pretty sure it started well before this damn Chaos. Donovan smoothed back locks of dark hair that had tumbled down his forehead, but his attention went from Arya to Autumn.

It was Brax who met my gaze first.

My heart skittered at the wild way he looked, though not a single hair was out of place. Like a god chiseled from stone, the feathers and beads entwined with the dark strands, mixed with a molten desire blazing in his arctic blue eyes, made him breathtaking.

Syr's lips quirked to the side as though he'd read my thoughts, and my face heated. He started toward me with Brax only a step behind, while Donovan stayed in place near the door as though he might bolt out of it at any moment.

Syr clapped his hands together. "Who is up for a board game?"

I blinked, choking on the words, "Board game?" Syr's grin grew like he wanted to say something else, but Brax lifted a brow in question.

"It's a game played with a map and cards or dice—"

I waved his explanation away. "I know what a board game is, I just don't know why we would play a game when Arya needs a doctor and I have to get back to my pack."

Donovan's jaw clenched so hard I thought it might shatter.

Syr stopped at the coffee pot, grabbed a mug from the cupboard right above it and poured himself a cup without hesitation. "None of us," he pointed to everyone but Autumn and Arya, "are leaving this cabin until the Chaos is over. We all agreed, and I've waited years, wondering if we were fated. I'm not just going to let you walk away from this without thinking it through."

My eyes widened. "You think you can keep me here?" I asked with deadly calm.

"Shouldn't be difficult between the three of us," Donovan said with a tilt of his sensual lips.

Stop looking at his mouth, I scolded myself, forcing my gaze back to Brax, then Syr.

The three men looked content to keep me locked up here with

them. I knew what they were doing.

While the Chaos pulled and pushed us together, I'd be defenseless. Little by little my reasons for not wanting to take a mate would fall away. Especially when they looked at me like I was a hot meal, and they were starving.

My mouth went dry as I glanced sidelong at Autumn who smirked into her coffee cup.

"Thanks for the support," I muttered, causing her to giggle. To Syr, I said, "You know we have to go back. My father is going to need every bit of help he can get in rebuilding Carvingwood."

"I wouldn't worry about that," Donovan answered before turning and walking back through the small living room. I set my mug down and marched after him.

"What the hell does that mean, Dickhills?"

He whirled right outside the bathroom door, staring down at me like I was an insect, but I didn't give an inch. Invading his space, I glared up at him, hating that I had to crane my head back just to meet his gaze.

"It means," he said in a voice so low and menacing that my breath caught, "that your father deserves what he has coming."

I launched myself at him, fist flying for his jaw, but he caught me by the wrist, spinning me and pushing my back against the door. My knee jerked up between Donovan's thighs, only for the asshole to block that too.

He threatened my father.

My *alpha.*

No one threatened my alpha and got away with it.

He had my other hand pinned before I could claw his eyes out, his lips a breath from mine. "As much as I'd love to continue this, I need a shower. Unless you'd like to join me, Little Wolf?"

"Only to make sure you fucking drown," I snarled.

Donovan chuckled darkly. Then he ran his tongue up my cheek. I jerked back, ignoring the unwanted throb between my thighs as every vile word I'd saved up for Donovan Dockhills came spewing from my mouth.

"You despicable, vulgar, pathetic asshole—" My fists rained down on the door, my rage preparing to break it to splinters.

Strong arms wrapped around my waist, hauling me back. I bucked, slamming my head back, but Syr anticipated it, dodging before dropping me to my feet.

"Come on, Carvingwood, you wanna fight? Let's go outside."

Though I had no reason to fight Syr, I snarled, "Fine." Maybe the training would loosen the tension in my body.

Syr put me through my paces until my breaths sawed in and out of my chest. Sweat coated my back. The baggy T-shirt I wore—tied at my hip so it was less of a weapon against me—stuck to my skin. We landed less blows than usual, and I expected that he was simply letting the brutality in my veins melt away.

Brax watched us circle each other, arms folded over his bare chest.

Syr faked a quick jab with his left hand meant to move me into prime striking range for his dominant hand. I didn't take the bait, kicking his arm away, then launching my foot into Syr's chest. He stumbled back with a grunt, and satisfaction roared through me.

I took the offense, stalking toward him as I let my fists fly. He blocked and dodged what he could, but the strain was evident in his face. My lips pulled wide, and I spun low, kicking my leg out to knock Syr down.

It worked, but instead of allowing me time to jump onto him, he tackled me to my back. I hissed out a breath that Syr covered with his mouth on mine. Jolting with shock, he held my wrists against the cool ground, but I didn't fight him this time. Syr's scent was all around me, and it cooled the violence and rage that simmered in my blood. His knee forced my legs apart and his hips settled between my thighs.

I melted into him, letting him take what he wanted from me. The intense, punishing strength of his kiss turned softer, his tongue flicking my lips, seeking entry.

And I opened to him, groaning slightly. He tasted like home. His hard, sweat-soaked body pressed against me felt far too right. Or maybe his kisses simply drugged me.

With Syr, whether we trained or just simply existed together, life was easy. I knew he'd be the one to break me down, and distantly, I was sure I'd hate myself for this later. But for now, the grinding of his hard length in his pants against my damp heat had me wanting to mewl like a kitten.

I heard Brax whistle low, but something about breaking away from my best friend seemed impossible now. The last time he'd kissed me hadn't felt like this. Where I'd assumed Syr lacked the necessary heat and passion that Donovan delivered, he stroked a deeper urge inside me that would easily be my ruin.

"What the fuck is this?" Donovan snarled. Then Syr was being torn off me. A cry of near desperation caught in my throat.

Syr knocked Donovan's hold off, glaring daggers at the alpha.

I got to my feet, my instant fury coming to a screeching halt at the sight of Donovan in just a towel.

A fluttering sensation in my chest had me growling.

He shook his head, looking me up and down, then fixing his attention on Brax. "What, were you just going to let them fuck in the dirt?"

For the first time, I caught a glimpse of Brax's usual, level-headed demeanor beginning to slip. His eyes flashed a brighter blue.

"She's in heat. Of course, I wanted it to be me she was kissing like that, but she needs this."

I swallowed thickly. In heat? I wasn't in heat.

Though my body felt feverish, and my clit throbbed so hard I wanted to rub it against something—anything—to find release.

Donovan's answer, was of course a smirk. He lifted his chin in a haughty gesture. "Need a ride, Little Wolf?"

I fucking hated the way my pussy clenched greedily at his words. "Go fuck yourself, Dockhills."

He bared his teeth. "I can smell your arousal. Your excuses and insults are wearing thin."

That was exactly why I needed to get away. If I stayed near these men for even one more moment I'd be in serious fucking trouble.

"Let's go inside and sort through this like rational adults, shall we?" Brax quipped.

I gazed over Donovan's shoulder to where the quiet, reserved man stood. He'd just watched me almost jump Syr's bones. I couldn't help but wonder what it would be like to have him join in. The feel both guys' hands on me.

Brax led the way back into the cabin and Donovan followed. Syr turned to me, lifting a brow in question at whatever he saw on my face.

I shook my head, hoping my cheeks weren't as red as they felt, but from the slight twitch of his lips, I guessed my embarrassment showed on my face. There was hope in his gaze too that I couldn't stand to see.

I didn't want to hurt Syr.

Though I feared I was already too late.

Inside, Autumn stood in front of Arya on the couch, slinging a backpack over her shoulder.

Her eyes locked on Donovan, a silent exchange of words passing between them before Donovan nodded stiffly.

To Brax, she said, "Thank you for allowing us to stay here while I rested. But I really need to get Arya to a human doctor so she can cast her leg and get her stronger pain relief."

Brax inclined his head.

Selfishly, I wanted her to stay, to be a buffer between me and the guys. "Can I help with anything?" I offered, hoping for anything that would get me away from here.

She smirked before sashaying toward me and pulling me into a hug. Her lips were next to my ear when she whispered, "Put Donovan in his place, but then fuck his brains out, okay?"

My stomach swooped, but I snorted a laugh to cover up my body's reaction to that statement. When she pulled back, I held her gaze for a moment. She winked, then spun, going to Arya.

"I'm going to shift, and they'll help you onto my back okay?" she said gently to her mate.

The frail girl nodded, looking nervous.

"I'll guide you safely around the traps," Brax said.

She nodded in gratitude before stripping off her clothes and shifting into her wolf form. Brax looked at Rogue lying on the kitchen floor, who lifted his head for his owner, tail flopping side to side in tentative excitement. Brax said in a commanding tone, "Stay."

The dog whined, laying his head back down. I felt bad for the hound and walked over to pat his head in comfort. Brax shucked off his pants, and though I tried to keep my gaze off the hard lines of his naked back, I couldn't help the momentary appreciation of his firm backside.

Donovan and Syr caught me stealing a glance and I averted my eyes just as quickly, rising to my feet. Autumn's wolf was a majestic red color, and Brax a shimmering grey that reminded me of pure moonlight. His dark, sapphire gaze met mine, a reassurance that he'd return soon shining in them.

I helped hoist the human onto Autumn's back, then she and

Brax took off. The moment he was out of sight, I felt the loss of his presence like a thousand tiny cuts on my heart.

It was stupid, and purely the Chaos that made me feel like I might not see him ever again—let alone the fact that I even cared, considering I wasn't going to take any of these men to be my mate.

I stood on the deck, stark red moonlight bathing the mountain top like a horror movie. Syr brushed a hand down my arm.

"Let's go inside, we need to talk."

I bit my bottom lip, then turned to face him. "I'm leaving, Syr. I can't stay, even for the night. Carvingwood needs me, and sooner or later the Chaos is going to strip me of my free will."

Syr reeled back like I'd slapped him.

Donovan huffed a mirthless laugh. "If you're leaving, then so am I. Whether you like it or not, we're still bound. And until Braxton returns, I don't think it's wise to just leave without saying a word. I don't particularly like the guy, but I respect him."

I knew he was right, but it felt like a trap. With all two of the three males here to keep me from leaving, I'd be at the mercy of the blood moon.

Sighing, I spat, "Whatever. But when he gets back, I'm going."

Syr let the words roll off him with ease, smiling broadly. "So now we play that board game?"

CHAPTER THIRTY

Dani

"Winner gets a kiss," Donovan said with a smirk as Syr laid out Monopoly on the kitchen table.

I narrowed my eyes at him. "And if I win?" I asked sweetly.

"Then you can choose who you wish to kiss," he answered.

I was mildly surprised by that statement but bobbed my head in agreement. "Fine."

It didn't take long for Donovan to dominate the real estate on the board, making me glare at the asshole. He'd cheated somehow.

He had to have.

It was how he always won the Pack Games.

When Syr declared that he was bankrupt, I threw my fake money down on the board. I wasn't far behind, but I knew the game was essentially over.

Donovan's grin was so smug, I wanted to punch him in the face. "That's right, Little Wolf, bring your sexy ass over here."

I got to my feet slowly. Unable to look at my best friend, I just hoped he'd look away. Instead, I felt him go utterly still beside me.

Walking around the table, my hips swinging side to side, a wicked grin curved my lips. Donovan watched, hunger blazing in his eyes.

I threw one leg over his lap, and sat myself on top of the bulge in his jeans, earning a grunt. Weaving my fingers into his hair, I cocked my head to one side, my lips ghosting just a breath above his.

His hands gripped my hips painfully, holding me firmly against him like he knew what game I meant to play. I snagged his bottom lip with my teeth, nipping it a little harder than necessary. Donovan growled. Heat skated through my veins.

If I didn't get off his lap, I was going to lose myself. Kissing Donovan Dockhills was a very dangerous game. One I would lose if he had anything to say about it.

One hand fisted in my hair, then his mouth claimed mine. Whatever fight I'd been intending to put up went out the window. The hot, brutal way Donovan kissed me had all thoughts fleeing from my brain.

I sucked and licked his tongue, trying to unravel him the way he unraveled me. But it was no use. When he tugged my head back, exposing my throat, he peppered kisses down my jaw, grazing his teeth lower. I whimpered.

The bulge I'd foolishly positioned at my apex was hard and throbbing. My body seemed to have a mind of its own, rocking against him and moaning at the friction.

"This is what you crave, Little Wolf," he snarled against my skin, sounding more wolf than man. "I'm not going to let you walk away from this twisted thing we have. You can pretend for tonight if it makes you feel better." He sucked lightly at the base of my throat, sending a jolt of lightning straight to my pussy.

"But when the morning comes, you're mine," he finished. His voice was harsh—rough.

He stole my answering words from my mouth by sealing his lips over mine again. I couldn't get enough of him. His smell. His taste.

The delicious friction of our bodies thrusting against one another drove me to the brink, and when he pulled away at last, leaving me panting, he smirked. Then, looking over my shoulder at Syr, he said, "Take her to bed, I'll sleep on the couch."

He lifted me off him, setting me on my feet before stalking away. I heard the bathroom door shut and the shower turn on. My legs were like jello, and I ached something fierce. For a moment, I leaned against the table, catching my breath, and hoping that the fire in my veins would settle. When it didn't, I looked to Syr with pleading eyes.

His irises were bright, but his body looked larger, and he wore a pained expression.

Had Donovan just been putting on a show to make Syr jealous? I couldn't process anything beyond Donovan's threat.

Seeming to shake away whatever thoughts he was lost in, Syr got to his feet, extending a hand for me to take. I did, and just the simple contact felt like my nerves were all going haywire.

He led me to the bedroom, and uncertainty flared through me. What I wanted and what I burned for were two different things, but in the light of the Chaos moon that streamed in through the window, those two were one in the same.

Syr seemed to sense it and stopped in the middle of the room, hands on my hips lightly. "I fucking hated seeing you kiss him," he said into the quiet.

I opened my mouth to speak, taking a step back. He followed, and then he was guiding me to the bed. "I'm sorry," I whispered, shame choking me. The back of my legs hit the edge of the mattress, but I forced myself to stay upright.

His gaze was distant, fixed on something behind me. Wanting him to be here with me, I lifted up onto my toes, pressing a kiss to his cheek. "You light up for him, Dani," he said, meeting my gaze.

I swallowed hard, not knowing what to say. It had been a game. He rattles me, and I rattle him back. But I couldn't say that it didn't mean anything.

Donovan knew how to piss me off better than anyone alive, but I couldn't deny that I wanted him any longer.

"However," he continued, pressing a kiss to my forehead, "you come alive at my touch too." He kissed my nose. One cheek, then the other. My eyelids fell shut and then his warm lips were on those too. I sighed, feeling the ache between my thighs intensify.

He laid me back on the bed, standing at the foot of the mattress before wedging himself between my knees. My brows pinched together as mischief alighted his swirling honey-brown eyes.

"He bowed out after the warmup act. Now I want to hear you

scream my name." Syr knelt on the floor, tugging my pants down with such force, I gasped.

My sex was borne and I knew he could scent as well as seen my arousal. A growl shook his chest, and I felt the vibration at my knees. It carried up my legs, making me desperate for his tongue on me.

His eyes dragged up my body, and whatever was left of the gentle, calm Syr was gone. "Take your shirt off," he ordered.

Smirking, I reached down, grasping the hem, and pulled the fabric up and off in one fluid motion. Before he could make any further demands, I shucked the bra off too.

Being completely naked around Syr had always been normal, but this time was different. My nipples were hard, my breasts heavy, and I found myself drawing my shoulders back, pushing my tits out as if in offering.

Syr's husky string of expletives made my lips curve with satisfaction.

"You're so fucking perfect, Dani. I've thought so since we were kids, but right here, right now, I'm thanking the Goddesses that you're *mine*." The last word was a rumble of thunder in the room.

"Yes," I breathed. "Taste me, Syr. I want you to."

He didn't hesitate another moment, wrapping his arms under my thighs, forcing them wider.

"Such a pretty cunt," he murmured.

I didn't have time to feel shock at his words before his lips pressed kisses to the insides of my thighs, growing closer and closer to my center. Gritting my teeth, I writhed—or tried to, but his grasp on my lower half was like steel bands.

"Syr, please," I begged.

He chuckled, and the sound was so unlike my best friend that it gave me pause. "I love it when you beg, baby."

The first lap of his tongue at my damp slit had my back arching. Everything was an explosion of sensation, but his mouth on my pussy was pure euphoria. He licked in long, languid strokes, drawing small cries from me that got louder and more guttural when his tongue swirled around my throbbing clit.

Releasing one of my legs, he ran a finger through my slick heat, and I bucked.

"Fuck!" I growled.

"Not yet," Syr admonished, nipping at the inside of my thigh again. When he plunged a finger inside me, I thrashed, my hips gyrating. I wanted to ride his finger into oblivion.

His tongue worked faster, feasting on me in between tiny sucks on my tiny bundle of nerves. My head fell back, unable to hold it up any longer. He fucked me with his finger, adding a second that provided the exquisite stretch I craved.

The building pleasure grew and grew until I was wild, fighting against my wolf for control.

My orgasm crashed into me so hard I screamed, back bowing off the bed. Syr pumped his fingers in a steady rhythm, forcing me to endure wave after wave of pleasure.

Until it began to abate, and he stilled.

Feeling drugged by the high I'd just experienced, I lifted my head, blinking the room back into focus. Syr grinned at me from the floor.

"You're the best meal I've ever had," he said with primal satisfaction. Rising, he climbed onto the bed, settling beside me.

I kissed him in thanks since my brain didn't seem capable of forming words yet. My taste was on his tongue, and it made my overachieving lady bits throb again. I groaned and Syr chuckled.

He pulled my body against his, so my face was buried in his shirt, with his chin resting atop my head. The scent of him like a balm on my soul. Despite my desire to climb on top of him, I liked that he was holding me like he used to.

We laid in peaceful silence for several moments, his thumb stroking lazily on my shoulder. Then he said, "I remember the first time I ever saw you. Your mother had forced you to wear a dress to the town meeting and you sulked the entire time. I remember thinking that you were so pretty, even when you frowned. But afterward, when you were climbing one of the trees outside, I climbed after you to ask you to be my friend. I just knew I wanted to make you smile. Hear you laugh."

I huffed out a laugh. "Yeah, I remember. You filled your pockets with muffins and brought them up to the top so you could give them to me after my mom said I couldn't have any."

He smiled into my hair. "And when the pack started to panic after the first year of no Chaos, you marched up to your father and said we'd all just have to play games until the Chaos came back…" His voice trailed off and my smile faltered.

"That's the day I decided I wanted to be alpha."

Syr was quiet a moment. "You'll make a great alpha. You're a natural born leader; fearless, kind, and dedicated to our pack. It's part of the reason I fell in love with you."

My chest tightened at those words, but I couldn't speak. Couldn't move.

"I knew it when you'd knocked John Marsten on his ass for touching you." He chuckled, and a small smile tugged at my lips. "You've always been such a violent little thing," he teased.

I leaned my head back so I could look up into my best friend's eyes. Biting my lip, I considered what I wanted to say. His smile faded. Then the truth spilled out of me. "I never wanted a mate because I didn't want the competition to be alpha, and I also didn't want to assert my authority over you. Because I love you. I don't want you to resent me later down the line."

He opened his mouth to speak, but I pressed my fingertips to his lips, silencing him.

"I love you, Syr. And I'm glad it's you. I just need to figure out what's going on with the other two before I officially make a decision, okay?"

Syr's lips tugged to one side in a goofy grin. He nodded, then pressed a kiss to my forehead again. "I could never resent you, Dani. And if you choose to have all three of us as your mates, we'll make it work. I don't know about Braxton but I'm pretty sure Donovan meant what he said earlier, and I know I'm not letting you go for anything or anyone." He sighed sleepily.

I had no way of knowing what time it was, but our game of Monopoly had lasted a long time. Regardless, I felt my eyelids grow heavy, and cocooned in Syr's warmth, I fell gently and swiftly into deep, blissful sleep.

CHAPTER THIRTY-ONE

Brax

When I arrived back, the Dockhills alpha was sitting in the dark on the couch, sipping dark-amber liquid from one of the only nice glasses I owned.

"They're safe," I said.

Donovan nodded before draining the last of the whiskey from his glass. "Thank you." He got to his feet. "Do you want the couch?"

I shook my head.

He nodded again, and I scented the air, trying to figure out what had him so out of sorts. The faint scent of her desire lingered in the air. My brows creased.

"Did she…?"

Donovan gave a soft, humorless laugh. "Not yet. She says she has to figure out where she stands with us before she makes a decision."

I thought for a moment. What decision was there for her to make? I decided to voice the question aloud. "Why should she choose between us? The gods gave her three mates for a reason."

Donovan's teeth ground together audibly. "I won't fucking share her," he growled.

I shrugged. "Then you'll lose her. If you weren't so desperate to bend her to your will, she'd likely be less cold toward you."

Donovan smirked, stretching out over the couch with an arm thrown over his eyes. His legs hung off the edge, but he didn't seem to care. "I'm addicted to her bite." He sighed. "Besides, if she knew what she was so desperate to defend was more corrupt than I am she wouldn't fight me."

I narrowed my eyes at him. "Is this about her family?"

He peered from under his arm at me. "What do you know of that?"

"Enough," I answered. "You should just tell her."

"She'd never believe me. It has to come from her father. And it will." His last words were a sworn vow. The guy was a calloused asshole, but I could sense that he cared for her.

As I did.

As we all did.

I gave another, single nod before heading into the hall. Tugging my clothes off, I tossed them to the floor, bringing my wolf to the surface.

Nosing the door open, I curled up at the foot of the bed. Her scent—her nearness soothed my nerves. I'd move the mountains just to make the mysterious girl breathing softly above me look at me the way I'd seen her look at Syracuse earlier today. And even at Donovan when he wasn't looking.

You'll be mine soon, Little One, I vowed silently.

Then I slipped into her dreams, keeping watch for anything that might harm her.

I was up early, pancake wrapped sausages packed for the journey. When Daniella stepped from the steam-filled bathroom, freshly showered and looking like a wet dream, I smiled at her.

"Good morning, Little One."

She blinked at me warily before a smile curved her lips too. "Morning, Brax."

Fuck, I love my name on her lips.

"Breakfast is ready. I think the other two might have mowed through most of the wraps already, but I made sure a fair few were set aside for you." My wolf almost seemed to preen at how we'd provided for her. Both in the night, and with food.

Her stomach rumbled as though responding to my gift. "Oh good, the other guys totally forgot to feed me last night." With a wink, she passed by me, her arm brushing against mine, sending sparks of desire straight to my cock.

Forcing down the growl that fought to escape, I followed her to the kitchen.

The awkwardness in the room the moment she entered it was palpable. I rolled my eyes, grabbing the brown bag filled with food for my mate, as well as a steaming mug of coffee that I held out to Dani.

She inhaled the scents deeply and moaned, making my back stiffen. Donovan and Syr stilled as well. Dani, seemingly oblivious to the three males starving for her, pulled out the first wrap and bit into it before stalking for the door.

"Alright, let's get out of here," she called.

When the door banged shut behind her, Donovan released a frustrated huff.

I couldn't help but chuckle at that. This was going to be a long day. We'd shave off plenty of time by running as wolves, but until we were out of the steep, treacherous mountains, it was safer to stay in human form.

It was strange to be guided by the light of a red moon, but we made it around the traps that encased my land without any further issue.

I found myself walking by her side at every opportunity even though she had the grace of a feline. Her silky, black hair reflected the eerie moonlight, but I couldn't help but admire her ethereal beauty.

Perhaps she was a descendant of the gods themselves.

She glanced back at me, catching me staring at her. "Where are you from, Brax?" she asked.

I cleared my throat. "Outside of the valley. A pack from the frigid north that was called Nightwoods."

Her brows lifted. "I've never been outside Chaos Valley. What's it like?"

My shoulders lifted in a shrug. "Much like here, but the Chaos isn't as strong. A mate bond can snap into place at any time."

Only the sound of the four of us breathing filled the quiet for several moments. "What made you come to Chaos Valley?"

My chest tightened. "Revenge." The images that filled my own dreams rushed through my mind.

Seeming to sense that I didn't want to talk about it just yet, she didn't push. The simple action gave me a rush of gratitude.

We slowly crept down the slope of loose rock, myself in front to catch Dani if she slipped, the two following behind her for the same reason. Rogue slipped several times, though he made a valiant effort to travel independently, but Syr took pity on him, and slung the almost-hundred-pound dog into his arms, carrying him down. By the time we made it to the next flat level—a road that led into pack territory—we all breathed heavily.

"Do you like being a lone wolf?" she asked after gulping down some water.

I grimaced, taking the bottle she offered and sipping it while I carefully selected my words. "It's something I've grown accustomed to." She stopped to lean against the rocky outcropping while the other two shared their own bottle of water. Donovan and Syr walked to the edge, pretending to look out over the forest below dotted with pack lands.

With a sigh, I pushed through my reservations and said, "Fifteen years ago, my pack was attacked by The Silver Vipers. They razed my home and killed my family. I never found my sister's body to bury her with the others. That was when I came to Chaos Valley. I vowed to avenge their deaths as well as hunt the assholes who have been destroying packs, kidnapping the women, and selling them at the auctions."

Dani let out a long breath. "I'm so sorry, Brax," she whispered.

I nodded. "Now, their deaths are avenged. But I don't think I'll ever be able to stop hunting the wicked men of this world. No one deserves to go through what I went through. What my family suffered…" I stopped just as my throat tightened. "It's why I wear these." Tugging at a plait that had an amethyst and a feather from it, I continued, "Each feather is a life I couldn't save. The gems represent the family I lost."

Her eyes welled with unshed tears, and she placed a hand on my shoulder. "I think that's a great way to honor them. But you know that it wasn't your fault, right? None of those deaths were your fault." Her gaze swept over the feathers and stones, no doubt counting them again. I wanted to kiss away the sadness on her face. "But I get it. You're a protector by nature." She shot me a half-smile. "I could feel you in my dreams last night. And the night before."

I cleared my throat, trying to find an excuse that didn't make me sound like a total creeper, but she held up a hand to stop me. "I've been waiting for the nightmares…I mean, I wasn't in there long, and nothing truly horrific happened to me, but there was this little girl, twelve, maybe thirteen, years old…" She swallowed hard, and brutal rage surged through my veins. "I don't even know where she is or if she's okay, and I can't help but feel responsible."

I'd made sure that every single male in the area that bore the silver snake on their forearm was slaughtered, but the sick fucks there to purchase stolen females weren't all dead. Once the Chaos had hit, my sole focus had been her. I wanted to track them all down and kill each of them slowly.

Make them beg for death.

She sucked in a deep breath before continuing. "Anyway, I felt certain I'd find myself back in those cells, but every time they've started to surface, I felt you there, fighting away my demons." She offered me a watery smile that broke my heart.

I wrapped an arm around her shoulders and pulled her against me, sucking in her scent until my blood only simmered. One of her small hands rested on my chest and I cursed the fabric Donovan had insisted I don for the journey separating me from her touch.

"If you wanted me to, I'd fight your every demon, slay every monster that came for you, waking and not. However, I know you're not the type to back down from a fight." I placed a finger under her chin, tilting her head back until our gazes collided. "Whenever you are ready to face those nightmares, I'll be by your side."

Her violet eyes pierced me so completely, they stole the air from my lungs. "I think I understand now," she said so softly I almost hadn't made out the words. Then she lifted up onto her tiptoes, brushing her lips against mine, feather soft.

Before she could pull away, I cupped her face in one hand, holding her where I wanted her. With the other hand, I held her hip, loving the feel of her slender body against mine.

I kissed her tenderly, letting her feel just how much I wanted her to want me. To choose me.

Her hand on my chest fisted my shirt, the other tangling in my hair. She deepened the kiss, tongue tasting me with sure strokes that I returned.

I knew this was just the beginning, but I felt her choice in that single kiss. The way we clung to each other like we needed the other for air. I tasted her desire for me on her tongue. My wolf howled inside my chest.

Our mate.

She was ours.

No matter what.

CHAPTER THIRTY-TWO

Dani

After Brax's heartbreaking story, I didn't even think before kissing him as if I could wipe away the horrors of his life.

Now I had three men who wanted me and had laid claim to me despite my reasons for pushing them away. Maybe it was the Chaos that caused the shift in me, but I was finding it harder and harder to push them away.

Donovan was easy. The second he opened his mouth, my hatred for him came rushing back. And I couldn't ignore his threat to my alpha. He'd been much more tolerable today though, which wasn't helping me sort through what the hell I was going to do.

Syr was my best friend. I'd loved him for years already, and being his mate would likely be the easiest of all them. And sweet, quiet Brax who kept watch in my dreams, so I didn't have to face the nightmares alone…

Yep, I'm fucked.

Shaking away the chaotic thoughts, Ivywood came into view at long last, and my heart soared. I was almost home. I ran harder than I had all day, pushing my sore body to go faster.

The alpha link snapped into place, and if it were possible to grin from excitement in wolf form, then that's exactly what I was doing.

We're coming, Dad, I said down the link.

But no answer came in the form of words.

Rage. Savage, feral, bloodlust.

I shared a glance with Syr who looked as concerned as I felt. Clearly, he'd experienced what I just had.

The smell of charred forest wafted through the trees. Stomach churning, I prepared myself for what I might see.

We burst into the wide clearing and I skidded to a halt. Buildings that once stood tall and proud were blackened and damaged. Some were reduced to bare timbers and mounds of furniture devoured by blackened tongues.

At first glance, it appeared to be a ghost town. No people milled about, trying to repair their homes. Snarls and the sound of snapping jaws stopped my heart cold.

I tore through the side roads, deeper into Carvingwood. A crowd of people were gathered in the town center, and without catching a glimpse of the wolves who fought in the middle, I knew in my heart at least one of them was my father.

Someone had challenged the alpha.

Cheers and whoops went out from the audience as a low whine reached my ears.

I slipped back into my human skin, grunting from the pain of a quick shift, but I only managed to grab a big T-shirt from the pack on Brax's back before pushing my way through the throng.

Evan Carvingwood was an impressive wolf. Even if he weren't my father, I'd have nothing but respect for him and the hard-earned loyalty of his people. His size was not as big as Brax or Syr, but his fur was a violent crimson, his eyes so dark, they were almost black. The way he fought was a thing of pure beauty.

Except his opponent was slightly smaller and shook so hard I wondered how his legs supported him at all. After a moment I recognized him as Michael, one of the pack's elders. Foam dripped from his maw like a rabid animal. Cocking my head to the side, I scented the air. A metallic tang tainted the space.

Yet, there didn't seem to be that much blood.

"He's been poisoned," Donovan said near my ear. "Silver."

My shoulder gave a phantom pang. Never again did I want to know what that felt like. I shook my head. "How would he have been poisoned?" I shot back.

His lips pressed into a tight line, but he didn't answer.

I watched my father circle the dying wolf, no doubt offering Michael a choice: swift death or banishment.

The moment my alpha sprung onto Michael, knocking him to the ground, I knew the fight was over. But my father didn't execute a painless death.

He dug his claws into the elder's chest. Blood matted his brown fur, and the weak whimper struck a chord in my heart that made me take a step forward.

Syr was the one to grab my shoulder, preventing me from inadvertently putting myself in the ring and challenging my father for the pack.

Michael's death was slow, and pained cries were nearly drowned out by the cheering crowd. I felt sick, but when my father at last turned to human, rising to his feet, he lifted a fist in the air, claiming the victory.

The pack roared its approval, but looking around, I noticed some looked on with rage and even disgust.

Just what the hell had happened while I was gone?

Donovan squeezed my shoulder before pushing by me, and my heart dropped. Then he said, "I challenge the Alpha of Carvingwood!"

"No!" I rushed forward, but Syr hauled me back.

My father eyed up Donovan like he was a nasty insect that needed to be squashed. "Stay out of this, Daniella."

Donovan sent me what I thought was supposed to be a reassuring look, but mixed with his usual arrogance, I almost hoped my father would kick his ass.

Yet, my chest ached at the images that flashed in my mind of his body bloodied and lifeless in the dirt. I couldn't let this happen.

I couldn't let my father get killed.

Or Donovan, though I loathed to admit it.

I looked over my shoulder at Syr. "We have to stop this."

His expression was grim. "It's too late."

Frustration roared through me like a bear disturbed during its slumber. My father and Donovan agreed to the standard fight until one yielded or was killed. Michael's body was cleared away for an outcasts' burial while my dad offered his hand for a friendly shake. I noted the way Donovan narrowed his eyes at my father's hand before stalking to the edge of the circle.

Was there any truth to Donovan's accusation? Did my father poison Michael? It's not like he had a silver dagger on him—silver was illegal in Carvingwood—though I knew from experience that the tiniest fleck of silver under your skin could cause a great deal of damage.

He had no way of using silver though, nor a way to even gain access to it. Most of Chaos Valley outlawed silver.

My father made his way to my mother, who stood almost across from me, looking teary eyed. They embraced; their love felt throughout the entire square. But Donovan watched them with mistrust in his golden eyes.

The pack stomped a slow, thunderous beat, indicating that the match had begun. My alpha didn't look worn out after the previous fight. He grinned broadly before they both became wolves yet again.

My own heart beat in time with the growing rhythm around us. There was no way to stop this fight, and I couldn't stand to watch bloodshed on either part.

So when my father launched himself at Donovan first, I gasped. The sound was devoured by the mass of wolves hungry for violence.

Boom.

Boom.

Boom.

The cacophony of stomps made it impossible to hear anything else. Donovan easily rolled away from my father's attack, and the two began to circle each other again. I saw the cold, calculating way that Donovan assessed my father for weaknesses he wouldn't find.

For a moment, I forgot that I held my breath, sucking in air when my father roared and leapt at the sleek black wolf that was Donovan. Teeth sank into the side of his neck, and Donovan rolled, flinging my father off. He charged next, incensed, and swiped his paws down my father's face.

He snarled, swinging his own paw for Donovan who spun away just in time. I fought my instincts to throw myself between them and demand that this match end.

Brax seemed to sense my struggle and took my hand in his, giving it a light squeeze.

They continued their dance of dodging and leaping for each other for what felt like an hour. Both breathed heavily. Even the gathered pack members chanted for it to be finished.

When my father struck out a paw yet again, Donovan roared in pain. But he jumped over the Carvingwood alpha, tearing through fur and muscle with his teeth. Collectively, an intake of breath went around the ring as my father collapsed at last.

Since there was no alpha link for mental communication, Donovan turned human, crouching over the crimson wolf.

Donovan's face was bleeding, three gashes running from his forehead, across his nose and down his cheek. Leaning low, he whispered something to my father, but I was unable to make out the words.

Silence descended, and when Donovan stood, Brax tossed him a shirt and pair of shorts that he slipped on. My mother sprinted to where my father laid, crouching beside him and speaking into his ear.

"I am naming myself the victor of this match based on sheer strength and cunning. However, Evan Carvingwood has long since used banned methods in order to secure his reign." Donovan spoke to those gathered like the leader he was, but still an outcry rose up.

And just like that I felt the alpha link sever.

It knocked the air from my lungs. Tears burned my eyes, but I blinked them away, refusing to let a single one fall.

Tomorrow I'd grief.

"No," I snarled. Heat licked through my veins and my wolf howled at the idea of bowing to Donovan Dockhills.

His eyes met mine, and he held my gaze for a beat. "Many of you were alive when my father, Aris Dockhills, lived in this area. He and Evan Carvingwood were best friends and vowed to rule their packs on joined territory, but as alphas of their own people. After all, the land is one of the largest in all of Chaos Valley."

Murmurs snaked around the pack.

He continued. "When Evan decided he wanted this territory all for himself, and meant to claim Dockhills as well, he challenged my father. It came to a draw, and Aris chose to take his people and retreat to the south. However, Evan left my father a little parting gift." He paused, taking in the silence like an addicting drug. "Silver poisoning."

The reaction was instantaneous. People booed and jeered at him, calling for his head, but he spoke over them, his breaths coming faster.

"It took him several years to die from it, but Evan got smarter. I can guarantee the results of the blood test from your deceased elder would show a toxic level of silver." His body trembled and his pupils ate away the gold in his irises.

What in the—

He grinned despite his one eye drooping, the swelling turning purple and nearly closing it. "I can feel it in my system now."

My mother gasped, her gaze whipping up to Donovan while she pressed a hand to hold the wicked gashes on my father's side closed. He gave a gurgled chuckle.

"Quite the story, Donovan," he rasped.

Donovan lifted the non-drooping brow, nodding to someone in the crowd before two of his men approached. One had what looked like tweezers and a jar in his hand, while the other took my father's free hand. He struggled, growling low.

My mother shrieked, "Stop it, he's injured! That's enough!"

But the other scraped what he needed into the jar. Tiny flecks of something dark fell to the bottom and my stomach fell to my feet.

Donovan took the jar and inspected it with his one good eye. He walked around the outside of the ring, allowing the pack to see my father's shame.

"Tiny specks of silver. Of course most of it is in my face now." The last part he tacked on with a rasping laugh. One of his henchmen slung Donovan's arm over his shoulders, helping him walk.

"They're just rocks," my mother insisted, her tone turning shrill. But no one paid her any attention but me. I stared at her in disbelief. Because I could see the guilt in her eyes.

My mother—the woman who held me and read me stories—

was a traitor.

And my father who had taught me to fight, priming me to take over the pack one day had committed the most foul crime of all time.

I stepped forward, catching Donovan when he stumbled. "Healer! Where's Faith?"

My mother began to sob that an alpha had the right to break rules in order to keep their pack safe.

I put myself in front of her, forcing her gaze to mine. Her lip trembled but I didn't allow myself to feel pity for her. She'd known. She might have even helped my father. Who knew how far the corruption ran within the pack.

"What he did was disloyal, Mom. No alpha should stoop to such lows. And the fact that you helped him makes you just as bad."

Her mouth opened, but I turned and walked back to Donovan, helping to support his weight just as Faith burst into the circle.

"How do you know she helped him?" Donovan wheezed. His skin had a ghostly pallor that made my stomach knot itself into a tangled mess.

"My mother loves my father, but if she had known he was betraying the pack's trust, she'd have left him to die on the ground." I didn't add the fact that when he'd embraced her, they'd clasped hands which I'd never seen them do before. Maybe it was reaching, but with how silent my father was, I knew.

I knew he was a traitor.

I'm the daughter of a traitor.

My head spun, but I sat at Donovan's side, watching as Faith tried to draw the nearly microscopic bits of silver from his wounds.

A single, silent tear tracked down her cheek, and I knew she wept for what would happen to my parents.

The pack bellowed out the need for a judgement, but Donovan's eyes slid shut and didn't reopen. I stood, expecting looks of hatred and disgust, but none were directed at me.

Clearing my throat, I said, "I can't speak for Donovan, but I think a situation like this requires that my parents both be exiled. Shall we call it to a vote?"

Murmurs of ascent answered, and I nodded.

"All those in favor of Evan and Angel Carvingwood being banished beyond Chaos Valley?"

A chorus of cheers, howls, and shouts sounded. It was deafening.

I spun, letting my parents see what they'd brought upon themselves. My upper lip curled as my mother threw herself at my feet, weeping uncontrollably.

"You helped Dad murder at least a dozen challengers by cheating. I'll always love you both, but I can't stand the sight of you. You're both banished from these woods and from all of Chaos Valley. I will not allow you to take anything but the clothes on your backs. Now be gone or suffer my own wrath."

The two people I loved most in the world had betrayed my pack. They'd betrayed me.

Yet, watching them scrambled from the square, my heart cracked even further. I'd never see them again.

They may have been willing to sell me for the good of the pack, but I'd have done it a hundred times over again.

Because my pack was my true family.

But now I had to wonder if Donovan would pull through. If Faith could get all of the silver out of him before it polluted his bloodstream.

I knelt beside Donovan, feeling the alpha link only weakly tethered. His face was a torn mess since Faith had to keep slicing into the wound to keep it from closing until she was sure the silver was gone.

Tears fell silently from her face, but she worked diligently.

Placing my hand over hers for a moment, I got her to meet my gaze.

"I'm sorry," I whispered. My mother had been her friend since she'd arrived in Carvingwood. Banishment was never an easy thing, especially when it was someone you loved.

Which was why I had no idea how I was holding myself together, but I knew that I needed Donovan to pull through so I could kick his ass for challenging my father knowing full well he'd be poisoned with silver.

Faith nodded, then went back to cleansing the wound as it bled furiously. Bile rose in my throat while I watched.

Syr and Brax stood behind me, their presences a comfort that both surprised and pleased me.

Brax squeezed my shoulder, saying quietly, "He'll make it. He's an alpha. He's too tough to quit."

Tears stung my eyes again, and I swallowed them down.

Maybe he was. But my dad had quit. He'd let my mother try to defend him. He chose to be exiled rather than to accept a swift death.

Syr knelt behind me and wrapped an arm around my shoulders. The touch was soothing, and I sagged against him while holding one of Donovan's limp hands. It was impossibly warm.

Live, you asshole, I thought bitterly. *Live and let me rail at you.*

We all stayed that way until Faith announced that she couldn't sense anymore silver in the wound, but that only time would tell if he would make it. She informed me that he'd taken silver in the raid on Carvingwood, and guiltily I thought about how I'd shot all three guys to try to escape them.

I tightened my hold on his hand and thought about the words I'd say to him when he awoke. It was all still a bit of a jumbled mess, but he'd challenged my father so that I hadn't faced him and potentially died from silver poisoning. I still wanted to believe my father never would have used such tactics on me, but after the whirlwind of events over the past few hours, I wasn't sure about anything anymore.

Donovan could have killed my father, but he left him alive. That might be in part due to the silver poisoning, but he could have delivered the fatal blow before proving his betrayal. In sparing him, he'd only shown the people of Carvingwood that he wasn't the enemy.

In fact, very few seemed put out by the shift in leadership. Donovan was an excellent leader, but he knew I wanted to be alpha.

And I'd have to fight him for it.

One day, I would.

I grew up with these wolves. I loved them in a way he never would.

"Should we move him?" Brax asked, jarring me from my racing inner monologue.

I opened my mouth to answer when Donovan's hand squeezed mine back.

"That won't be necessary," he rasped.

CHAPTER THIRTY-THREE

Donovan

I awoke to searing, aching pain that felt skull-deep. Though I imagined it was dulled by whatever foul smelling salve the pack healer had coated my wounds with. Still, my one eye throbbed, and for a moment I wondered if I'd be able to see out of it again.

Daniella's much smaller fingers twined through mine grounded me. I gave her hand a squeeze, letting her know I was grateful to have her near.

I heard Brax ask if they should move me, and I managed to croak, "That won't be necessary."

My Little Wolf sucked in a sharp breath, and I heard the steady rhythm of her heart pick up its pace. A grin pulled at the corners of my mouth, but the burst of pain swiftly killed it.

"How are you feeling?" Dani asked.

"Like I had my skull cracked open and stitched back together," I answered, trying and failing to open one of my eyes more than a crack.

"Excellent, then you won't even feel this," she answered. Then she punched my arm.

I winced. "What did I do now?"

"You challenged my father knowing that he was going to poison you with silver all so you could make a point! That's what this whole thing was about, wasn't it?" Her tone grew more and more shrill with each word. I managed to open my good eye enough to see her waving her arms.

"What thing?" I asked. Fuck, my mouth was dry.

"The Tying Ceremony, showing up here with some mysterious device and offering my father a deal he couldn't refuse. That's why you said you knew his secret. That was his secret. It all led up to the moment you challenged him and—" she broke off, a deep, shuddering breath that sounded like she was on the verge of either tears or a panic attack. Maybe both.

I sighed, pushing myself up to sitting, though every bone in my body protested the movement. Dizziness pummeled me, but I had to make her see the truth on my face. She had a death grip on my other hand, but I let her keep it.

"At first, yes," I answered simply. "But make no mistake, I've wanted you for years. This just gave me the excuse I needed to ensure you couldn't say no. Or rather, that your protests went unanswered." My throat bobbed as an unexpected and unpleasant emotion flooded me. I'd taken what hadn't belonged to me, simply to hurt Evan. Now his pack was mine, and looking at his daughter, even knowing we were fated mates, I wanted her to choose me. Even if that meant sharing her with Brax and Syr.

The way I chose her the first time she got in my face, not at all afraid of the nine years or foot height difference I had on her, nor the fact that I was alpha, and she was her father's beta, cursed to forever live in his shadow.

Her voice was mournful as she said, "I sent them away. Since you didn't finish my father off, I banished them both from Chaos Valley."

I wasn't sure why she was volunteering that information. Perhaps it was because her hands shook, and she didn't know how to process what I'd told her." I nodded slowly—gingerly—since everything fucking hurt.

Part of me knew it was killing her inside to know she'd never see them again unless she sought them out. But I'd seen the disgust on her face when she learned the truth about her father. Wolves were intensely honor-bound. A challenge for leadership was meant to be earned on strength and wit alone.

And while some packs might not find the use of silver poisoning unforgiveable during a match, I knew she valued skill and strength in an alpha.

It's what made her the best candidate for running Carvingwood. I didn't intend to keep the northern pack—her home, or her people. Only to show her what tactics her father used to keep his power. And what she might have faced, had she challenged him.

"I'm sorry," I told her, taking her other hand in mine. "For what you lost today."

She nodded stoically.

"And when I'm healed, I intend to hand over Carvingwood to you."

Her eyes widened. "You *want* me to fight you?"

I smirked as much as my sore face would allow. "And just so you know, I don't take it easy on pretty girls."

Standing across from my mate, I couldn't suppress the urge to smile. She lifted her chin, though I saw the excitement that lit her eyes.

"You're sure you're completely healed?" she asked for the fourth time that morning. "Because I don't want to hear you whining about how you got your ass kicked by a girl while you were still injured."

I snorted a laugh. I'd spent all of yesterday recovering, I couldn't rest any longer or I'd go crazy. "First of all, it was my face. Secondly, why don't you tell me?" Taking a step closer, our bodies almost touching, I saw her throat work nervously. Heat surged through my veins. The full, crimson moon still hung high in the sky and it called to my wolf. Thunder rumbled in the distance, the occasional flash of lightning barely illuminated one half of the sky. The storm lumbered closer like a bear on the hunt.

Every urge that told me to pull Daniella's hard, slender body to me and kiss her until she was mindless with desire became a dull roar in my mind. Her eyes narrowed as if she could sense my inner struggle.

"May the best wolf win, *Dickhills*," she said sweetly,

before putting a step between us again and offering her hand.

I shook it, loving even the simplest contact with her.

"Now, with the Chaos still in effect, if anything should happen that would require us to step in, you sound this alarm," Syr said, handing Dani a small, compact device that would let loose an awful screeching sound should she press the button.

She nodded, placing the cord over her head so it hung just above the swell of her breasts.

Brax stepped forward and said, "As this is not a fight to the death, nor grounds for banishment, only a few select pack members will be placed throughout the trees. The two of you will run the perimeter of Carvingwood, where you will then fight until the other yields or until one is unable to do so."

I growled slightly at that. We would be fighting, no holds barred, with the exception of true harm. Brax ignored me, surveying Dani.

He cupped her cheek for a moment. "Ready?" he asked her.

She nodded, giving him a crooked smile that spoke of her love for violence. He pressed a kiss to her forehead, then stepped back. Syr turned to me.

"Ready?"

I rolled my eyes. "You better not kiss me, Milton."

He sighed. "On your mark." Dani took her place beside me, a readying stance. "Get ready. Go!"

She took off like a shot. I followed at a leisurely pace. It wasn't technically a race, and exerting too much energy too soon would only hinder me in the long run.

I followed her scent, letting it guide me between the trees until it was my only focus. My wolf tried to burst free. To hunt her.

Find her.

Fuck her.

Claim her, it urged.

Her shallow breaths were barely audible with thunder rumbling all around us. Rain began to fall steadily between the trees and dampened my fur. I saw her ahead, still weaving through the trees to try to confuse her scent.

I picked up my pace, giving her path a wide berth until we were parallel, but far enough away that she couldn't see me unless she looked closely.

The call to complete the bond was too strong, and my form became as fluid as the raindrops rolling off the canopy above. One minute I was a wolf, then it was my hands and feet that hit the hard earth. Twigs cracked, adding to the symphony of sounds.

And her breathing. Soft pants that I wanted to hear beneath me.

Her heart racing while her back bowed, and my name spilled from her beautiful, kiss-swollen lips.

I leapt out from between the thick copse of trees and tackled her shimmery, silver wolf.

She twisted, attempting to kick me off. But then she smelled the electric lust vibrating around us. Her arousal was almost instant. She softened beneath me, and then she was human again, her violet eyes still flaring brightly.

"Donovan," she murmured.

Whatever else she was going to say, I stole from her lips in a punishing kiss. My cock was so stiff, aching for her. The frenzy was too much, so while I was still mildly in control, I grated, "Will you let me claim what is mine?"

Her hesitation stretched out for only a heartbeat, but it felt like minutes.

Then she nodded.

Satisfaction tore through me, and I bowed to the Chaos.

CHAPTER THIRTY-FOUR

Dani

Hearing Donovan ask my permission was a shock, but I was grateful for his moment of clarity because all I felt was hot, pulsing desire.

My insides were molten, my hands roving over bare flesh. Our tongues and teeth clashed in an act so savage it could only be the Chaos driving our needs now.

Once upon a time, I fucking hated Donovan Dockhills.

But not anymore.

I wanted this battle of physical dominance to stretch on forever, but I also wanted him to know how much I wanted him.

My hips thrust against the velvety rod between my thighs again and again. Donovan reared back, a hand landing on my throat. I'd never seen his eyes so wild.

It was like he was wholly beast inside while wearing the sex appeal of his human form.

I grinned, trying not to purr with desire.

"I always knew I'd fuck you in the wild," he drawled, one hand palming my breast. His fingers rolled the nipple, pinching and lightly tugging it until I was seeing stars. He pressed kisses down my neck, in the valley between my breasts.

And lower still.

My fingers wound into his dark, damp locks, breath hitching when his hot breath caressed my sex. The cool droplets hitting my feverish skin had me bucking and trying to squirm away.

Donovan grabbed my hips with both hands, forcing me to endure this delicious torture. Without wasting another second, he licked me from slit to tip.

I cried out, clawing at his back and snarling. "Just fuck me already."

Donovan growled in warning, snapping his gaze to mine, and holding it for a breath. I saw the need in his eyes. The need to taste me.

The need to make me scream his name.

With slow strokes from his tongue, he teased my clit. I rode his mouth, chasing the climax that was building into a wild whipping wind, threatening to carry me away.

And I would let it.

When he plunged his tongue inside me, an animalistic noise escaped me. He did it over and over again before flicking my clit.

All at once I was consumed.

Clawing at the ground. His back.

Screaming his name to the treetops, not to be drowned out by the raging thunder. Rain fell harder, soaking us both.

"Just like that, Little Wolf," he said with a twist of his lips.

Then he yanked me up onto his lap. His cock pressed at my entrance, but Donovan stilled, staring down at me. One last question.

I nodded. "Don't hold back."

That was all the encouragement he needed before thrusting into me, hard. I pulled him to me, my nails raking across his back as I cried out.

He pumped into me with wild abandon, giving himself over to the Chaos. My head fell back, and I met his strokes, fucking him right back.

His teeth scraped over my shoulder, eliciting a shiver from me. Tilting my head to the side to grant him better access, I readied for the sting. For the pain.

He licked up my throat, grunting with each hard thrust. "You're mine, Little Wolf," he breathed against the shell of my ear.

"Prove it," I answered with a small grin.

He growled, then his teeth sank into my neck. The pain was burning and hot. But after a moment it cooled.

Like stepping into a trickling stream flowing with freshly melted mountain snow, pleasure surged around me. Through me. I came again, my cunt clenching Donovan's cock. I rocked back and forth on him, savoring every last drop of this high.

My own canines lengthened, and I felt the pull to bite him back. Without another thought, I wrapped my lips where his shoulder met his neck, and bit down.

His ragged sigh of relief was heady, and I felt him lengthen even further, stretching me. I whimpered at the exquisite bite of pain paired with unparalleled pleasure. He bellowed to the storm raging above, spilling his seed inside me. His arms were banded so tightly around me that I felt cemented to his front. Our hearts hammering in unison.

And then I felt it.

The bond. The link. It was different than the alpha bond. I didn't have to reach for it. Instead, it felt like a tapestry within my mind, curled ever so gently around me. Unsure exactly how it worked, I projected my sheer bliss through the link.

Donovan stiffened, leaning back to look down at me. He cupped my cheek, smiling. The expression was so vastly different than the snarky, arrogant looks he often wore. It was genuine happiness.

And I savored it, soaking up his heat despite the cool forest.

"Mine," he rasped, as though he couldn't quite believe it.

Resting my head on his shoulder, I slid a hand between us, running it up his hard, muscled torso, stopping where the beat of his heart drummed under my palm.

"Mine," I replied, feeling inexorably sleepy.

He cleared his throat, rising to his feet, and taking me with him. In a much louder voice, he said, "I yield Carvingwood pack to Daniella Carvingwood."

I gasped, my heart soaring for the second time tonight.

And like it was always meant to be there, a swell of strength and power coursed through my veins. I flexed my fingers, taking a step back from Donovan.

Still grinning, I said, "Thank you."

He inclined his head. "You look sexy as an alpha."

I smirked, feeling the pulse of desire between my thighs again. Images of his head between them again, his fingers fucking my pussy or teasing my ass until I came again and again filled my mind.

As if knowing exactly where my mind had wandered, he took my hand, leading me out of the forest. "Let's get cleaned up and find somewhere a little warmer to continue this."

CHAPTER THIRTY-FIVE

Dani

My parents' home had little damage, but I found that I couldn't stay there. Too many memories, and the pain of their banishment still too fresh.

Syr and Brax had been waiting for us just outside the forest, but I had no doubt they'd heard everything. They held out towels and clothes for both of us. I needed a shower, and the rain had turned to a sprinkle, managing only to make me look like a drowned pup. Most of the pack had gathered as well, curious about the leadership change.

"I vow to you all that this is the last of Carvingwood's instability. I know my parents' betrayal is still fresh for most of you, but I intend to rule justly and honorably for as long as you'll have me as your alpha."

They cheered and clapped, Donovan squeezing my hand and flashing me a wink. Syr took the three of us to his house which had only sustained serious damage to the garage.

Not exactly what I had in mind, Donovan said inside my mind as Syr showed me to one of the guest rooms. Brax and Syr were paired up, and despite Donovan and I now being bonded mates, Syr was reluctant to give us a joint room. In fact, he put Donovan in the room on the other side of the house, making the muddy alpha mutter obscenities under his breath.

I chuckled. *Guess you won't be having me on every surface in this house*, I teased.

Donovan's gaze bored into me with fiery intensity.

Brax cleared his throat. "So, I'll cook dinner or whatever meal it is currently, and you two can grab showers?" he offered.

Syr glowered at Donovan like a father ready to lay down the law regarding his daughter. The thought almost had me busting up laughing.

My lips twitched and Donovan followed suit before nodding to Brax.

See you at dinner, he said, flashing me his signature grin before turning and striding down the hall to his room.

I headed for the main shower, moaning when I finally stepped under the hot spray. The water swirling brown from the mud and grime, sticks and leaves falling to the floor. I had to scoop it all out twice to keep from blocking the drain.

Washing my hair for the second time, I paused with my head tilted back when I heard Donovan's voice in my head.

I have to leave tomorrow. I've already been gone from Dockhills too long, and with Autumn away, my pack will be restless.

I swallowed thickly. *But what about me and my pack?* I asked. Surely we hadn't made a mistake by forging a bond.

A tendril of reassurance came through the link, as though he'd heard my private thoughts. *I wanted to offer your pack a permanent residence near Dockhills in person, but I couldn't wait. With Carvingwood's territory destroyed, it'll take you months to rebuild. If you brought them all south, there'd be plenty of space for them. You'd remain alpha, and we wouldn't have to be apart.*

Plus, he added, *I think a few days alone with Milton and Braxton will give you the push you need to complete the bonds with them as well.*

My cheeks heated, but I let myself wash the shampoo from my hair before saying, *Meet me in here in two minutes.*

Only Donovan's rumbling laugh answered.

And two minutes later, the door creaked open, and Donovan stepped into the steamy bathroom donning only a plush grey towel around his middle. I smiled at him through the glass door and crooked a finger for him to join me.

He dropped the towel, making my mouth go dry. Then he opened the door and stepped into the soothing heat of the shower.

"Yes, Little Wolf?" he crooned.

I reached up on my tip-toes and kissed him hard. *Is three days sufficient*? I asked.

"On second thought, it might be too long," he rasped against my lips.

I smiled, kissing him slower. Sadly, we didn't have the time for anything more, as I switched off the shower.

"I'm fairly certain Syr will be in here with a knife if we don't hurry," I whispered, smirking.

Donovan growled. "Fucking let him see what he's missing out on."

I slipped out of the shower with a sly smile, blowing Donovan a kiss before rushing through the hall with only a towel around me as I entered my temporary room.

Spying the stack of clothes one of the guys had obviously brought over folded neatly on the bed made me smile.

I dressed in pjs, too tired for anything else, and headed down the stairs to the scent of spices and beef. My stomach rumbled loudly when I entered the kitchen, causing Brax to laugh.

Everything for tacos was spread out on the counter, and I strode to the cupboard that I knew kept plates.

Donovan entered behind me only a moment later, my need for more of him pulsing between my thighs. I nearly groaned out loud, but one look from Syr told me my arousal was vibrantly on display within the room.

His mouth was a hard line, his eyes narrowed on the tomatoes he angrily chopped. My legs carried me toward him without another thought, and I pressed a kiss to his cheek.

He didn't react, and I wanted to tell him that I intended to make him my mate too. Before I could do or say anything, he turned away, grabbing a tub of sour cream from the fridge.

Trying to not let my hurt show, I moved to get cutlery when Brax reached out an arm, snagging me around the waist and yanking me to him. "I'll take one of those, Little One."

I smiled at that and raised myself up to press a kiss to his cheek, but he moved at the last second, and suddenly my lips were on his.

Need overtook my sense of rational thought, and I melted against him, gripping his shirt to try to anchor myself. Our tongues tangled, and the rush of sensations stole my breath. He was so hot beneath my palms. So firm. I wanted to lick each dip and curved plane of his muscled body.

Brax broke the contact first and shot me a wink while I blinked, dazed.

We tucked in to eat our dinner and Donovan announced his plan to return to Dockhills. Syr crushed the taco he held in his hand into a dozen pieces when I interjected with what I wanted for Carvingwood.

"You want to uproot a pack far older than you or I and force them to start over down south? Are you insane?" he snapped.

I narrowed my eyes at him. "We can either rebuild Carvingwood or start fresh somewhere else. Many people will want that after the attack."

He scoffed. "This is just so you can be close to him and you know it."

"In part, but by that logic, Dockhills could move here, but that would mean a great deal of expansion. They already have the space and most of the housing. It's perfect."

Syr flicked the lettuce and salsa from his hand, onto the plate before shooting to his feet and storming out of the kitchen. I heard him march up the stairs, and sighed.

"He'll come around," Brax said.

I nodded. "I hope so."

He heaved in a heavy breath, and I watched him, knowing he had something more to add. "My...work will take me all over Chaos Valley, and even beyond. I think it is best that I leave tomorrow as well."

"No!" My explosive reaction had his eyes widening. I shook my head. "Please. Not yet."

His brows creased sympathetically, but at last he relented. "Alright. I'll wait until the Chaos is over, then I'll go."

Fine by me, I thought to myself. *By then, we'll be irrevocably tied, and you'll have to return to me.*

It was a selfish thought, I knew, and I was thankful Donovan hadn't heard it. But being around Brax for the past few days—having him to watch over my dreams—was something I knew I didn't want to live without.

I helped clear up the dinner, saving Syr's plate of tacos as I ascended the stairs with it. I'd kissed Donovan goodnight, then Brax pulled me in for another intoxicating kiss before I stumbled out of the kitchen.

Standing outside Syr's room, I paused. I wanted a completely level head when I went in to calm the boy I'd grown up with.

We'd screamed at each other, sparred, and even kissed with a fire that could consume one's soul, but this reaction from him tonight, I knew was a fork in the road. He'd assumed I didn't choose him, but I needed him to know that it was my own, stupid, indecision that kept me from accepting him the minute the blood moon rose into the sky.

How I'd ever thought for one moment that I didn't need all three of these men, I didn't know.

I knocked, but no answer came. Pushing the door open, I saw Syr sprawled out on his bed. The size of him made the massive thing look almost too small, but I knew from experience just how perfectly we fit together.

Setting the plate of tacos on his side table, I climbed onto the bed behind him, wrapping an arm around his middle.

We laid like that for several minutes. I enjoyed the steady beat of his heart, the warmth of his body.

"Will you look at me?" I asked.

A moment's pause, then Syr slowly turned over.

When his sad, golden eyes met mine, I cupped his cheek.

"I remember when you made me a doll out of old fabric scraps your mom had lying around. You even sewed buttons on for the eyes and drew a smile on it." I smiled, recalling little eight-year-old Syr presenting me with the ugliest rag doll I'd ever seen.

But he'd made it for me, and I took it without hesitation. I snuggled it during thunderstorms, or when I was sad. And when I grew up, it sat beside my bed, keeping watch over me.

"It's the most precious thing I own," I said at last. "And the summer we decided we wanted a tree house, you fashioned your own materials and tried damn hard to build it yourself until your grandpa took pity on you and did it himself. You insisted that it have an open area for me to see the stars at night."

A burning in the back of my throat told me I was close to tears, but I couldn't stop. "You were the first person I ever told that I wanted to be alpha. And you said that I'd be the best there ever was. It was after you said that, that I trained harder and longer. You trained with me every morning from then on."

A tear slipped down my cheek, and Syr wiped it away with a soft brush of his thumb.

"It might have taken me longer to figure it out, but I've always loved you, Syr. I want you to be by my side. Always."

A muscle feathered in his jaw. "As your beta?" he asked harshly.

I shook my head, pressing forward until our lips brushed. "As my mate." My whisper was barely audible; the heavy silence that followed making my heart pound. "As my equal."

When I thought he wouldn't respond, I turned over, preparing to get up, when he caught me by the waist.

"You're sure?" he asked, sounding far more hopeful than I'd ever heard him.

I spun back to face him, and nodded, brushing another errant tear away.

He smiled. Then he was kissing me, and I kissed him back. The rush of emotions was so strong it overcame us both like a hurricane. We ripped and tore at each other's clothing, unable to get the other undressed fast enough. My mouth pressed kisses to his hard chest, and lower.

The bulge straining in his boxer briefs caught my attention and I ran my hand up and down it, earning a hiss of breath.

Smiling, I pulled him free of the fabric, stroking the smooth, hard length. Part of me wanted to go slow, to savor this, but the other part of me felt like he was going to disappear at any moment.

"I love you, Dani," he rasped, just before I licked the tip of his cock. He groaned, jerking in my hold. "Fuck!"

The taste was divine. I did it again, this time slower. Then from the base of his shaft all the way to the slit. A bead of moisture pooled there, and I licked it off, humming at the taste of him.

"As much as I really want to fuck your mouth right now, I need you on my cock more," he said, pulling me up so I was straddling his hips.

My pussy was already wet, the hunger for more impossible to resist. I rocked against him, earning another groan.

He held my hips in place, then forced me to meet his gaze. "We don't need to rush this, okay?"

I nodded in complete agreement, and when he finally let me slide down on his cock, I moaned a guttural, animalistic sound.

Syr propped himself up on his hands, using his tongue to do all sorts of wicked things to my nipples. It made it impossible to go slow, and before I knew it, I was riding him full force, loving the fullness of his cock buried inside me.

His pupils stretched, and I felt that same inescapable pull to bite. My canines lengthened on cue, and when we both shattered together, we bit down, solidifying the bond instantly. The pleasure rocketed through me, causing me to erupt again and again. Tears streamed down my face from an overwhelming sensation of love and happiness.

Daniella, he said reverently in my mind, and I grinned, my body like jelly against him. He laid us back, covering us with the sheet and we laid there together in perfect bliss.

I trailed my fingers up and down his chest while we talked and Syr finally ate his dinner. We used the night to acquaint ourselves with each other's bodies. I tried to memorize every groan or sigh.

But when we collapsed together, slick with sweat, a smile pulled at my lips. I'd have forever to figure out every little thing that drove him wild. Forever to fall asleep beside him, and Donovan, and Brax.

Syr pressed his lips to my damp forehead, and I let sleep take me into its waiting embrace.

CHAPTER THIRTY-SIX

Brax

"Keep or donate?" Syr asked, holding up an ugly lamp.

"Donate," Daniella called back, lost somewhere in the mountains of boxes and stuff.

I continued tugging hangers from the clothing in the closet and dropping them into separate boxes. She was handling the whole situation far better than any of us expected.

Donovan had left right after breakfast, and Dani—unable to keep still—had dragged Syr and I to her childhood home where she insisted we donate her family's belongings to the wolves who lost much in the fire.

The agitation in my veins was near to consuming. There were only two more days of Chaos left. She bonded with Syr and Donovan, which left me feeling like a caged animal. I wanted to run. To hunt.

I wanted to drag her into a far-off room and draw every whimper, sigh, and scream from her lips, like the ones I heard through the walls all night long. I *needed* to be the one to drive her as mad as I was feeling.

My movements grew jerky, my cock stiff and aching as I tossed hangers in one box and clothes in another. Over and over, my wolf tried to push through.

My breathing became labored; vision zeroing in until I dropped the hanger in my hand. Nails elongated to claws, I backed away from the mess, before turning and running from the room.

I heard Dani shout after me, but I didn't stop.

Tearing through the house, I made it to the door, scraping the wood as I fumbled for the handle.

"Brax!" Dani shouted, sounding closer.

My heart pounded like the drums of war. I needed to move faster. Her footsteps followed me, and I wondered if she felt it too.

Distantly, a horn blared into the constant night and I slowed.

"Someone is coming!" Dani sped ahead of me, to the entrance of Carvingwood. I tailed her, grateful for the momentary distraction. Though being downwind of her scent was intoxicating.

She stopped short at the mouth of the town, as two figures loped closer. One was a black wolf that I knew to be Donovan. The second was a girl—not so much a girl as a woman. Her skin was a rich brown like my own; a thick scar crossed her face, and others covered her exposed arms. The wind kicked back, carrying three distinct scents toward me.

One was my unbonded mate, and Donovan's with it, but the other…

A swirl of a thousand memories bombarded me. A million nightmares. Recognition hit me so hard, my knees collapsed out from under me, a guttural cry wrenching the air.

But how?

No. It's not possible.

She's dead; she died in the fire.

She's dead, it's not her. It can't be. You're seeing things.

But there was no denying what my wolf unequivocally knew. Her scent was different—changed by the years away. If there was a heart buried somewhere between my ribs, I swore it laid on the dirt road. Shattered all over again after fifteen years.

Donovan and the woman stopped. Dani whirled to face me, before turning back to the woman who plagued my thoughts constantly.

"Emmy," she breathed, both in relief and in realization.

"Emmy. Esme. My sister." I didn't know if I whispered the words or screamed them.

Dani ran for her, wrapping my frail sister in a tight hug and the two of them cried, but my sister's gaze kept returning to me. When Dani pulled back, she turned to face me as well, smiling. Her hand slid into Esme's and she led her to me as I rose to my feet.

She appeared apprehensive. Vaguely, I wondered if she even remembered me. But I couldn't stop myself from reaching out for her.

She flinched away, her gaze falling to the ground in submission for a moment, then rising back up as if forcing herself not to cower. Dani wrapped a comforting arm around her. "It's okay, Emmy, he's your brother."

I died a little inside. What has she been through to fear me within the first five minutes of seeing each other again? Who had scarred her skin so heinously? Why hadn't I searched for her? I should have fucking looked for her. Not finding her body haunted me still. I cleared my throat, trying to find the words to speak.

"Esme." It came out in a rasp.

She squinted slightly. Something shone in those deep blue eyes, a more vibrant shade than my own. Perhaps a memory.

Dani cleared her throat. "Emmy was one of the…" she glanced sidelong at Esme, as though looking for confirmation on something.

"Servants," Esme said at last. This time she held my gaze with renewed courage. "I met Daniella at the auction." She lifted her chin as if to defend herself, but I wouldn't have it. There was nothing she could say—no shame too great—that would make me turn away.

I shook my head. "I'm so sorry, Esme. I want to hear everything you remember. Whatever you're willing to tell me. I thought you were fucking dead—" my words cut off abruptly at the invisible hand that clamped around my throat.

Her gaze softened slightly, and she nodded.

"I'll make you two some tea so you can talk. Catch up," Dani offered, taking a step back toward Donovan, when Esme grabbed her arm, stopping her.

"Join us. Please."

Dani nodded, smiling sadly. I wondered if what they

communicated silently between themselves was that Esme didn't want to be left alone with me yet. Not that I could blame her if she had been kept as a slave for The Silver Vipers.

Turning to the black wolf that still stood a few yards away, Dani stared at him, no doubt speaking into his mind through the bond. I couldn't help but watch for a moment, transfixed by the wonder of bonded mates. My own wolf seemed to want to howl mournfully that Daniella was not yet ours.

At last, Dani nodded once, then turned, a bit reluctantly, and Donovan met my gaze. I gave a subtle incline of my head, letting him know I was grateful for finding my sister and returning her to safety. He returned the gesture, then was gone, disappearing back into the thick forest.

We sat at the breakfast nook in Syr's house, holding mugs filled with steaming tea. The floral scent was a mixture of calming herbs. Esme took a sip, looking unsure of herself.

"What happened after I left you?" Dani prompted gently.

Esme sat the cup down, though she didn't release it. "We made it to the forest, but several men chased us. Myself and several others tore them to pieces. Then we kept walking until we happened on a human town where some of the women were from. A bunch of the others stayed too since most of the locals were happy to help arrange transportation and accommodation for those with homes farther away. One of the packs let me camp on the outskirts of their territory to rest, and some healer brought me food. They offered to let me stay, but I just couldn't." She shook her head as if recalling something to mind. "I felt this urge to keep moving; it was strange."

Dani nodded slowly. "And you made it this far north by chance? How did you find Donovan?" Her words weren't spoken like an accusation, but I couldn't help feeling like even the tiniest of threats to my sister might tear her away from me again.

Esme shrugged. "I'm not really sure. With the Chaos moon my only guiding light, I had to rely on my wolf instincts alone. And since I haven't been able to reliably shift ever, they were not the best of instincts." She smiled sheepishly. "They led me close to here, but I was so dehydrated by the time I got close that I collapsed. The black wolf brought me water and carried me the rest of the way here."

My hands were balled into fists under the countertop. Dani must have seen or sensed the anger directed at myself because she rested a hand atop one of mine. Just her touch was able to draw the tension from my tightly coiled muscles. I was still irate at myself for not taking care of Esme like I should have, but I knew there was no way I could have known. It was simply a miracle from the gods that led her straight to me.

"Can I cook you something?" I asked my sister. She was far too thin. Did they ever feed her in that house of tortures?

Esme started to object, when Dani piped in, "Could you just grab a selection of cold cuts, crackers and cheeses?"

I nodded, heading for the fridge. Instantly, I missed my mate's comforting touch, but I needed to get up and do something or I was going to lose my mind. While the two of them talked, I listened in as best I could. Dani kept away from heavy topics unless Esme brought them up, which she didn't, other than to say she wasn't sure how old she was. Only that she'd tried counting the winters.

I interjected then, meeting my sister's gaze. "Twenty-three. You were taken when you were eight. That was fifteen years ago." The fact that I managed to say it without my voice cracking or destroying the block of cheese I squeezed in my hand was a small mercy.

Fuck.

Fifteen birthdays had passed without her knowing.

How was I going to make up for fifteen years of abuse and slavery to a trafficking ring?

Esme's eyes lined with silver, shining with tears she refused to let fall. I admired her strength. How she wasn't completely broken after fifteen years I didn't know, but I hoped to find out.

I set the completed tray on the counter before grabbing two plates and sliding them toward Dani. She began loading one up while talking about life in Carvingwood—the training she could benefit from and the ability to control on-demand shifts—before setting the heaping plate before Esme.

She eyed the selection with apparent hunger, and as soon as Dani made herself her own plate and began to eat like she never had before, Esme followed suit.

Making her feel at ease like that only made my desire for my mate grow. I set a glass of ice water in front of the frail girl, watching with satisfaction when she chugged half of the glass.

Already her coloring was improving.

"So if you want, you can take a shower or a bath here, get cleaned up and I can take you to Faith—our resident healer—for her to just do a quick welfare check. Get you any vitamins and supplements you might need.

"But even if you just want to sleep for the day, that's fine too," Dani added. "As I explained, we're all getting ready to head south so I'm going to finish packing up my old home. Faith is great company though, if you wanted to stay with her. It's totally up to you."

Esme shrugged. "I might just sleep, I suppose. Can't remember the last time I was able to get more than a few hours."

Dani's smile brightened, though I could tell it was forced. "Excellent! I'll show you to a room you can use."

The two got up from the table, as I said, "Wait."

They both looked to me while I pulled the dull golden locket from my pants pocket and slid it across the counter to Esme.

She picked it up cautiously before prying the small door open. Her gaze became watery again as she stared down at the image inside that I'd committed to memory.

A small girl smiling wide with her arms wrapped around a beautiful woman.

Our mother.

I didn't know if she remembered much of her, but it felt right for her to have the one and only keepsake that had survived the fire.

"I want you to have it," I said around the thick ball of emotion stuck in my throat.

A tear spilled over Esme's dirt-covered cheek, and she met my gaze before nodding. "Thank you," she murmured, and I offered her a small smile.

Dani hugged her again before they vanished up the stairs while I stood there, reeling. Fifteen years of nights haunting me. I'd relived my entire family's slaughter, believing Esme had perished with them.

I'd dug through the rubble for her body until my hands were charred and bloody. In the end, I'd buried the only dress that was not entirely burned to ash. I visited her grave every year.

A grave for a girl who had lived in slavery. Stolen from the house before it collapsed.

How had I not fucking known?

There were so many scents already, I'd just assumed it was the Vipers pillaging our town. Raiding my home.

And they had.

They'd taken something far more precious than jewels or gold.

My grip tightened on the counter so hard, I heard the solid stone crack. I shook my head, feeling the same desire to hunt the fuckers down and kill them again. But Esme needed me here.

However, once she was settled, I'd hunt for those who sought to wrong the innocent of the world. Any sick and twisted being who tried to control another being. I'd be the last thing they saw.

I would become justice for Chaos Valley and beyond.

Dani came back downstairs a little while later, looking drained. I didn't move as she approached, though I tracked her every movement. She glanced at the counter, noting the split.

But her eyes held no pity. For which I was grateful. Folding her arms across her chest, she said, "She's going to be fine, Brax."

I nodded.

She drew in a deep breath before running a hand through her

hair. Then, she gestured toward the door. "Let's get back. I've already asked Faith to be here when she wakes up."

I slid around the counter, snagging her by the waist and pulling her sharply toward me. A small sound of surprise escaped her lips, and I kissed them hard, pouring out my thanks and my desire.

After only a moment, she kissed me back just as fiercely. Hands seeking, winding into my hair, the gemstones clacking together in soft whispers.

Our desperation became too strong, and I forced myself to break away. I wouldn't take my mate on the kitchen counter with my abused sister right upstairs.

"The other house." My words came out sounding like a snarl.

She nodded fervently, grabbing my hand and we practically sprinted the short block over to Syr's place. We barely crashed through the door before we were on each other again. My cock pressed against her apex, savagely grinding while our hands tore through the fabric that separated our connection.

My wolf was alive in my veins, the urge to pin my mate and claim her near overwhelming. But Dani was a warrior too. Every nip and scrape of claws only had her moaning and arching into me.

I shredded the thin lace of her bra, freeing her breasts before taking one in my mouth. Licking and sucking, I groaned at the taste of her.

She was sin and heaven on my tongue. Her hands worked my jeans down before gripping my cock through the fabric of my boxer shorts. I hissed, nipped her breast and she rewarded me with a low moan.

All that was left was her jeans and I made short work of shoving them down, then pinning her to the wall while I yanked each leg free of her pants, tossing the fabric far enough away so she couldn't get to them easily.

There was no way I wasn't claiming my mate right here and now in the fucking foyer of Syr's house.

I knew he was upstairs and could hear everything, but I didn't care. My cock was aching to be buried inside her, and as soon as my boxers were slid down, Dani had my length in her hand, guiding it to her entrance.

She panted as I slowly eased it inside her, the stretch of her pussy so exquisite, I couldn't help the low growl that shook in my chest.

When I was seated to the hilt, I allowed a second for her to adjust to me. She clawed at my back, urging me on.

"Don't. Stop," she said through gritted teeth.

Flashing her a devilish smile, I pulled out to the tip before plunging in full force. Picture frames rattled on the walls and Dani locked her legs around my hips, trying to keep me there. With a smile, I nuzzled my nose into the crook of her neck, drawing in her scent and letting it drive this wild, animalistic hunger in me.

I slammed into her over and over, drawing sexy little cries and moans from her that had my claws sinking into the walls around her head, caging her in.

My canines lengthened and I gently scraped them down the column of her throat. She shivered under me, a breathy moan escaping before I thrust into her again.

She shattered on my cock, her cunt squeezing it so hard it took everything in me not to spill my seed inside her so quickly.

I licked the hollow dip of her throat before clutching her hips for better control. Her screams grew louder as I drove up into her with feral need. The feel of her was almost too much, too perfect. I snarled against her skin and the wolf in me took over. My fangs sank into her as she came again, and I with her. She too bit my shoulder, the combined ecstasy drawing out our orgasms. I rode her through the aftershocks, emptying myself inside her until all that was left were our mingling, heavy breaths.

The new link that stretched between us was a visible, tangible thread in my mind. One I intended to cherish for my entire lifetime.

Slowly, I let her feet slip to the floor, and I took her mouth with mine again, but this time, sweeter. I wanted her to taste the same triumph and euphoria coursing through my veins.

She was mine at last.

The girl who'd slipped into my dreams, pulling me from the horrors I once lived night after night.

And in turn, I vowed to protect her always. To battle by her side whenever the need should arise. And to chase away her demons if she wished me to.

My mate.

My salvation.

And for the first time in fifteen years, the dark, lost bits of my soul stitched themselves back together. I took that first ragged breath as a new man.

A whole man.

CHAPTER THIRTY-SEVEN

Dani

We made it to Dockhills on the first proper sunrise after the Chaos. The light cresting over the shimmering lake in the distance, and the wide expanse of city and countryside dispelled any anxiety I'd felt about settling so far from my homeland.

Donovan met me at the edge, smiling that twisted grin that sent my heart fluttering. I had all three of my mates back in one place. And from the civilized nods they granted each other, I got the feeling that somehow—by some crazy twist of fate—this was all going to work out.

The "house" Donovan showed all five of us felt more like a mansion. Emmy got an entire wing to herself, leaving me with my guys in the western wing.

Donovan explained his plans to knock out the wall between the two suites at the end, expanding the room so the four of us could stay together most nights. They had their own rooms as well, but I wanted to have my three mates with me as often as possible.

Even with the Chaos over, the need to have them close, to have them inside me was insatiable. Before Donovan left to attend a council meeting, we snuck away, tucking into a linen closet for him to take me hard and fast. His heated kisses lingered on my skin when I emerged.

Syr smirked at me when I rejoined him outside to help find the allocated housing for our pack members. I shot him a wink in return, promising him his own pleasure soon.

But what I really wanted was the three of them at once. Their hands roving over my body. Three cocks plunging inside me.

I sucked in a sharp breath to try to cleanse away the throbbing in my clit until later. Fortunately, no one commented on my sudden shift in demeanor. Not that it was anything to be embarrassed about when you were newly mated.

It was a beautiful sight to see so many mated wolves in one place. The recent Chaos would ensure a population growth for our people.

The sun was hotter here; sweat beaded on the back of my neck, slowly soaking into the fabric of my tank top. But I loved the warmth. Loved the cool pools deep in the eastern forest we'd passed on our way into Dockhills land. They reminded me of home.

Syr's fingers threaded through mine and my heart swelled with happiness. Carvingwood wolves fanned out before me, awaiting my updates. With Donovan approaching in the distance, I stood out on the large porch overlooking the grassy plains of Dockhills territory—now Carvingwood territory.

“Thank you all for gathering, I know you’re getting settled into your new living spaces, but I just want to take another moment to appreciate every single one of you for following me so far from Carvingwood territory. As my way of thanking you, I’m proud to announce that Dockhills will be hosting the next round of Pack Games in just a few days!”

Cheers went up, and I smiled out at the crowd. Pride for my people filled me. Everyone had been through a lot. Lost so much and gone through plenty of uncertainty. They needed this chance to get out some of their frustrations and bond with the members of Dockhills while letting loose.

Donovan leapt over the railing before coming to my other side and sliding a hand around my waist. I tried to suppress the urge to grin up at him like an idiot, focusing on going over donations that were still available to those who might need them, as well as the rules in place that would hopefully ensure a seamless transition for shared territory.

We were to respect the laws of Dockhills, show respect to our neighbors and to bring all inter-pack disputes to the appropriate pack’s council.

Donovan had assured me the diner and shops within Dockhills would have employment opportunities aplenty, as well as room for growth should anyone else wish to start their own business here.

I dismissed my wolves, catching sight of Brax and Esme

approaching. They climbed the steps, Esme pulling me into a hug that momentarily separated me from Donovan and Syr.

"Hey, wanna check out Grace's Place? I overheard someone saying they're playing a movie there tonight," Emmy said. "We could grab dinner and watch whatever it is, even if it's lame."

Donovan snorted. "It usually is, but it's quite the hang out spot."

Emmy's big blue eyes widened while she batted her long lashes. With her stunning features, I feared for whatever wolf or wolves got her for a mate.

I laughed, looking to Syr for confirmation. He nodded, golden strands falling over his forehead. My fingers itched to push them back, but I refrained. "Yeah, that sounds like fun," I told Emmy.

She made a gleeful squeal before throwing her arms over my shoulders again, and I embraced the slender girl, catching Brax watching me with a look so tender it nearly stole my breath.

"Until then, you and I are going to work on shifting some more," Brax said, then pressed a kiss to my forehead and turned, but not before shooting both Donovan and Syr a look I couldn't decipher. Emmy groaned, but followed after him, back around the side of the house.

Pivoting on my heel, I leaned into Donovan, placing my hands on his chest. "More meetings?" I asked.

His lips twisted into a smirk. "Missed me, Little Wolf?"

I lifted a brow, an attempt at sass. My desire to feel him inside me again was almost overwhelming but I loved it when he lost control. "Wouldn't you like to think so?"

He chuckled low, leaning in until the tip of his nose brushed the shell of my ear. "You might have two other mates making you cum at every opportunity, but I can sense just how bad you want me to fuck you again, so why don't you be a good girl and go upstairs to wait for me?"

The thrill sent a shiver up my spine, making my toes curl. Syr pressed in behind me, sandwiching me between the two men as he lightly pulled my hair aside to kiss on my neck. I stiffened when Donovan didn't move back or react beyond grinning down at me.

What the hell is happening? I asked them both through our internal link.

Go upstairs, Little Wolf, Donovan demanded in his gruff, sexy tone.

I'll be right behind you, Syr assured me.

Stepping out from between the two of them, my gaze flicked back and forth, trying to figure out what was going on. There was no way in hell Donovan and Syr were going to fuck me at the same time.

They may have figured out a peaceful truce for my sake, but I wasn't sure they'd ever be okay with sharing me in bed. Syr and Brax, however, I could easily picture worshipping my body at the same time, lavishing me with their kisses while filling me with their cocks.

"You don't…" I started, my mouth going dry at the images conjured. "We don't have to do *that*," I said, but my words fell flat.

Syr smiled while Donovan just smirked.

Without another word, Syr pressed a kiss to my lips, lingering for just a moment. *Just trust us, Dani.*

I nodded slowly, feeling certain I was about to combust. My

path through the house was nothing but a blur in my haste to figure out what was going to happen.

Sitting on the double-super king bed was a strip of black satin, and near it, a note. I picked up the piece of paper, reading the handwritten words as my face flushed hot. Tingles spread through my body.

I followed the instructions to the letter after having a quick shower to make sure I was free of sweat and dirt. Lying back on the stack of soft pillows in nothing but the blood red lace panties and bra I'd chosen this morning, I waited, my eyes covered with the blindfold.

I heard the faintest creak of the door, followed by a strong, purposeful stride.

Syr.

My tongue darted out to moisten my lips just before the foot of the bed dipped slightly. I stilled, breath caught in my throat.

Syr prowled up the bed like a lion seeking to devour its prey. Yet, I was practically naked and couldn't see a damn thing. The easiest kind of prey.

He didn't speak, saying more with his lips on mine than words ever could. I kissed him back, feeling the rush of desire taking over.

Without warning, he pulled back, getting off the bed entirely. A sound of protest escaped me. Then the bed dipped again, and he crawled toward me once more.

The mouth that claimed mine was different this time, and I gasped, taking in Donovan's scent as I did.

My pussy throbbed. Whatever game they were playing, I was

clearly losing.

Rough fingertips I knew all too well slid the straps of my bra down my shoulders, then the lacey fabric was shoved beneath the swell of my breasts, exposing them to the cool air. My nipples were hard peaks jutting toward the ceiling.

Donovan continued to kiss me, making me breathless, while Syr's lips sucked one of my nipples into his mouth. I gasped and my back bowed of its own accord.

"Such a wanton thing," Donovan said in apparent praise.

Fingers skated up my thigh, moving toward my damp core. I writhed, drunk on the heady sensations coursing through my body.

"Can I see you now?" I asked as Donovan kissed down the side of my neck.

A tongue licked above my knee, running higher and higher. I gasped, then paused, taking stock of how many bodies were near me.

Not two.

Three.

"Brax," I breathed.

The three men chuckled, and one moved. I felt the ties of the blindfold being undone. Impatiently, I helped rip it away, finding all three guys in nothing but their jeans.

Shirtless, beautifully chiseled men surrounded me on the bed.

Oh, bloody Chaos. This is what fantasies were made of.

"What is this?" were the only words that I could vocalize.

Donovan smirked. "You projected an image of all of us worshipping you."

"So we agreed to try it out," Syr added.

My entire face felt like it was on fire, but I hid my embarrassment with a laugh. "I didn't mean to project that. It was just…I don't expect—"

Brax took up position between my thighs and crouched low like the predator he was. His full, sensual lips twisted. "Oh, Little One, what kind of mates would we be if we didn't keep you thoroughly satisfied?" His hot breath ghosted over the sensitive flesh I so desperately wanted to feel his lips on.

I swallowed hard, watching with rapt attention. "What about Emmy?"

"I have her doing some chores to prepare for the Pack Games. She's well looked after."

The knot of worry in my chest began to loosen, and I reached for Syr and Donovan on either side of me. "You guys are cool with this?"

Donovan's eyes flashed with primal lust and hunger, which was answer enough. I looked to Syr who cupped my face gently. Reverently.

"As fun as it is to have you all to myself as often as I can, I have to admit this setup is kind of hot." He winked and I swear my heart fluttered.

I grinned, pulling his face down to mine and kissing him to show my gratitude. This was going to work. They were all putting in an effort, and something like this was worth cherishing.

Brax placed gentle kisses on my thighs while Donovan kissed my shoulder, my chest, over the swell of my breast.

When his teeth grazed my nipple, Brax sucked my clit between his lips, and I moaned into Syr's mouth. He smiled against me then lowered himself to my other breast.

My eyes closed and I lost myself to the pleasure, feeling all three of my men sucking and licking me. I trembled under their touches.

Then one of my hands were winding into Syr's hair, the other reaching for Donovan's jeans. He chuckled, releasing my nipple with an audible pop before raising to his knees. I undid the button with one hand, tugging his jeans down until his thick, hard cock was free.

I wrapped my hand around it and gave a gentle tug to bring him to my mouth. Donovan made a grunt of approval as I licked the head. My mouth watered.

I was so hungry for them all.

My tongue swirled around the head in playful motions before he jerked slightly, and I took him in. Suckling on just the tip, Donovan growled low. My gaze lowered, finding Brax watching me. The black ate away the midnight blue in his eyes.

I felt the wild, animalistic lust filling the room. Donovan must have seen Brax watching too because he thrust deeper into my mouth. I pistoned my tongue on the underside of his cock, slowly bobbing my head.

Brax was the one to growl next. His tongue lavishing my cunt had my muscles coiling tight. The pressure built as Syr nipped at one stiff peak while pinching the other.

Then Brax slid a finger into my greedy pussy, and I exploded, clamping down on him and screaming onto Donovan's cock. He fucked my mouth harder, not allowing me to move off him for even a second.

When the aftershocks subsided, I groaned. Donovan pulled out of my mouth, causing drool to run down my chin.

He stroked my cheek lovingly. "You're so pretty with a cock in your mouth, Little Wolf."

I tried not to preen, but it was impossible.

Brax sat up, wiping my juices from his lips. "Have you ever had your ass fucked, Daniella?"

I bit the inside of my cheek and shook my head. "Not technically. I've done it to myself with toys."

As wolf shifters, we were hypersexual creatures. I'd had a threesome before, but other than a finger in my ass, I'd never let a guy do that. Something about wanting to save it for a potential mate, which at the time I'd never thought possible.

Now I had three ravenous guys in my bed, and I wanted them all to fuck me in every way possible. Looking at Brax I said, "Since you were the last to claim me, I want you to do it."

He smiled, nodding.

Donovan pulled his pants the rest of the way off and maneuvered me, so I was straddling his hips. The press of his hard, rigid cock against my clit had me rocking on it instinctually.

Syr knelt in front of me, above Donovan's head, kissing me again. I was so consumed with him that I didn't feel the hard length massaging my tight asshole right away.

Donovan held my hips, guiding me down on his cock. I whimpered, already feeling another orgasm building. Syr undid his jeans, and my hands wrapped around the silky-smooth steel of his cock.

Brax began to rock against me while Donovan slowly thrust in and out of my pussy. All that was left was to take Syr into my mouth. And when I did, Donovan reached between us, rubbing my clit.

It helped ease the sting of Brax sliding into my ass. I was somewhat familiar with the pain, but the exquisite pleasure of being so full had my body relaxing completely.

"Fuck, Little One. You're taking it all," Brax said with no shortage of pride.

Syr's fingers wound into my hair. I could sense him watching Brax slide slowly in and out of my ass by the way he jerked and pumped into my mouth harder and harder. I loved how he didn't treat me like I was breakable.

I let him fuck my throat, fighting for breath when I could. And like a hurricane sweeping us all up, suddenly my men were fucking me with pure abandon.

"Is it everything you imagined?" Donovan asked through panting breaths. "Being filled with three cocks?"

I nodded, unable to speak. It was all I could do to stay upright. My arms shook and fire of the most delicious kind licked through every nerve-ending. I was awash in ecstasy with these men.

They'd come together for me. Worshipped my body and put aside their reservations to fulfill all my desires.

My orgasm hit so hard I screamed, writhing between them, but Donovan and Brax held me still, continuing to fuck me. The pleasure went on for so long I tipped over into another, even harder orgasm that was almost painful.

Then Donovan roared beneath me. Brax was muttering curses

in a language I didn't know, and Syr's salty hot seed shot down my throat.

They filled me with their cum while I rode out the last dregs of my energy. Finally, I collapsed, sweaty and spent.

Donovan wrapped his arms around me and pressed a kiss to my temple.

"You were incredible," he whispered for only me, though I know the other two heard it.

"So were you," I said, then giggled. Clearly, I needed food and sleep. But it would have to wait.

We'd already spent too much time away from our packs. Pulling apart, I kissed Brax, then Syr, thanking them.

Brax waved it away. "I plan on many more interesting events such as that."

My stupid post-orgasm grin grew. Syr pulled me close and nuzzled against my neck where his mark was.

"I love you," he breathed.

My breath hitched and I closed my eyes. "I love you too," I said.

"Go shower, we have to leave in a few hours if you want to snag a spot at Grace's later," Donovan said, sitting on the bed looking more relaxed than I'd ever seen him.

I hurried from the room and started the shower. The hot spray of water washed away the physical evidence of what we'd done, but everywhere I rubbed soap was a reminder of the kisses, the touches.

I closed my eyes and smiled to myself. Never had I imagined I'd be lucky enough to score one mate, let alone three.

If this was what I had to look forward to regularly, then I was the luckiest girl alive.

Grace's Place was an adorable little diner. The logo was of a strawberry milkshake on a pale pink background.

Oldies played over the speakers inside, and I knew instantly I'd find myself here often.

Outside, I plopped down on the outstretched plaid blanket beside Esme, holding out one of the bags filled with hot, fragrant food. Brax carried sodas and milkshakes, Syr and Donovan with enough bags to feed a pack of hungry wolves.

Which, I guess is exactly what we were.

"Did you know they have a waterpark here?" Esme asked with wide eyes.

I peered at brochure she held in her hands. It held images of water slides and laughing children splashing in fountains.

"It's small, but it keeps the kids occupied all summer. Plus, there are lap pools for the more aquatic wolves." Donovan said, sitting across from me.

Brax sat on the Esme's other side, and Syr on my left.

"There's even a library?" she asked, her tone excited.

Donovan chuckled. "Again, it's small. Dockhills has been self-sufficient for many years, and our borders have always been open to humans since we're right on the edge of Chaos Valley."

My pulse skittered. Leaving to find my parents one day might be easier than I thought. Emmy set the brochure aside to dig into her food.

The heat of the sun dipping into the horizon behind us warmed my back. It didn't take long for the space to fill up, dozens upon dozens of Dockhills and Carvingwood members intermingling easily. It was comfortable, and it warmed my heart.

A motorcycle roared down the road and into the parking lot. It came to a stop outside the diner, and Donovan paused, sitting straighter.

When the male pulled his helmet off, I caught sight of dark, loose waves of hair that toppled across his forehead, and vibrant, emerald-green eyes. He was well built and rugged looking in his leather jacket. Beside me, Emmy went still.

"Who is that?" I asked.

Donovan got to his feet, meeting the man in the middle.

"Donovan," he greeted. The two shook hands, though it looked tense. The wolves around us settled into a watchful quiet.

"Jericho, what brings you to Dockhills so soon?"

The man, Jericho, looked to our blanket, eyes sliding to Emmy, where they stayed fixed for a heartbeat.

"The Pack Games, of course," he answered. "And to ask if you've seen my brother."

Donovan frowned. "Rhyland? No. Mind you, I've been away for a short while. But my wolves would've mention if he'd paid us a visit."

Jericho nodded, seeming to anticipate Donovan's response. He gave a tight smile. "No matter."

But there was a darkness in his expression that I couldn't quite pinpoint. Emmy shifted uncomfortably next to me, and I took her hand in mine. Did she recognize him from somewhere?

Looking sidelong at Brax, I tried to search for any hint as to who this man was. His eyes were narrowed, as though he too were trying to piece the puzzle together.

Behind us, someone whispered, "Isn't Rhyland the Dark River Alpha?"

My brows furrowed. I knew nothing about the Dark River Pack. They had never participated in the Pack Games as far as I knew. Most of their territory sat outside of Chaos Valley. They were unknown.

"Well, you're welcome to join the movie night if you'd like. There's plenty of food to go around." Donovan gestured to our blanket. There wasn't much room left with the five of us on it.

Jericho's lip curled slightly, as though that idea was utterly revolting.

Part of me wanted to sock the asshole in the face, but I simply fisted the blanket instead.

Catching sight of what I was sure was an epic glare of mine, Jericho smirked. "I see the Chaos was good to you." Then he looked to Syr and Brax. "Or maybe not. Seems you were only worthy of a third of a mate."

I sprang to my feet then, preparing to knock Jericho on his ass. Syr and Brax were at my sides in an instant, though smart enough not to touch me. Donovan's smile was tight. "You're mistaken. She was worthy of more than just one mate."

His smug smirk only grew, eyes shining with mischief. "I'll just stay in my usual cabin. Be seeing you, Donovan."

He lowered his gaze to Emmy yet again, before turning, dismissing me in an instant. There were two things I was utterly certain of in that moment.

The first, I was going to keep Esme out of his sights for the next two weeks. And second, we were going to kick his ass in whatever competitions he decided to enter.

As Donovan came back to us, chatter started anew. Jericho mounted his steel beast and it roared to life before he spun it around, zooming back the way he'd come. Donovan dropped back to the blanket and gave me a small smile.

"So that guy is a douche," I grumbled.

He nodded. "If you think he's bad, you should meet his brother."

Emmy shivered beside me, and I wrapped an arm around her slender frame. "So, they're competing in the Pack Games?"

Donovan shrugged. "I guess. They haven't before."

I bit the inside of my lip just as the last of the golden rays of summery sun vanished, giving the navy-blue sky above its nightly reign.

The old black and white film played, though I barely paid attention. I was too busy snuggling against Syr with Emmy laying her head on my shoulder. Though she was older than me by a year, I felt a surge of protectiveness for her that I associated with all of my found family.

Brax's fingers tangled with mine, and Donovan's head rested on one of my thighs.

Sighing, I drew in the clean, crisp air. My nerves had settled at last, and I allowed myself to enjoy my new reality.

No matter what came for us, we'd face it together as a family.

BONUS CHAPTER

Autumn

I paced the hall waiting for news. The sterile smell made my nose itch. I hated hospitals. Every time the double doors yawned open, my head jerked toward them. But the surgeon had yet to inform me of Arya's condition.

The reset of her femur by Brax had been completely undone by the time I made it to Ivywood's hospital. Arya had passed out from the pain, and she'd been rushed into surgery. Words like plates and screws had been thrown around, but all I could do was stroke my beautiful mate's terrified face.

I'd only just gotten to meet her, and there was chance she could die in the operating room. Yeah, it was a miniscule chance, but one that had my wolf itching to burst free. I paced back and forth, trying to keep my impatient snarls locked inside my chest, but the occasional glance from people seated outside the rooms told me I wasn't doing a bang-up job.

"Miss Lefair?" A white-haired nurse stood behind me, and I whirled.

"How is she?" I asked in a rush.

The older woman smiled, the lines around her eyes crinkling. "She's doing splendidly. The operation was successful. They didn't have to use any metal hardware, which is good news, but she will of course have to be back for a follow-up scan to make sure it's healing properly in a week."

I nodded, not caring about anything else she had to say. "Can I see her?"

"She's resting at the moment. But as soon as she's awake someone will come and fetch you."

"Please," I said, my voice bordering on pleading. "Can I just sit with her? I won't disturb her."

The nurse's lips pursed. Finally, she released a long sigh. "Alright then, come on."

My heart soared as I followed the old woman down the hall and into a room enclosed only by a papery sheet on hooks.

The space was small, and when the curtain was drawn back, revealing my Arya, my breath caught.

She was pale and looked so small under all the blankets. A monitor beside her kept a constant record of her vitals.

Swallowing down the lump rising in my throat, I took a seat in the only chair situated by the bed. The nurse drew the sheet back across the rail, giving me what little privacy they could offer.

I reached for her, deciding to rest my head next to her arm. My thumb brushed slow strokes back and forth over the thick blankets covering her hip. I could hear the steady beating of her heart, and reveled in the magnificent sound.

She was so fragile. I wanted to wrap her up in bubble wrap and keep her locked in my bedroom for the rest of her short life.

I had to change her.

Our bond was one-sided with her as a human and I hated that. There was no way I'd watch her grow old and die while I lived several lifetimes.

The assurance that she was fine—the rhythm of her heart and the soft breaths she drew, lulled my eyelids lower.

I only realized I'd fallen asleep when I felt her stir and jerk upright. For a moment, I wasn't sure where I was. But the astringent scent of alcohol-based cleaners filled my nostrils, and it all rushed back to me. The auction. The male that chased Arya. The pit. Her leg snapping filling my ears and her screams wrenching my heart in two.

Arya's dark eyes fluttered open, taking in the tiny space, and then me. Her lips twitched like she wanted to smile, but the expression died before it even fully formed.

"Hey," I said gently. "How are you feeling?"

She took in a deep breath, trying to sit up, and winced. Her hands peeled away the layers hiding her broken leg, and when the cast from her upper thigh to ankle was revealed, I pulled in a long, steadying breath. Arya whimpered, eyes filling with tears.

"They didn't have to use any plates or screws, which is good," I told her.

She nodded, and I could tell she was trying to be brave.

I bit my lip, considering my next words, but still they spilled out of my mouth before I could catch them. "If I were to change you, your leg would be—"

Arya shook her head wildly, eyes so big, they appeared cartoonish. "No, no, no, no, no…" She muttered the word over and over. Her heartrate spiked, making a beeping sound, and instantly, the curtain was thrown open. A nurse charged inside, different than the older woman from before.

"What is going on?" she asked, then looked to me, frowning. "Who are you and what are you doing in here? Visiting hours are over."

"We're family," I said firmly, rising to my feet as though to protect my mate.

The nurse simply turned the beeping off, and began murmuring something to Arya. She inhaled a slower breath, then exhaled. Though she sounded slightly winded, her breathing didn't sound panicked, and her heartrate monitor no longer bounced all over the small screen.

I backed away, toward the curtain.

Arya glanced my way for only a moment, and I saw the fear still lingering in her dark eyes. She thought me a monster. That my kind were unnatural.

She'd never accept me.

I dove under the hanging sheet and hurried down the hall. My feet carried me farther from the only one I desired to be near while my soul felt like it was being cleaved apart.

Why had fate chosen a human for my mate? A frail and petrified one, no less.

I burst through the front doors, gulping in the still night air. The electrifying crimson light above seemed to glare down at me in judgment.

We were only two days into the Chaos, but still, I didn't feel as though I'd be able to convince her in time. Which meant I'd have to wait for the Chaos to roll back around—and no one could even guess as to when that might happen, if ever.

My drumming pulse began to slow, and a feeling of determination took over in the place of panic and helplessness. Arya might fear becoming a wolf right now, but I had five days to change her mind.

I took my time heading back up, stopping in the café for a coffee as well as the gift shop for flowers and a stuffed white bear. It was cheesy, but if I was going to sweep Arya off her feet in less than a week, I had to make every minute count.

The nurse in the post-op wing informed me that she'd been moved to her own room, and I made my way there, trying to brace myself for how she'd react to me being near again. But she was asleep once again when I pushed the door open.

I set the flowers and bear on the wide windowsill as silently as I could manage. A large armchair sat by the window, though the curtains were drawn, blocking out the moon painted in blood. Humans were wary of it. And they had every right to be.

Arya had almost been sold to some sick fuck, and her escape had ended up with her in a massive cast, lying in a hospital bed.

My fingertips gently caressed the side of her face, her full, plump lips tempting me to lean down and press my own to them. But I didn't want to do anything without her consent. My wolf instincts were shredding my humanity apart with the need to claim her, but she was broken and hated what I was.

And that alone allowed me to pull away from my mate and glide into the bathroom, exhaustion weighing on me. I splashed water on my face and attempted to brush my teeth with the overnight pack sitting on the edge of the sink.

I crept back out into the room, finding Arya awake, staring at the gifts I'd left in the window. Another step closer had her head snapping in my direction, as though she sensed me.

She went still, but didn't scream.

"Are you in pain?" I asked.

She shook her head.

I gestured to where her attention had been before I'd interrupted. "I brought you some flowers. Apparently, they help with the overall healing process." I tried to force a smile to my lips, but it fell flat when she didn't react.

"Why are you still here?" Her voice was hoarse, but her tone was biting.

I flinched. "I had to make sure you were okay."

She looked away from me, leaning her head back and letting her eyes fall shut. "Well I'm fine now, so you can go."

The air in my lungs seemed to go stale. Shoving my hands into the back pockets of my jeans I took another step closer. "Do you have anyone that can come get you? Which town are you from?"

Arya was silent a moment, but I saw the slight tremble of her shoulders as she fought back tears. "No," she answered in barely a whisper. "No one is coming for me."

I straightened. "Then you can come home with me when you're ready. Or we can stay here for a while. Do you have any belongings you want to get?"

"I just want to go home." A tear tracked down the smooth skin of her cheek.

"Where is home?" I asked, trying to sound gentle. It was like trying to coax an abused animal from a corner.

"Blood Hollow."

My eyes widened. "That's a long way away."

She didn't answer me, but her eyes fixed on mine, and I saw her unasked question in them.

I nodded. "I'll take you there."

"*Not* on your back," she added. "I'll hitchhike my way back if I have to."

Forcing a steadying breath through my lips, I said, "Don't worry, I'll get us a car."

Arya leaned back into the bed, seeming content with my answer, and I let her slip back into unconsciousness. I waited until her breathing was a steady, slow rhythm before sinking into the armchair where I curled up, letting sleep claim me as well.

We made it to Blood Hollow two days later. Arya had spent the entire time either staring listlessly out the window or sleeping in the back seat. Too far away to touch. It drove the wolf in me crazy.

The most she spoke was when she gave directions in the small town to her rundown cabin. My lip had curled at the scent of mildew and cat urine as I carried her up the faded, wooden stairs.

The door was rickety and the lock wouldn't keep a mouse out, but I vowed to have them fixed for the short duration of our visit. My nerves frayed more and more with each glance out the filthy window. The blood moon hanging in the sky served as a constant reminder that time was running out.

I watched Arya sleep on her tiny mattress. The room itself didn't look too bad. Clearly she'd gone to a great deal of trouble to make this place feel like a home. A soft grey rug covered most of the dingy floor in the small room, and there were hints of pink and gold everywhere I looked. But it was the picture frames that drew my interest.

One showed an older couple that looked much like the young girl standing in front of them. It was Arya at maybe ten years old or so. Her parents?

I wondered what happened to them. Arya was clearly all alone now, and I hated that she was barely scraping by. The next frame held a worn picture of a slender woman in a tutu, artfully posed with her face downturned. But I knew instantly it was Arya.

Two more frames held pictures of her dancing, one with other girls, and one with a man I didn't recognize. The burn of jealousy at the sight of his hands on her waist had my fists clenching at my sides.

A few medals and ribbons hung from the frames. Awards won

at competitions and the like. My eyes widened. I turned to scan the room, but saw that Arya was awake, watching me.

"Hey," I said, feeling hesitant and wary of my mate.

She pulled herself upright, wincing slightly, then looked past me to the picture behind me. "Hey."

"I didn't know you danced." The words felt lame because of course I didn't know that about her. I didn't know a single thing about my mate besides the few details I'd managed to glean over the past four days.

Tears filled her eyes. "I taught ballet. But now…" She gestured down at her leg as a wretched sob broke free.

"Hey," I whispered soothingly. Striding across the room, I knelt beside her on the bed to cup her cheek. Her chocolate kissed eyes lifted to meet mine, as tears spilled over her smooth, beautiful skin. "If I turned you, your wolf form would heal your leg so completely, it would be as if the break never happened."

This time, the words didn't bring forth fear and loathing. Hesitation showed clearly on her stunning face. "But the change… would hurt, wouldn't it?"

I bit the inside of my lip. "The first time sucks pretty bad, but I think it could help."

Arya shook her head. "I'd rather just heal as I am…at least for now."

My heart sank. "If it heals completely in your human form, the damage may be irreparable."

A steely look of determination crossed Arya's face. "Then that's just how it'll be."

I didn't argue, but I nodded in defeat. Pressing my lips to her cheek in a lingering kiss, I silently hoped she'd change her mind.

I could claim her as a human, but we'd never have the mental link wolf mates inherently had. We'd never be able to run together. She wouldn't be a part of my pack. So many things seemed to slip through my fingers each time she rejected my request to turn her.

Arya's breath caught. "How much longer will the-the Chaos last?" she asked. I suppressed a smile, loving the faint smell of her arousal in the air.

"Only a few more days," I responded, pressing another kiss to her throat.

She swallowed hard and my pussy clenched with the need to taste her. To fuck her. I licked up the column of her throat, growing as wet as she was.

"Autumn," she breathed, spurring me on.

"What do you want, babe?" I asked.

She ran a hand through my hair before clenching it in her fist and pulling me down to her mouth. Her kiss was hot and seductive, her tongue tentatively tangling with mine.

I ran a hand up her torso, slipping it under her shirt to cup her breast over the delicate lace of her bra. Swirling a finger over a taut nipple, I drew a moan from her sweet lips that I swallowed down like it was my oxygen.

"You," she gasped when I trailed kisses down her jaw, her throat.

I pulled her shirt off her head gently and tossed it in the corner of the room. Pausing, I took in the sight of her in just a white lace bra, the worn quilt pooled at her tiny waist.

Meeting her nervous gaze, I let my adoration for her shine through my eyes. Holding her stare, I slowly lowered my head until my lips were only a breath above one of her hard nipples. The dark skin barely shone through the fabric. Wrapping my lips around the firm bud, I flicked my tongue over it.

Her back arched as she moaned my name. She pushed the quilt down further, exposing the red silk panties she had on beneath. The breath stilled in my lungs.

She was so fucking beautiful.

My wolf eagerly clawed beneath my skin, wanting to take her in ways that were too much for her as a human—especially with her broken leg.

My gaze locked onto her sex, hidden from me by the scrap of fabric I wanted to tear off her. I trailed my fingers up her bare thigh, teasing my way closer and closer to her apex. She trembled beneath my touch and I wanted to taste her so fucking bad I ached everywhere.

Sliding the thin material of her bra aside, I claimed her nipple with my mouth, lavishing hot, languid kisses to it and she shuddered.

I brushed a single finger over the damp fabric between her legs, coaxing another sound of pure pleasure from my mate.

She's ready, I thought eagerly. But I wanted this to last. I'd have her taste on my tongue and her cries ringing in my ears the rest of the fucking week.

Part of me knew I'd have to hold back slightly, but I didn't care as long as my mark was on her tonight.

I released her nipple with a pop, then lifted myself up to free the other, showing it the same treatment as before. Her writhing body beneath mine was like a drug I was already hooked on. Tentatively, I felt her hand on the back of my thigh, roaming up over the swell of my ass.

Fuck it gelt so good to be touched by her.

"Take your jeans off," she ordered shakily.

I huffed a laugh, but slid off the bed before sliding my pants down in a slow, teasing manner that had her throat bobbing.

Next, I gripped the hem of my shirt and slid it up over my head. Tossing it aside, I smirked at Arya. "Now we're even," I purred.

The tiny whimper that escaped her had me back on the bed in an instant. I straddled her, taking care not to bump her leg as I kissed her hard and possessively. She rocked her hips against mine, the heat of her pussy rubbing into me. A growl shook in my chest and I peppered her throat with my kisses, savoring her thundering pulse beneath my lips.

I nipped slightly, testing her reaction.

"Yes," she whispered.

Trailing lower, I cupped both of her breasts, kneading them before licking each tip. Her supple body was a feast for all of my senses, and I couldn't get enough.

"Let me try," she breathed just before I meant to slide down her body.

I lifted up, gazing down at her. A smile curved my lips, and she returned the gesture. Though hers held an innocence I hadn't possessed in years. I held still as she wrapped her arms around me, unfastening my bra.

Cool air kissed my skin, brushing over my achingly hard nipples. Her head lifted and I adjusted so she could take them into her mouth.

Tentatively, she licked one nipple, keeping her eyes on me to gauge my reaction. I bit down on my bottom lip as she ran the length of her tongue over the other.

A hiss escaped me, and Arya smiled. "Do you like that?"

I nodded, not trusting myself to speak. With one hand she cupped my breast, rubbing it and rolling my nipple between her fingers in a way that had me moaning. She suckled on the other and the sight alone nearly made me cum.

Moving to the other, she gained confidence, licking, and nipping until I was wild with the urge to taste her pussy.

"I need to taste you," I ground out.

She drew back in surprise, but smiled at my words. "And then I'll taste you?"

A non-committal grunt from me was all she got. "Spread your legs, Arya," I commanded. And my sweet little mate obeyed.

Kneeling between them, I clenched the sides of her panties in both hands, then tore them in half.

She gasped, but I was fixated on her exposed cunt, slick with desire. It was the prettiest shade of pink, and I wanted to worship it.

Running a finger through her wet heat, I heard her inhale sharply. I brought the finger to my mouth and tasted her while staring up at her. She watched with wild eyes, not daring to move or even breathe when I pressed the flat side of my tongue directly to her clit, then pulsed it up and down.

A wild sort of noise tore from her and she fought to move away. But I couldn't let her hurt herself. Clamping my hands around her waist, I held her still, licking her pussy until she relaxed into it. Her head fell back, and she moaned.

I craved each sound, each slight buck of her hips, knowing she couldn't move too much in her cast.

With her sufficiently distracted, I brought a finger to her entrance and slowly pushed it inside. She was so tight I groaned at the same time as her. I couldn't help but imagine all the filthy ways I'd take her and make her scream as soon as she was healed.

My gaze flicked up, zeroing in on the smooth column of her throat. Canines lengthening, I rasped, "Arya."

She blinked down at me, lust coating her every feature.

I sank my fangs into her uninjured thigh.

And she screamed her released, her pussy gripping my finger over and over as though she desperately wanted me to fill it with more.

I'd give her everything.

Anything.

Because she was *mine*.

Mine. The possessive word came out as a growl, and I felt the link that stretched between us.

Arya's eyes snapped open, her orgasm just barely subsided. She scooted back up the bed, suddenly shaking.

"What did you do?" she gasped.

The mark left on her thigh—my mating mark—would forever scar her skin.

“What did you do?” This time she screamed the words.

I knelt on the bed in front of her, reaching for her. To her credit, she didn’t cower. Instead, anger filled her eyes.

“I can’t believe you! You didn’t even ask if I wanted this.”

The euphoric sensation of claiming her began to fade, and my throat tightened. “I-I didn’t mean to. It just came over me, I couldn’t stop it,” I said, but before I could say anymore, she jerked a finger at the door.

“Get the fuck out, you monster!”

My jaw dropped. “Arya, please.”

Tears filled her eyes again, and then she said the only words that could shatter my entire soul. “I reject Autumn Lefair as my mate.”

To be continued…

WOLVES OF CHAOS VALLEY SERIES

Dive into the next Chaos Valley book today!

Captive Omega by Eva Brandt:

http://mybook.to/CaptiveOmega

Alpha Maddox by Emilia Rose:

https://books2read.com/u/bPXP81

Fated In Chaos by Moni Boyce:

https://books2read.com/FatedInChaos

Onyx Awakened by Quell T. Fox:

https://books2read.com/u/bWPgo7

Rogue Desire by Leeah Taylor:

https://books2read.com/u/47NzLg

Soul of the Chaos by Miri Stone & K.O. Newman:

https://books2read.com/u/m2RP7R

Chaos Bitten by Raven Woodward:

https://books2read.com/u/3LRKPX

Rogue Alliance by Lia Davis:

https://books2read.com/u/bQJ65D

Broken Moon by Ainsley Jaymes:

http://books2read.com/brokenmoonchaosvalley

Destined to Rule by Jessica Feyden:

https://books2read.com/u/mZeNdD

Feral Breed by Nikki Landis:

https://books2read.com/FeralBreed

MORE FROM THE AUTHOR

The Scondeladian Chronicles:

Marked for Darkness (https://books2read.com/u/3RJAwE)

Chained to Darkness (https://books2read.com/u/bojxVp)

Queen in Darkness (Coming November 2021)

Urban Mafia Kings Series:

Auctioned Virginity (https://books2read.com/u/md7xVx)

The Christmas Nibbles Anthology

CPSIA information can be obtained
at www.ICGtesting.com
Printed in the USA
BVHW040934070721
611241BV00017B/1438